"Why did you buy me a man?" a panicky Beth asked her two friends.

"It's just one night with him. A date. You'll have fun," Cindy promised. "Todd Graham's an okay guy. Not as flashy as the newspapers say."

"Todd Graham?" Beth gasped. "*The* Todd Graham? Local millionaire? You bought me a date with *him?*"

Mike looked confused. "Is that bad?"

"I'm a thirty-eight-year-old mother of two," Beth explained. "I have breasts. Hips."

"Most guys actually appreciate those things," Mike observed.

"Not when they're this old. Todd Graham wants a twenty-year-old fashion model. What am I supposed to do now?" Beth whimpered.

"Go out with him," Cindy said gently. "Hey, it's for charity. And it's just one night...."

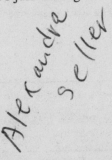

Dear Reader,

As you head for your favorite vacation hideaway, don't forget to bring along some Special Edition novels for sensational summertime reading!

This month's THAT'S MY BABY! title commemorates Diana Whitney's twenty-fifth Silhouette novel! *I Now Pronounce You Mom & Dad,* which also launches her FOR THE CHILDREN miniseries, is a poignant story about two former flames who conveniently wed for the sake of their beloved godchildren. Look for book two, *A Dad of His Own,* in September in the Silhouette Romance line, and book three, *The Fatherhood Factor,* in Special Edition in October.

Bestselling author Joan Elliott Pickart wraps up her captivating THE BACHELOR BET series with a heart-stirring love story between an amnesiac beauty and a brooding doctor in *The Most Eligible M.D.* The excitement continues with *Beth and the Bachelor* by reader favorite Susan Mallery—a romantic tale about a suburban mom who is swept off her feet by her very own Prince Charming. And fall in love with a virile *Secret Agent Groom,* book two in Andrea Edwards's THE BRIDAL CIRCLE series, about a shy Plain Jane who is powerfully drawn to her mesmerizing new neighbor.

Rounding out this month, Jennifer Mikels delivers an emotional reunion romance that features a rodeo champ who returns to his hometown to make up for lost time with the woman he loves... and the son he never knew existed, in *Forever Mine.* And family secrets are unveiled when a sophisticated lady melts a gruff cowboy's heart in *A Family Secret* by Jean Brashear.

I hope you enjoy each of these romances—where dreams come true!

Best,

Karen Taylor Richman
Senior Editor

Please address questions and book requests to:
Silhouette Reader Service
U.S.: 3010 Walden Ave., P.O. Box 1325, Buffalo, NY 14269
Canadian: P.O. Box 609, Fort Erie, Ont. L2A 5X3

SUSAN MALLERY

BETH AND THE BACHELOR

Published by Silhouette Books

America's Publisher of Contemporary Romance

 SILHOUETTE BOOKS

ISBN 0-373-24263-8

BETH AND THE BACHELOR

Copyright © 1999 by Susan W. Macias

This edition published by arrangement with Harlequin Books S.A.

® and TM are trademarks of Harlequin Books S.A., used under license. Trademarks indicated with ® are registered in the United States Patent and Trademark Office, the Canadian Trade Marks Office and in other countries.

Visit us at www.romance.net

Printed in U.S.A.

Books by Susan Mallery

SUSAN MALLERY

lives in sunny Southern California, where the eccentricities of a writer are considered fairly normal. Her books are both reader favorites and bestsellers, with recent titles appearing on the Waldenbooks bestseller list and the *USA Today* bestseller list. Her 1995 Special Edition title *Marriage on Demand* was awarded Best Special Edition by *Romantic Times Magazine*.

Dear Reader,

People often ask me where I get my book ideas. Sometimes a line from a song inspires me, or I overhear a part of an interesting conversation. (This happens most often in restaurants and department store dressing rooms. I'm a shameless eavesdropper!) But the unique ideas, and sometimes the most inspirational, come from my life. Such is the case with *Beth and the Bachelor*.

While real life isn't as tidy or well plotted as a book, it is certainly as romantic. But sometimes things happen and our journey takes an unexpected turn. The death of a loved one or a divorce can leave us in the uncomfortable position of starting over.

I had seen this happen to friends, but I'd never thought it would happen to me. And then it did. I was single again and it wasn't at all what I thought it would be. Dating as a teenager had been hard enough, but as a grown woman, it was even more difficult and awkward and scary.

While the heroine of this book, Beth, and I had very different dating experiences, we did share the same fear of getting involved again. We both worried about making fools of ourselves. The thought, *Dear Lord, I'm way too old to worry about whether or not this guy is going to want to hold my hand,* had crossed both our minds. Giving up and living alone forever seemed like a much more viable option.

But then I met a wonderful man who was funny and smart and patient, and suddenly I was in a relationship, acting just like one of my heroines. It was terrifying…and the best time of my life.

So this book is for those of you who are starting over, or have started over again. It was so much easier at nineteen, but when a relationship works now, it's even more satisfying because we know how blessed we are to have a second chance at a happily-ever-after of our own.

Regards,

Susan Mallery

Chapter One

"**Y**ou bought me what?" Beth Davis asked as she stared at the couple sitting across from her in her living room. A thunderstorm filled the late-afternoon sky.

Maybe she'd been hit by lightning and hadn't noticed. That would explain why she thought Mike had said what he had. She shook her head, trying to clear her obviously confused hearing. He couldn't have said that. Something was very wrong.

"It's not so awful," her friend Cindy told her. "Really. I didn't know he'd done it, but now that I think about it, it's kinda sweet."

Beth tried to laugh, but the sound that came out was more of a moan. "Sweet. Of course. I'm sure that's what he meant." She turned her attention to Mike, Cindy's husband. "What did you mean?"

Mike grinned. The handsome bodyguard turned security agent wasn't the least bit upset by her reaction. If Beth had to put money on something, she would bet that he was actually amused.

"I thought I was doing you a favor. You've been talking about it for a long time. Cindy's mentioned it several times. So I figured I would help things along."

Beth rose to her feet and crossed to the floor-to-ceiling windows that lined the wall of her family room. Outside, a storm raged, but its wildness couldn't compare to the panic growing inside of her. "You've always hated me. I see that now. Was it something I did?"

"Beth, don't," Cindy said. "If it's really going to be this horrible for you, you don't have to do it."

"Actually, she does," Mike told her. "Hey, it's for charity."

Beth spun around and faced her two friends. She read the concern, along with a healthy dose of amusement in their expressions. She told herself they were trying to be helpful. They cared about her. She wouldn't have made it through the past eighteen months if it hadn't been for them. "But why did you have to buy me a man?" she asked.

"I didn't buy you a whole man. Just one night with him. A date. You'll have fun," Mike promised.

Beth made that moaning noise again. She sank into the nearest wing chair. "This is impossible."

"No, it's not." Mike's voice was firm. "It's dinner at a fancy restaurant. He picks you up, you talk for a while, eat some nice food, come home. No big deal. I've met Todd Graham a couple of times and he seems like an okay kind of guy. Not as flashy as the newspapers say."

The slender thread of composure that had been holding her together snapped. Beth stared at Cindy, who was suddenly shifting uncomfortably on the sofa. "Todd Graham?" she asked.

Cindy nodded. "I've heard that he's—"

"Todd Graham?" Beth repeated, cutting her off. "*The* Todd Graham. Local millionaire, charter member of the bimbo-of-the-month club?" She turned to Mike and glared at him. "You bought me a date with Todd Graham?"

Mike looked confused. "Is that bad?"

"Not when compared with dating a serial killer."

"I don't understand," he said. "Why does this make it worse?"

"I'm thirty-eight years old," Beth said.

Mike leaned toward his wife. "Is that significant? Is this a female thing and am I missing the point?"

Beth sprang to her feet. "I'm a thirty-eight-year-old mother of two. I have breasts and hips."

Mike flinched. "At the risk of being yelled at, most of the time guys actually appreciate women having those things."

"Not when they're this old. Todd Graham doesn't want a woman, he wants a twenty-year-old fashion model, with a skinny body and no stretch marks. I can't believe you did this, Mike." She pointed at Cindy. "I can't believe you let him. What am I supposed to do now? Go out with him?"

"That was the point," Cindy said gently. "Beth, you're overreacting. It's just one night. A date for charity."

Beth slumped back in her chair. How could she explain this without coming off sounding like she was crazy? She drew in a deep breath—maybe it was too late to prevent that from happening. "It's not that I don't appreciate the thought," she said. "I know you're both worried about me and you think it's time for me to start dating. Maybe it is. Maybe I need a jump-start. But not like this. I don't need the public humiliation."

"There isn't going to be any humiliation," Cindy said earnestly. "You're a very attractive woman, Beth. He's going to adore you."

"I'm middle-aged, I've gained twenty pounds since Darren died, Todd Graham and I have nothing in common. I don't want to meet the man. I don't want to be compared with postadolescents who look younger than my daughter. Besides, he's rich. I hate that in a man."

Mike rose to his feet. "That's it. I'm outta here." He crossed to Beth, bent down and kissed her cheek. "This is about to turn into female talk and you're going to say things I know I don't want to hear. Beth, I bought you this date because I thought it would be fun for you. If you don't want to go because you feel it's morally wrong, I'll respect that. If you're just scared to get out there, then you're going. If you don't, I'll never come over and fix a leaky faucet again."

She glared at him. "I've learned to fix my own faucets."

He didn't answer, he just raised his eyebrows.

"Fine," she said. "I think it's very rude of you to point out the fact that I messed up the last time. I take this moment to remind you it was a small flood."

"I mean it," he said. He smiled at his wife. "See you soon," he told her, and left.

"He really meant well," Cindy said when Mike had left. "He worries about you. We both do."

Beth wanted to bury her head in her hands, but she felt she'd already humiliated herself enough for one day. "I know. It's just I can't do this. I'd feel ridiculous. Like I had to buy a man."

"It's worse for him. He was the one for sale. Think of him as slave labor."

Beth knew Cindy was trying to help. Unfortunately no words were going to undo the knot in her stomach. "I'm not ready."

"Yes, you are. You're just afraid. You pushed me to

start dating for months after my divorce. You were doing it because you cared about me. I'm returning the favor."

"I should have kept my mouth shut," Beth mumbled. She looked at her friend. Cindy's expression was one of concern. "I know you worry about me, but you don't have to. I'm fine."

"You said you wanted to start dating."

"I lied."

"You can't stay in mourning forever."

"Yes, I can. I like it here. It's safe. I have a very full life. My children, my work, the community, my friends."

Cindy tucked her short, light brown hair behind her ears. "You're lonely." She held up her hand. "Wait. Let me finish. I know how you feel because I remember what it was like after my divorce from Nelson. If you were a different person, I wouldn't be pushing. But you're the kind of woman who wants to be part of a couple. You need that."

Beth pulled one knee up to her chest. "I don't," she said fiercely. "I don't need any more than I have. I'm very content." She paused, half expecting some of the lightning from outside to leap indoors and strike her for lying.

Cindy didn't say anything—she didn't have to. The women had been friends long enough for each to be able to read the truth.

"Not him," Beth said quietly. "You're right. It's time for me to get out there and do whatever it is when people date these days."

"I don't think it's changed all that much."

Beth didn't even want to think about that. "Not this way," she continued. "Todd Graham is way out of my league. I would feel horrible the entire evening. He would be bored, I would probably forget where I was and start cutting his meat for him."

Cindy grinned. "Nice try, but it's not going to work. Both your kids are teenagers. They haven't needed you to cut their meat for years." Her smile faded. "I'll admit that Todd Graham isn't anyone's idea of a simple first date, but that's part of what's so great about this."

Beth blinked. "I'm sorry but you're going to have to explain that to me a little more."

"It's practice," Cindy told her. "He's not your type and you're not his. So nothing's going to happen. You already know that. Think of it as a trial run for a real date—one that matters with someone you might like to be involved with. If you were to meet the perfect guy, you would want to have a little experience under your belt, right?"

Beth mulled the idea over in her mind. She didn't think there was going to be a perfect guy for her. She'd already had a wonderful eighteen-year marriage. She'd done the "in love" thing. If she were to get involved with a man, it would just be for companionship.

"I am out of practice," she admitted. "I started dating Darren when I was in high school, and we got married just after I turned nineteen."

"That's my point. Todd will be your transition guy."

Beth smiled. "One date does not a transition guy make."

"Fine. He'll be your first practice session. No expectations."

"I'd like not to throw up during the meal."

Cindy laughed. "Great goal. I'm sure Todd would appreciate it, as well. So there you are. You're going to find out how much dating has changed by going out with a man you'll never see again. Your assignment is to carry on normal conversation for the two or three hours you're with him and to not throw up. You can do this."

Beth wasn't so sure. "If it was anyone else but him, I

would agree. Todd Graham. What kind of name is that? It sounds like something made up by an escort service.''

"And you would know this how?"

For the first time since hearing the news about Mike's little gift, Beth laughed. "I'm generalizing."

"Say you'll go," Cindy urged. "If nothing else, next time a well-meaning friend bugs you, you can tell him or her that you're dating."

"That has appeal," Beth admitted.

What she wanted to do was run screaming from the room. Unfortunately that wasn't an option. Cindy would hunt her down and talk and talk and talk until Beth acquiesced, just to be left in peace. She'd dealt with Cindy's tenacity before. And if Cindy didn't convince her, Mike would be back.

She thought about Darren, her wonderful husband. *Why'd you have to go and die?* She'd asked the question dozens of times in the past eighteen months and not once had there been an answer.

"I'll go," she said.

"You won't regret it," Cindy promised.

Beth nodded even though she had a bad feeling that her friend was very, very wrong.

"I'm a cow," Beth said the following Saturday as she stared at her reflection in the full-length mirror in her bathroom.

Jodi, her beautiful sixteen-year-old daughter, met her gaze in the reflective glass. "You're lovely, Mom. And you know you shouldn't think like that. You're always telling Matt and me to have positive thoughts."

"Good point." Beth tried to turn the litany of negative images around. "I'm not an ugly hag," she said.

Jodi groaned. "No, that's not good, either. How about—

I'm an attractive, vital woman and any man would be lucky to have me.''

"Easy for you to say," Beth told her daughter as she kissed her cheek. "Because it's completely true. Any man *would* be lucky to have you."

"Mo-om."

"Okay, okay." She squared her shoulders and returned her attention to the mirror. "I'll try to think more positively."

In honor of her first date in over twenty years, she'd had her short, red hair trimmed a whole week early. Despite the April humidity, it had fluffed nicely after her shower and her fringed, slightly spiky bangs were even. She'd used a tad more makeup than usual—a smoky shadow that accentuated her blue eyes—and she'd even dug out some old lip liner to help her lipstick last longer.

After eight changes of clothing, including trying on her red dress twice, she'd settled on an old favorite, a cream-and-navy dress with a matching cropped jacket. The round neck flattered her face, and it was cut high enough to not even hint at cleavage. Cindy had been after her all week, advising "if you've got it, flaunt it" but Beth had decided her nearly forty-year-old breasts would be more comfortable behind a couple of layers of clothing.

She'd vacillated between pearl earrings and gold hoops, finally settling on the pearls. A simple gold watch, sheer stockings and navy pumps completed her outfit. Cindy had loaned her a small navy clutch.

Her gaze turned critical. There were tiny lines around her eyes, but her skin was still pretty tight, and as clear and pale as it had been at twenty. She would never see a size eight again, but at five feet eight inches, the twenty pounds she'd gained since Darren's death were fairly easy to hide. If she started her walking again and cut back on the chocolate, she could drop it in a couple of months…or six. Or she might just stay a size twelve.

"You're beautiful," her daughter said, giving her a hug.

Beth took in Jodi's copper hair and bright, *young* smile. "Thanks, kid. My entire goal is not to make a fool of myself, so I'll think cool, elegant, sophisticated thoughts."

"Hey, Mom, you clean up pretty good."

Beth turned and saw her youngest, fourteen-year-old Matt, lounging in the bathroom doorway. While Jodi had inherited her rich hair color and blue eyes from her mother's side of the family, Matt was his father's son. Medium brown hair, brown eyes and glasses made him look like a much younger Darren. Beth's heart still ached when she looked at her son. At first, seeing him had made her miss her husband more, but now being able to see Darren's reflection in his son's expression gave her comfort.

"Thank you," she said, then grinned at Jodi. "That will be my affirmation for the evening. 'I clean up good.'"

"I'm ignoring you," Jodi said as she leaned toward the mirror and began experimenting with eye shadow.

"So what time are you going to be home?" Matt asked. "Because we're having this really big boy-girl party. I've ordered three kegs and Jodi promised one of her friends would be the stripper."

"Ma-att." Jodi spun toward her brother. "Don't joke about that. Mom's nervous enough." She gave her mother a comforting smile. "There isn't going to be a party. Sara is coming over and we're going to study for our trigonometry test next week. I don't know what Matt is going to do but he'll be doing it alone."

Matt raised his eye brows. "I plan to annoy my sister and her friend because Sara always wears really tight clothes and I want to look at her body."

"You're disgusting," Jodi announced, and turned her back on him.

"I'm fourteen and I'm honest. According to my health teacher, boys my age are awash in hormones. I'm just being normal. You're just jealous because you don't get to your sexual peak until you're almost forty."

Matt's gaze turned speculative. Beth knew how his adolescent mind worked and she did *not* want to have a conversation with her children about the fact that she was just two years shy of forty and therefore close to her supposed sexual peak.

"Did you write your paper for English?" Beth asked.

Matt groaned. "Yeah. I just finished it and left it on the kitchen table. You can look it over, then yell at me in the morning about all the grammar mistakes."

She smiled. Her kids were the best part of her life. "Sure thing." She headed out of her bathroom and started for the kitchen. "The tuna casserole is going to be ready in about twenty minutes. There's ice cream and some cake."

She paused by the counter. Matt and Jodi had trailed after her. "Jodi, I rented a couple of movies for Matt. He can use the television and VCR in my bedroom so you and Sara can study in the family room."

"Great," Jodi said. "We'll be fine. I'm sixteen, and even though Matt's still a baby, he's sorta mature."

Matt assumed a boxing stance. "Say that again, sister, and I'll show you mature."

Jodi dimpled. "You can't hit me. I'm a girl."

Matt groaned. "Come on, Mom. Just once let me hit her. Just once. Please?"

Beth ruffled his hair. "Sorry. No. You can't hit women."

"But she deserves it."

"So do you sometimes, but I don't hit you."

He straightened. "That's because I'm the same height as you and I'm a tough guy."

Beth stared at her baby, who actually *was* almost her height. Jodi had reached five eight and stopped, but Matt was going to easily pass six feet.

Matt took a step back. "She's got that look, Jo. The one where she starts talking about how cute we were when we were little. You'd better run for it."

The sound of a car engine distracted them all. Beth felt her stomach dive-bomb her toes. Dear Lord, she *was* going to throw up.

"He's here," Matt called as he raced to the front of the house. "It's a limo, Mom," he yelled back. "Black and really cool looking. So how rich is this guy anyway? You think he wants to buy me a car?"

Jodi touched her arm. "You'll be fine. You look great. Just smile. If there's a lull in conversation, ask about him. Guys love to talk about themselves."

"How do you know all this?" Beth asked.

Jodi grinned. "I'm repeating the advice you always give me. It works."

Beth could feel her chest tightening. She was going to pass out or something equally embarrassing. "At least I raised my kids right," she said as she kissed her daughter's cheek.

She walked slowly toward the front door. Matt knelt on the sofa facing the window and motioned for her to come look out with him. "The driver is turning the car around at the end of the cul de sac. You can't see in the windows or anything. This is so great. Maybe you could really date this guy, Mom. I'd pretend not to like him and he'd give me money to change my mind. What do you think?"

She bent over and kissed the top of his head. "I think you have a great imagination, which is why I push you so hard when you write those English papers. I know what you're capable of.''

''I wonder if the driver is in a uniform and everything,'' Matt said, ignoring her comment. ''How much do you think Mike paid for this date?''

Beth didn't want to wonder about that. She didn't want to think about the fact that she wasn't ready for this at all. She didn't want to think about the fact that Todd Graham was going to take one look at her and run in the opposite direction, or at least wish that he could. He went through postadolescent models the way other people went through tissues, tossing them into the trash when they got a little used.

She reminded herself this was for charity. That if Todd hadn't wanted to go on a date, he shouldn't have been in the bachelor auction to begin with. Then she repeated Cindy's words that this was just practice…nothing more. Better to get the first-night jitters over with someone who didn't matter. And if it got really, really horrible, she would just walk out of the restaurant, get a cab and come home. She'd made sure she had enough cash in her purse.

She drew in one deep breath for courage, walked to the front door, flipped on the porch light…and waited.

Chapter Two

Todd Graham glanced out of the tinted limousine window and realized that, until this particular moment in time, he'd never been in the suburbs before. Looks like he hadn't missed much.

Two-story brick houses lined the residential street. The architecture was all similar, with the painted trims ranging from white to ivory. The trees lined up perfectly, there were minivans and sedans parked in the driveways. So this was Middle America. Who would have thought it was only twenty-five minutes away from his high-rise penthouse?

His driver drew the vehicle to a stop in front of a house that looked much like all the others on the street. Todd decided that despite the sameness to the construction, the neighborhood wasn't unappealing…in its own way. If only he could say the same about his date. Middle-aged women were not his style, but he'd been coerced into the charity bachelor auction and he couldn't think of a good excuse to back out of his date.

He already resigned himself to a long and boring evening. At least he had a seven-thirty golf game the following morning, which gave him the perfect excuse to cut things short. They were going straight to the restaurant, then straight back here. He ignored the flicker of guilt that reminded him the price paid for an evening with him should at least include going somewhere nice for drinks, either before or after, but Todd didn't think he could stand that much insipid conversation.

R.J., his driver, opened the rear door and Todd stepped out into the humid Texas evening. Even though the sun had set nearly an hour before, several people were still outside. The sound of laughter drew his attention. He glanced to his left and saw a father wrestling with his son on the front lawn of their house. The boy looked maybe five or six. They were both having a great time.

Todd paused in midstride to stare. The stab of loneliness was so familiar, he barely registered the pain. There had been a time when he'd longed for a relationship with his own father. But the old man had never had time for anything but the newest Mrs. Graham, whomever she might be that month. Certainly he'd never bothered to notice he had a son growing up in his house.

Todd dismissed the emotion, looked away from the family and headed toward the front door of the brick house. The sooner he got this date started, the sooner it would be over.

"Mr. Graham?" R.J. said from behind him, then handed Todd a box of long-stemmed red roses.

"Thanks." Todd had nearly forgotten. He didn't see the point in bringing flowers, but his secretary had insisted and he didn't often argue with her.

He rang the bell and waited. Less than ten seconds later the door opened. He was face-to-face with his date for the evening.

He gave her a quick once-over, returned his attention to her face and offered her a smile. "Good evening, Beth. I'm Todd Graham."

She was much as he'd expected. Maybe a little younger looking, but not by much. Her dress was navy and cream. It hinted at a full figure, not fat, but more curvy than he was used to or liked. The red hair was interesting, although he preferred blondes. She had great eyes, a nice deep blue. She looked like what she was—an attractive suburban middle-aged woman. It was, he reminded himself, only one date.

"Nice to meet you." Her voice was low and a little tense. "I, um—" She hesitated. "Would you like to come in?"

He absolutely didn't want to, but he was determined to be polite. "Sure. Just for a minute. We have reservations in town."

"How nice." She stepped back and motioned him inside.

He moved into a small foyer. He had a brief impression of uninteresting furniture, smallish spaces, not much in the way of decorating. Again, about what he'd expected. "These are for you," he said, and handed her the florist's box.

She opened it and stared at the long-stemmed red roses. "How lovely. Thank you." Her smile was as tight as it was insincere. "I'll just go put them in water."

Her heels clicked on the hardwood floor as she headed for what he assumed was the kitchen. He glanced around again, taking in a bag with in-line skates by a hall closet door. Beth didn't strike him as the in-line skating type.

Then he stiffened. The woman had children. Of course. Most women her age did.

He wasn't sure what to think. Children. He hadn't been around them since he'd been one himself. Some of his friends joked that his string of female friends were young enough to be classified as children, but he knew their comments all sprang from jealousy.

Beth returned. "I've put them in water. Thank you again. They're lovely." She picked up a small handbag from a table by the door. "Shall we go?"

"Certainly."

He waited while she locked the front door, then escorted her to the car. R.J. held the rear door open for them. Beth slid onto the seat, and kept moving until she was practically pressed into the far corner.

Todd settled into the soft leather, then motioned to the champagne chilling in an ice bucket. "May I offer you a glass?"

Beth shook her head. "I'm sure it's nicer than anything I've ever had but…" The car started moving. She clutched at the door handle to her left. "I just don't think I should."

Todd frowned. Was she afraid he was trying to get her drunk? "Beth, you are perfectly safe in my company."

Her blue eyes widened. She gave a little laugh that turned into a strangled moan. "Like I don't know that," she said.

"Then I don't understand."

She angled toward him, although he noticed she was careful to keep herself anchored in the corner. "I mean this in the nicest possible way, Mr. Graham, but I really don't want to be out with you tonight."

He was so stunned he could barely speak. "You don't want to be on our date?" He couldn't believe it. While it was fine for *him* not to want to be there, he couldn't believe that *she* wasn't thrilled.

"I think I would rather have a root canal…without the painkiller."

That was telling him, he thought, and longed for the respectful, often shy, young women he dated. "Then why did you bid for me at the auction?"

"I didn't." She drew in a deep breath. "Some very well-meaning friends bought this evening for me. They thought it was time for me to start getting out into the world, and this seemed like an easy way to make that happen." She shook her head. "Easy for them. They aren't the ones who are going to throw up in the car."

Throw up? He inched back slightly. "Would you like me to roll down the window?"

"No. I'm fine. I meant that more in an emotional way than physically, although it's why I don't want to risk the champagne." She looked at him "To be honest, I haven't been on a date in twenty years. I don't remember what to talk about, or how I'm supposed to act. I don't imagine I'm your idea of the perfect partner anyway, what with me being well over twenty-five." The last comment was delivered with a slight smile. "From what I've read, younger would be your preference."

He didn't like the direction this conversation was going. "So you know who I am."

"It's hard to live in Houston and not have heard about you, Mr. Graham."

"Then we'll agree that I'm the expert in this dating situation?"

Her gaze narrowed. "Maybe."

She didn't trust easily and she wasn't a fool. Despite her obvious nerves and the fact that she was so ill at ease, she was saying awful things about him, Todd had to respect her honesty. "I'm going to give you some dating advice.

Use my first name. Mr. Graham makes me feel like I'm the high school principal."

She stared at him, opened her mouth to speak, then closed it. A flush of color crept up her cheeks. "I *have* been calling you that, haven't I?" She shook her head. "I don't think I should do this. I wasn't good at dating when I was young and I know I haven't improved since then."

He liked her vulnerability. Maybe this evening wasn't going to be so horrible after all. "It's like riding a bike— everything will come back to you."

"You say that like it's a good thing. I'm not so sure. I distinctly remember being tongue-tied and incredibly nervous in high school. I don't want to go back to that."

"How about if I handle the difficult parts? I'll introduce topics of conversation and keep things running smoothly. All you have to do is remember to breathe and respond where appropriate."

Some of the stiffness left her body. "Should I take notes?" she teased, as she flashed a smile that momentarily made her quite attractive.

"I think you're smart enough to remember the highlights."

"Keep the instructions in single-syllable words and I'll be fine." She leaned forward a little. "Actually, I do have a few dating questions, if you wouldn't mind answering them."

"Not at all."

"Do you like all the dating you do? Don't you get tired of all those different women? And how on earth do you keep their names straight? I've always wondered about that. Do you use a common endearment? Are they all honey, or in this case because they're so young, baby?"

Todd's first instinct was to be insulted. If one of his male friends had asked him the last question, he would have decked the guy in about two seconds. But Beth wasn't one of his male friends, and as he gazed at her, he realized she wasn't trying to be rude.

"I'm only asking because your life is so different from mine or from anyone's I know." Her mouth turned up at the corners. "I was married, all my friends are married. The most romantic excitement at my house is when there's a good love story on television."

"Flash cards," he said, pretending seriousness. "I have my secretary write out flash cards on each of the women I date, then I memorize the information. If I start to get confused, I just pull it out for a quick review. Of course it gets more difficult in the bedroom, what with me not having access to my pants pocket. In that case, I either tuck it between the mattress and the box spring, or under the pillow."

Beth stared at him for a long time, then she smiled again. The smile broadened and soon she was laughing. He joined in. His gaze drifted over her face. She was prettier than he'd first realized. Her blue eyes seemed to signal her emotions in the most charming way.

"Flash cards," she said. "What a great idea. Should I ever find myself in your situation, I'll remember that. Although the odds of it being a problem are quite slim."

"I think you'll do fine. You're all right now, aren't you?"

Her hands rested in her lap. He stared at her long, bare fingers and could easily imagine a slender gold wedding band on the ring finger of her left hand. Beth was one of those women born to be married.

"If I'm not fighting nausea, it's because of you," she said.

"A compliment to warm my heart."

She returned his smile. "I'm being serious."

"I can tell."

"No, really," she insisted. "I never thought it would be like this." She motioned to the limo interior, then to him. "I didn't think everything would be so nice or that I would be able to talk to you."

"What were you expecting?"

"I thought you would be kind of a snob, and that you would be angry that I wasn't some young girl…you know, a bimbo."

Todd couldn't remember the last time someone had insulted him so completely, all the while apparently unaware of what she was saying.

"Oh, no," Beth said quickly. "You have this tight look on your face. I said something horrible, didn't I? I'm sorry. I didn't mean to upset you."

"I'm not upset," he told her.

"Then what?"

He looked at her. "You don't have a very high opinion of me. So far you've implied that I date younger women, that I call them all baby because I can't remember their names and that they must be bimbos."

Beth covered her face with her hands and made a sound low in her throat. "I should never be allowed out on my own," she moaned. "Especially not in a situation like this."

She raised her head and stared at him. Remorse darkened her eyes. "I'm really sorry. I didn't mean to be insulting. That's not even what I was thinking. I guess it's because I don't think of you as a real person. I mean I've read about you in the newspaper and everything. You're like a movie star or a celebrity—very much larger than life. I don't think of you as being like everyone else."

He wasn't sure how to take that. In a way, her opinion was flattering. He liked the fact that she saw him as larger than life, but he didn't want her to be intimidated. But before he could figure out how to respond to her, the limo pulled to a stop in front of the restaurant.

Beth glanced out the window, and read the discrete lettering on the awning. "I've heard about this place," she murmured. "It's very expensive."

Todd leaned close. "I can afford it," he whispered.

She looked at him. Their faces weren't that far apart and he had the sudden urge to kiss her. Startled by the impulse, he pulled back.

A uniformed doorman reached for the rear handle and opened the door. Todd stepped out, then paused to assist Beth. He took her hand in his as she stepped out, then released her.

"I'm sure you meant to reassure me when you told me you could afford a place like this," she said as she walked next to him toward the double doors. "But it didn't work."

"So you think this would be easier if I was a truck driver or maybe a schoolteacher?"

She tilted her head slightly as she thought. "Maybe. Although I can't imagine dating ever being fun. But yes, I would like it if you weren't so..."

"Successful? Rich? Incredibly good-looking?" he offered helpfully.

She came to a stop on the walkway and stared at him. "Not to mention modest."

But there was a smile tugging at her lips and she wasn't as tense as she'd been before. Todd bent his arm, then drew her hand up to the crook of his elbow. "You'll be fine," he promised. "I won't let anything bad happen to you."

"You don't know how much I want to believe you."

They headed toward the wide double door. A young woman held it open for them. Once inside, they were greeted by Lucien, the owner of the restaurant, who knew

Todd on sight and quickly showed them to their table. Todd nodded at the several patrons with whom he was familiar. For a moment he didn't know what to do. Should he introduce Beth? If she'd been someone he was dating, he would have paused to talk with his friends. But she wasn't a real date. She was… He frowned as he realized he didn't know what she was. A fulfillment of an obligation?

But as he took the seat across from her and stared into her wide and wary blue eyes, he realized she was much more than an obligation. Despite the fact that he'd dreaded the evening and had wanted to think up an excuse to cancel, now that he was with her, he found himself having fun.

"Well, that confirmed everything," she said, when the waiter had placed the napkin on her lap before retreating to give them a few minutes to discuss their drink order.

"What do you mean?" Todd asked.

"Just that if I hadn't been completely sure I wasn't your type, all those interested stares and raised eyebrows just confirmed the truth."

Annoyance threaded through him. Not at her—everything about this situation was designed to make her feel uncomfortable—but at his supposed friends who had looked down at her.

"Now it's my turn to apologize," he said. "I should have picked a different kind of restaurant."

"Fast food?" She raised her eyebrows. "I assure you, I know which fork to use."

"Not at all. Just a place where we could get a quiet booth in the back and talk." He motioned to their seats in the center of the room. His usual table put them on display. Normally he enjoyed that, but not tonight.

He found himself in the unusual position of actually liking Beth. He thought she was bright and funny. She had dreaded their date as much as he had, yet she was being a good sport about everything. He liked that he could hold a conversation with her, which he realized didn't say much about the other women he dated. He didn't really think of them as younger, although he was starting to realize that while he'd gotten older over the past fifteen or twenty years, the age of the women he'd dated hadn't changed at all. Maybe he was going to have to do something about that.

"What would you like to drink?" he asked Beth.

She'd opened her menu and was staring at the selection. She leaned toward him. "There aren't any prices."

"I didn't ask you what anything cost, I asked if you would like a drink."

Her hair was short and layered, with wisps of bangs across her forehead. Perhaps as a child she'd had freckles—most redheads did—but hers had long since faded until her skin was pale and creamy.

"But I've never ordered from a menu that didn't have prices," she persisted. "I have to know how much I'm spending."

"Why?"

She opened her mouth, but no sound emerged.

"Are madame and monsieur ready to order a cocktail?" the tuxedo-clad waiter asked as he silently reappeared by their table.

"Beth?"

She stared at him. "I don't know. Maybe a glass of wine?"

"I thought I'd order a bottle with dinner. Would you like something else before?"

She shrugged helplessly. "I guess." She lowered her voice. "I suppose a margarita would be tacky, but that's the only cocktail I drink."

"How about a Cosmopolitan," Todd offered. "I think you'll like it."

"Fine."

He ordered that for Beth and a Tanqueray on the rocks for himself.

They sat in silence for a few minutes, until the drinks were delivered. Beth stared at the reddish-pink liquid in the martini glass. "I was worried about not being sophisticated, but I guess my drink is sophisticated enough for the both of us." She took a sip, then pressed her lips together. "Actually it's very nice. Thank you for suggesting it."

"You're welcome."

The waiter hovered. "Would madame and monsieur like to hear about the specials?"

What Todd wanted was a few minutes of conversation with Beth…alone. But that wasn't going to happen anytime soon. "Sure," he said.

The well-trained server spoke about the appetizer of the day, then the soup. Todd watched as Beth visibly blanched at the mention of bone marrow flan as an accompaniment with the *boeuf du jour*.

When the waiter had left them to discuss their choices, she swallowed hard. "Did he really say bone marrow flan?"

"It's just a side dish with the roast beef."

"Just a side dish. Great. Maybe I could get my entrée delivered on a plate that has never been contaminated by bone marrow anything." She shuddered. "I was going to tease you by saying I just wanted a hamburger, but I wouldn't trust this place with something like that. Who knows what they would put in it."

He grinned. "The salmon seems safe enough."

"Right. It's probably decorated with little fish teeth."

"I don't think fish have teeth."

"Sharks do."

"Then don't order the shark."

Her gaze held his. Despite her complaints, he could see the humor lurking in her eyes. "I don't get out much," she said. "But you get out way too much."

"Maybe."

"There's enough jewelry in this room to send my daughter's entire grade to college for four years."

He glanced around the room. He hadn't noticed before, but Beth was right. Many of the women wore large, glittering stones set in earrings, bracelets and necklaces. In contrast Beth was simply dressed. Her only jewelry was a pair of pearl earrings.

"It's okay to state the obvious," she told him. "I don't fit in here."

"Of course you belong here," he said automatically, and knew it was a lie. Even though he didn't want her to be, he knew she was right. "I should have planned something different," he said, then realized he hadn't planned this at all. He'd asked his secretary to make reservations somewhere nice. He hadn't cared enough to participate in the planning more than that. But now he was sorry. He wanted Beth to be having a better time.

"We could start a food fight," he offered. "That would change the atmosphere."

"I don't let my kids do that at home, so I'm not going to let you do that here." She pushed back her chair and rose to her feet. "Excuse me, Todd. I'll be right back."

He watched her cross the carpeted floor as she headed for the ladies' room. If someone had told him just three hours ago that he would actually care about the outcome of his blind date with a middle-aged housewife, he would have laughed in his face. But now he found himself in the uncomfortable position of wanting to make Beth happy for the evening and not having a clue as to how to make that happen.

Beth told herself to keep breathing but the instruction wasn't helping. She could feel herself panicking. She didn't belong in this restaurant. "Or with that man," she murmured, trying to ignore the fact that the lounge of the ladies' room was not only better decorated than her house, it was also about the same size as her living room.

The walls were papered in an expensive print and the furniture looked custom-made. She didn't want to think about how nice the actual bathroom area might be. It was all too depressing.

She faced the mirror and pretended to fix her makeup. Several women came and went as she wasted time and tried to gather the courage to face Todd Graham again. What on earth must he think of her? Not only was she completely unprepared to be anyone's date, let alone that of a notorious bachelor like himself, but she'd put her foot in her mouth at least a half dozen times. She still couldn't believe that she'd confessed she might throw up in the car, or the fuss she'd made about the menu not having prices, or her horror at the mention of bone marrow flan. Of course the latter explained why so many rich women were thin. If that's all they had to eat, starvation was a far more pleasant state of being.

He probably thought she'd never been outside of the Sugar Land city limits, let alone out of the state. Her only saving grace was that she didn't actually have hay in her hair.

They had nothing in common. She'd suspected they wouldn't. But suspecting and *knowing* were two very different states of mind. She'd never felt so out of place in her life. These people were different. Even the waiter intimidated her. The worst part was Todd was being so nice. If he'd stayed true to character—a jerk only interested in sleeping with young women—she might have survived the experience. But he was kind and funny and that made her want to make a good impression on him. Something that wasn't going to happen anytime soon.

If only he weren't so rich...or so good-looking. If only she hadn't felt heat clear down to her ankles when he'd pulled her hand into the crook of his arm. The old-fashioned gallant gesture had made her feel special and important; then his nearness had nearly taken her breath away. For a moment she'd felt sixteen again, and about as polished.

She gazed at her reflection. Men like him weren't interested in women like her. Plus, she was a widow. She didn't have any right to be attracted to another man. It was wrong, not to mention indecent and incredibly disloyal. How would she survive drinks, let alone the meal? With her luck, she would choke on the entrée and end up dying right there on the plushly carpeted floor.

"I can't do this," Beth murmured to herself.

She reached into her small evening bag and pulled out a tissue. Then she wrote quickly. She was rude and insensitive and fifteen different kinds of coward. She was also leaving.

Todd impatiently tapped his fingers against the table. Beth had been gone nearly fifteen minutes. Had something happened? Should he have the waiter send a female member of the staff into the rest room to check on Beth?

Just as he was about to flag the man over, the waiter appeared and pressed a limp tissue into his hand. "Madame asked me to give you this," he intoned in a voice that dripped with disapproval.

Instantly Todd knew what it was going to say. He opened the note and read it just to confirm his gut's intuition.

Sorry, Todd, but I'm just not ready for this whole dating ritual. You've been kindness itself and I really appreciate that. As far as I'm concerned, you have fulfilled your bachelor auction responsibilities completely. I hope my leaving doesn't cause you any embarrassment. Some of us aren't meant to leave the suburbs and I guess I'm one of those people. Please accept my apology.
Beth

"Is there a problem?" the waiter asked.

Yeah, there was a problem, Todd thought to himself. For the first time in his life, he'd been stood up.

Chapter Three

Beth paid the cabdriver then stared up at her two-story house. It was barely eight o'clock. Both her children were going to know that something was up. She would never have returned this early unless there was a problem. However, the idea of lurking in the shrubbery for two or three hours was even less appealing than confessing all, or at least part, of what had happened, so she headed for the back door.

As per her instructions, it was locked. That made her relax a little. While her lone foray into dating had ended in disaster, at least her kids seemed to be growing up into wonderful, responsible teenagers. Given the choice, she would pick her kids' success and happiness over her own, any day.

She inserted her key and turned it, then opened the door and made her way to the family room. "Just me," she called.

Her daughter, Jodi, and her friend Sara both looked up at her in surprise as she stepped into the room.

"I know I'm a little early," she said, careful to keep her voice bright and breezy. "Everything is fine. I told Todd I would prefer it if we ended our date quickly."

Jodi frowned at the VCR clock, then returned her attention to her mother. "A *little* early? Did you two even have time to eat?"

While Beth was willing to stretch the truth slightly, she wasn't going to out-and-out lie. "We had drinks."

"I thought he was supposed to be buying you dinner."

Beth crossed the hardwood floor and kissed her daughter's forehead. "He offered and I declined. I'd rather be home." She grabbed a cookie from the plate between the studying girls. "I'm going upstairs to get changed. Don't worry about me."

With that she was gone. One down and one to go, she thought, pleased Jodi had accepted her explanation so easily. Of course if she knew her daughter, they were going to be talking about this in more detail in the morning. Between now and then, Beth would think of a way to make things sound better than they were.

At the top of the stairs, she slipped out of her pumps and carried them. As she pushed open the half-closed door to her bedroom, she remembered that she'd given Matt permission to watch movies on her television so as not to disturb Jodi and Sara while they studied.

The sounds of an action movie assaulted her as she stepped into the dark bedroom. Matt lay on the bed, his head propped on top of all her pillows and a bowl of popcorn on his stomach.

"Hey, kiddo," she said as she walked toward her closet.

"Mom?" Matt set the bowl on the nightstand and sprang to his feet. "You're home early. Are you okay?"

She put her purse on her dresser and turned to look at him. "I'm fine. Yes, it was a short date, but Todd and I settled for drinks instead of dinner."

The twinge of guilt at her semi-lie surprised her. Why should she feel guilty about what had happened? *Maybe because she'd left a perfectly nice man in a potentially embarrassing situation,* a little voice in her head whispered.

Matt stood in front of her. He was a gangly teen with serious eyes behind his wire-rimmed glasses. Right now, worry pressed his mouth into a straight line.

His too-big hands curled into fists. "Did something happen? Did he—" His voice cracked and he flushed. "Did he try something?"

It took Beth a moment to figure out that her youngest, the boy she still thought of as her baby, was concerned about her safety and planning to protect her. Pain and pride battled for a place in her heart. Pain that he was already so grown-up and it wouldn't be long before he was gone, and pride for the man he would be when he left home for good.

She cupped Matt's face in her hands. He wasn't shaving regularly yet and he still had the blotchy skin of an adolescent, but since the death of his father, he'd done his best to be the man of the house.

"Thank you," she said quietly, and kissed his cheek. "Thank you for worrying about me. Yes, I'm home before I planned, but that's because I didn't stay to have dinner with Todd. Nothing happened."

At least nothing in the way Matt thought, Beth reminded herself. If anyone was guilty of behaving badly, she was the one in trouble, not Todd.

"You sure?" Matt asked.

"I swear." Beth dropped her hands and made an X over her heart. "Now let me get changed and I'll watch the rest of the movie with you."

Matt grinned. "You'll hate it."

"Probably," Beth said as she moved into the bathroom and the closet beyond. "But I'll get to make fun of it and annoy you with my sarcastic comments, so that will be entertaining."

Fifteen minutes later, she curled up on the opposite side of the bed. The large bowl of popcorn sat between them. While Matt lost himself in the movie, she tried to do the same. Unfortunately not even the sight of bare-chested navy SEALs was enough to keep her from thinking of Todd. Had he stayed in the restaurant for dinner? she wondered as she crunched popcorn. Or had he left? Did her abrupt departure make him feel embarrassed? She hoped not. She doubted that he would have felt anything but relief, but she wasn't sure, and that bothered her.

Beth knew she had her faults like everyone else, but she wasn't a deliberately cruel person. Guilt nibbled away at her until she thought it might have been easier to just endure the entire evening.

But that was part of the problem, she admitted to herself. Being with Todd hadn't been that difficult, and spending a few more hours in his company wouldn't have been all that tough to get through. Her uneasiness and discomfort had been about the strangeness of the situation, not to mention the snobby restaurant, not the man himself.

Later, when both her children were in bed and asleep, Beth paced the downstairs. It didn't matter that she'd told herself to put the evening behind her, nor did telling herself that what she'd done hadn't been so bad make her feel any better. When she finally crawled between her cool sheets, her mind still whirled. Questions of what she *should* have done versus what she actually *had* done followed her into her dreams.

* * *

Beth awoke to the smell of cinnamon and baking bread. Jodi must have put the ingredients for cinnamon rolls into the bread maker before going to bed the previous night. "You always were my favorite daughter," she said aloud as she headed for the shower.

Twenty minutes later she stood in her kitchen brewing coffee. The day looked clear. Except for a storm a few days ago, there had been nearly three weeks without rain, which meant she was going to have to continue watering by hand. The neighborhood prided itself on green lawns and lush plants. While Matt had taken charge of the mowing, trimming and raking, he wasn't much for watering.

"Morning."

Beth turned around and saw her daughter leaning against the doorway to the kitchen.

"Morning, yourself. It's early for you." She glanced at the clock on the wall and raised her eyebrows. "Barely nine and on a Saturday, too. Whatever is the world coming to?"

"Yeah, yeah." Jodi had pulled on shorts and a T-shirt, but hadn't showered yet. Her long red hair lay tangled on her shoulders. "I wanted to talk to you."

"About what?" Beth asked with studied casualness, although she suspected the topic. She poured a cup of coffee for herself and juice for her daughter, then sat at the round kitchen table and set the juice in front of the chair across from hers.

"Last night," Jodi said as she stumbled into the seat.

"What about last night?"

Beth was stalling and she knew it, but she did *not* want to have this conversation with her sixteen-year-old daughter…or with anyone else.

Jodi tucked her hair behind her ears and took a drink of

juice. "You said you and Todd just had drinks last night. That he offered you dinner and you declined."

"Yes, that's what I said." It was a lie, Beth thought guiltily, but a small one. On the lie scale, it should barely register.

"But you came home in a cab."

Beth silently cursed the beveled glass front door that allowed someone in the family room to see down the length of the house to the street. In the dark Jodi wouldn't have been able to identify a specific car but she had obviously seen enough to know the yellow cab Beth had taken home was nothing like the dark limo she'd driven in earlier.

She drew in a deep breath. "Nothing bad happened," she began slowly. "The date wasn't working, so I left early. It's not a big deal."

"Did he try something?"

"No. Matt asked me the same thing. What is it with you two?"

"We're worried about you, Mom. You haven't been out with a man before. Well, you dated Daddy, but that's different." Jodi shifted in her seat. "You know what I mean. You're not prepared for what really goes on when men and women date."

"Something you're expert at?"

"Of course not. It's just I have friends with divorced parents. The kids tell me what it's like for their moms. Men expect certain things. You're not that kind of woman. I just want to be sure that you're okay."

Beth didn't know whether to laugh hysterically, hug Jodi close and never let her go, or burst into tears. She settled on a sip of coffee.

"I appreciate the concern. Really. And I swear that Todd Graham was a perfect gentleman. He took me to a very exclusive restaurant." Briefly Beth filled Jodi in on the details, including the lack of prices on the menu and offer of bone marrow flan as a side dish for her *boeuf du jour*.

"That's gross," Jodi said, and shuddered.

"Tell me about it. All I could think of was that whatever I ordered would be served on plate that had once held bone marrow flan. It made my stomach queasy."

"But Todd was nice."

"Very nice."

"And you guys talked?"

Beth thought for a second. "Actually we did, and that surprises me."

"Was he having a good time?"

"I have no idea," Beth said. "If I had to guess, I'd say yes. We got along."

"So why did he let you leave early?"

Beth sprang to her feet. "Gee, I wonder if the bread is ready yet?"

"Mom?"

Beth hurried to the bread machine. Darn. There were nearly twenty minutes left on the timer. Maybe if she—

"Mom? Why do you have that funny look on your face? What are you hiding?"

Exposed by her own child. Beth wondered how she was going to talk her way out of this one. Then she reminded herself that she was the adult in the relationship.

"I'm not hiding anything. Todd didn't say anything about me leaving because I didn't give him the chance. I excused myself and sent a note to the table."

Silence.

Beth cursed herself for raising children who had opinions and were allowed to voice them as long as they were polite and respectful.

"You left him alone at the table and took off?"

She turned to face her daughter, took one look at Jodi's

outraged face and wished she hadn't. "You make it sound awful. It wasn't like that."

"How was it different from what I'm saying?"

"I'm sure Todd was relieved to have me gone. I'm not his type. He dates women closer to your age than mine."

"But you were on a date, Mom. If Matt or I tried to do something like that, you would ground us for a month."

Beth tried to ignore the fact that her daughter was right, just like she'd tried to ignore her own guilt from the night before. "I had my reasons. I..." Her voice trailed off. She returned to the table, sank into her chair and buried her face in her hands. "Oh, Jodi, you're right. It was a slimy thing to do and I know better." She raised her head. "I just couldn't stand it. The restaurant was so upscale. I felt like some hick from who-knows-where. The women Todd dates appear in the society pages. I didn't fit in."

Jodi still looked shocked, which made Beth feel worse. She hated disappointing her children, not to mention setting a really crummy example for decent behavior.

"I was in the wrong and I'll apologize," she said quickly. "I already did in the note, but on Monday morning I'll arrange to have flowers sent to his office."

Jodi's gaze turned speculative. "What was he like?"

"Different than I'd imagined. Nice and charming. I thought he would make me feel that he was hating every minute of the date, but he didn't." She remembered his teasing comments that he was the expert at dating and that she should let him give her advice. "He went out of his way to make me feel comfortable with what was obviously an awkward situation for both of us."

"So you liked him."

Beth smiled at her daughter. "Don't even go there. I thought he was a pleasant man, and that was unexpected.

I liked him the way I would like an acquaintance, not the way you would like a boy at school.''

Jodi grinned. ''Sure, Mom.'' She stood up. ''I'm going to shower. Can you finish the cinnamon rolls?''

''Not a problem.''

When her daughter had left the room, Beth stared out the window at her backyard. But instead of seeing the hedges, plants and grass, she saw Todd's face. He was a good-looking man with nearly perfect features. His dark blond hair had been conservatively cut, barely brushing the back of his collar. Cool blue-gray eyes added to his air of mystery. He'd had a straight nose, firm mouth and a body that filled out his clothes in a very nice way. Either he had the best set of genes this side of the Mississippi or he worked out regularly.

Jodi's comment still echoed in the quiet of the morning. *So you liked him.*

Was that the problem? Had she left her date early because she'd found herself interested in the man? Beth didn't want to think that was possible. Surely she wasn't such a coward. But she had an uncomfortable feeling that was exactly what had gone wrong. If she found him charming and attractive, what was not to like? She wasn't in a position to get involved with anyone—not that Todd would want to get involved with her. She also wasn't interested in getting hurt. She was thirty-eight years old and she had a bad feeling that like everything else in her body, her heart would take a lot longer to heal than it had at sixteen.

''I did the right thing,'' Beth said aloud. Leaving him like that had been tacky, but getting out of the situation had been exactly right.

She walked to the front door and opened it. Her newspaper lay on the step. She glanced at the house across the street and for once was grateful that Cindy and Mike were gone for the weekend. At least she had a couple of days reprieve until she had to tell her best friend about her evening. She didn't want to think about Cindy's response or how Mike would laugh when his wife confessed Beth's transgressions.

As Beth brought the newspaper inside, the bread machine chimed to let her know it had finished. Upstairs she heard Matt stirring and the running water of Jodi's shower. Her morning was already underway.

She wouldn't think about Todd any more today, she told herself. First thing Monday, after the traffic died down, she would drive into the city and find a florist close to his office. She would have them deliver a personal note of apology along with a bouquet of flowers and then she would put the whole thing behind her.

The scent of roses filled his office. Todd stood staring at the large spray of flowers sitting on his credenza. He'd sent hundreds of flowers over the years but this was the first time he could remember a woman sending them to him.

There was a greeting-card-sized envelope tucked in the greens instead of the usual small florist's card. He recognized the handwriting—after all, he'd spent much of the weekend reading and rereading the note Beth Davis had left him when she'd walked out on their date. So she'd delivered the note herself to—he checked the address on the delivery notice—a florist just down the street. That was a lot of work for a woman who had stood him up less than seventy-two hours before.

He opened the card and scanned the contents. It was all a repeat of what she'd written on Friday night. That she was sorry to have left without saying goodbye. She appreciated his kindness and hoped he would understand why the situation had been so difficult for her.

"Actually, I don't understand," he said aloud as he walked to his desk and settled into his leather chair.

She'd walked out on him. Todd still couldn't believe that had actually happened. He liked to think that while he had a healthy self-esteem, his ego wasn't overly inflated. But facts were facts. She was some middle-aged woman from the suburbs and he was a rich, single man. Women threw themselves at him, fawned over him and generally made it clear that he could have them whenever and wherever it was convenient. How could she have left their date early?

He told himself to let it go. She and the circumstances didn't matter. Except he couldn't think about anything else. Although he'd expected to be bored out of his mind, he'd actually enjoyed talking with her. She'd been nervous, obviously freshly divorced and completely out of her league, but she'd charmed him. He liked that she wasn't impressed by him. Her being unsure of the situation had been because of her inexperience, not his reputation. Her honesty had startled him, but he'd enjoyed knowing she would say what she thought, not what he wanted to hear.

His phone buzzed. "Mr. Graham, the marketing team is ready for you."

He pushed a button and spoke. "I'll be right there."

He rose from his seat and crossed to the door. Beth Davis had occupied more than her share of his time. His marketing meeting was scheduled to last all afternoon. When it was over, he would give the flowers to his secretary, toss both notes and never think about Beth again. Maybe he needed to get away for a few days. New York? It was April, the weather could be beautiful there. Or even Paris. He could call up one of his on-again off-again companions and make a mini-vacation of it. He would make up his mind when he left the meeting.

That resolved, he headed down the hall, leaving the flowers, and thoughts of Beth, behind.

Two hours later he cursed himself and the confusion of street names that was Sugar Land. He was lost. He hadn't bothered paying attention when R.J. had driven the limo down here and he'd only briefly glanced at his Key Map before leaving work.

What the hell was he doing? he asked himself again. He'd walked out of a meeting with only the barest of explanations, he'd driven for nearly forty minutes in the middle of the afternoon, and for what? He told himself it was because he wanted to hear Beth's apology in person. He told himself that it was about being right, and not anything more significant than that. He almost believed it, too.

"She's not my type," he grumbled as he pulled to the side of the road and pulled out his Key Map. He located the right page, then found the street. Up ahead was a sprawling mall. He should have turned left on Austin Parkway instead of right.

"She's not my type and we have nothing in common."

She was too old, too intelligent and too sincere. The woman had children. He didn't like children. At least he didn't think he did—after all, he didn't spend any time around them.

Todd turned right at the corner and found himself on Beth's street. Once again he was struck by the similarity of the houses. He studied the address, then pulled up across from the right one.

A young woman stood in front, watering some plants. She was tall and curvy, wearing a T-shirt and shorts. Todd was startled to realize Beth's daughter was so old. Beth must have gotten pregnant at sixteen.

He got out of his car and walked up the driveway. "Excuse me,'' he called over the sound of running water. ''Is your mother home?''

The girl spun toward him. Todd found himself staring into Beth's startled blue eyes. Her hair was mussed, her face free of makeup. While she couldn't pass for someone in her twenties, she looked surprisingly attractive in her casual clothes.

Her mouth dropped open. ''What are you doing here?''

''I came to see you.''

She took one step back, then another. Todd glanced down and saw the potential for disaster. ''Watch out for the sprinkler head,'' he warned.

But he was too late. Beth's bare heel came down on the edge of the metal. She shifted immediately, stumbling as she did so. The hose bounced wildly and a stream of cool water danced across the front of his pants, dousing his thighs and his crotch.

Chapter Four

Beth looked horrified. Todd hoped her expression came from her spraying him with water and not because he'd shown up unexpectedly, but he had a feeling she wrestled with both facts.

She dropped the hose to the ground and hurried to the tap. When the water was off, she brushed her hands against her shorts and turned back to face him. "You're here."

"I know." He sighed and pretended distress. "I thought things would be different in the suburbs, but I'm not sure I approve of your welcome ceremony. Given a choice though, I guess it beats a baptism of fire."

Her gaze drifted from his face, down his body to his soaking trousers. She swallowed. "I'd offer to toss them in the dryer, but I'm guessing they're not made out of a wash-and-wear fabric." She shook her head. "I really didn't mean to do that. I'm so sorry, Todd."

"No problem." Now that he was here, he was more

interested in seeing her again than angry by the accident. "Although I wouldn't mind being able to towel off some. I'm dripping."

"Oh. Yes, of course you'll need a towel." She glanced at the house, then down the street. Two women stood about a half block down the street. They were talking to each other and obviously interested in the goings-on in Beth's front yard. "We'd better go inside."

He could feel the cold water running down his legs and pooling in his shoes. No doubt his trousers were ruined. But he couldn't find it in himself to care.

Beth led the way to the rear of the house. As she held open the back door, she sighed. "Payback," she murmured. "I'm not the least bit surprised."

He was about to ask her what she meant when he stepped into the house but she disappeared, leaving him standing in the kitchen. On Friday he'd spent about thirty seconds in the foyer. He'd formed an impression of smallish spaces and average decorating. But everything looked different from his new vantage point.

The back door led into a bright kitchen, and he could see a family room beyond that. A baseball cap sat in the center of the round kitchen table. Books lay scattered across a wet bar. He could see a bike helmet, a letter jacket from a local high school and textbooks. All proof that Beth had children.

The information wasn't news, and if it was, it should have sent him running for cover. Instead, he found himself wondering about her kids. How old were they? How many? What were they like? He'd never much thought about having children of his own, nor had he been interested in other people's. But the thought of her children made him curious.

Beth reappeared carrying several towels. "I guess you

can blot yourself dry, then take a couple of these with you to protect your car seat.''

"Thanks.'' He took the towels from her and began patting himself down. He thought about offering her the job, but figured she would probably faint at the idea.

She shifted awkwardly from foot to foot. "Um, you don't want coffee or something, do you?''

"What a gracious invitation. I would love some coffee.''

She flushed. "I'm sorry. I don't mean to be rude. It's just...'' She waved helplessly. "You're here. I soaked you with a hose. It's not my finest hour. I've been praying for the earth to open up and swallow me whole, but we don't get many earthquakes here in Texas, so I guess I'm going to have to see this through.''

"Is that so horrible?''

Her blue eyes darkened. "That depends on why you're here.''

"How about that coffee?''

"Would you settle on iced tea? I just brewed some.''

"Sounds great.''

While she poured him a glass, he settled into one of the wooden chairs at the table. Beth offered him sugar, which he declined, then reluctantly took the seat opposite his.

She tried faking a smile and failed miserably. Todd almost found it in himself to feel sorry for her. Almost. "What did you mean when you said this was payback?'' he asked.

She cupped her hands around her glass. "It just is. For years I was so smug and happy with my life. I wanted exactly what I had—no more, no less. I felt sorry for women in unhappy marriages, I teased my suddenly single friends and never once thought that my turn would come. Here it is, whether I want it or not. Now people are talking about me. I'm one of the single friends.''

His parents had each married and divorced so many times he'd forgotten that musical partners wasn't a normal state of being. He wondered about her ex-husband. Was the man still in her life? Did he see his children? The thought was oddly unsettling.

"How long have you been divorced?" he asked.

Beth stared at him. "I'm not. I'm a widow. My husband died eighteen months ago." Her smile was sad. "Until then, we were one of the lucky ones. Our marriage was very happy."

Todd didn't know what to say. "I didn't realize. I'm sorry."

A widow? Beth? He looked at her, at her pretty face and bright red hair. In his mind, widows were elderly women all dressed in black. She still had school-age children. She wasn't supposed to have a husband die on her. He couldn't say why finding out about her being a widow was so startling, but it was. He didn't like the information.

Divorce he could handle, but death was very different. Her marriage hadn't ended because she'd fallen out of love with her husband, or he with her, but because he'd been taken from her.

She released her glass and pressed her fingertips against her cheeks. "I still miss him. Isn't that silly? But I do. It was unexpected. A car accident."

She gave him more information than he wanted. "You loved him." It wasn't a question.

She straightened. "Of course. I'd married him. We had two children together."

Love. He heard about the emotion. Every time one of his parents married someone new, they swore it was true love which would last a lifetime. Instead, the relationships generally lasted about two years. Then there were the loud fights, the accusations. Months later, he got a phone call saying the divorce was final. A year later, an invitation to another wedding.

"How long were you married?" he asked.

"Nearly eighteen years."

That was practically a lifetime. He wasn't sure he knew anyone who had been married that long. His parents' marriage had lasted nearly five years and the entire family thought that was a great accomplishment. What did people talk about year after year? How did they coexist without making each other crazy?

"I don't think you drove all the way out to my house to talk about my widowhood," Beth said. "So why are you here?"

He was still reeling from finding out she was a widow. It took him a moment to remember what had motivated him to walk out on his meeting and drive down to see a woman who by all rights he should have forgotten the moment their date ended.

"While the flowers were very nice, I wanted to hear your apology in person."

Beth blushed the color of the tomatoes ripening on the windowsill above the sink. She closed her eyes tightly and ducked her head. "I swear I've never done anything like that before in my life, and I'm never going to do it again." She looked at him. "Really. I'm a nice person. I have good manners, I tip great, I have taught my children to write thank-you notes for presents. I can't believe I just walked out on you like that."

"Me, either."

"It was just—" She waved her hands in the air, then slapped them on the tabletop. "I couldn't stay. Everything was wrong. The people at the restaurant were so rich and sophisticated. I felt like they were laughing and pointing. I thought you were bored and hoping to end the evening early. And no, I'm not pushing responsibility on everyone but myself. I didn't like the idea of a date from the beginning. I let myself be talked into it. I should have listened to my instincts and told you the truth. I don't usually mess up this badly. I apologize for my behavior and I'm very sorry if you were embarrassed or in any way inconvenienced by what I did. I mean that."

Sincerity softened her mouth and darkened her eyes. Despite her age, her lengthy marriage and having had two kids, she obviously hadn't learned how to hide what she was thinking. He found he liked that quality.

"I accept your apology. The flowers were a nice touch. No one has ever sent them to me before."

Beth smiled. "I thought about baking you cookies, but that seemed so motherish."

He tried to remember if his mother, or any of his stepmothers, had ever bothered baking cookies. He thought not. Several of the housekeepers had baked, but that wasn't the same thing.

She leaned forward and rested her elbows on the table. The front of her T-shirt gaped a little, but the neck was too high to show off any cleavage. Todd found himself hoping for a hint of exposed curve.

"So was it too horrible when I didn't come back?" she asked.

He shook his head. "I told the waiter there had been a sudden illness in the family."

"I'm sure he believed you. After all, you're not the kind of guy who gets stood up much."

Rather than agreeing, he took a drink of his iced tea.

"Can I reimburse you for the drinks?"

Her unexpected question nearly made him spit. Irritation sharpened his voice. "I understand that you weren't willing to spend an evening in my company, but please don't insult me further.''

Beth hunched forward as if he'd threatened her physically. ''I'm doing this all wrong. Please, Todd, I wasn't trying to be insulting. I really do feel badly about everything. I'm trying to make it better, but I see I'm just making it worse. Obviously I shouldn't be allowed out of the house with a member of the opposite sex until I take a remedial course on how to deal with men.''

Her discomfort eased his annoyance. He found himself leaning forward, as well, getting closer to her…wanting to touch her. ''The class isn't a bad idea. You're really out of practice. I shudder to think how you would have trampled on my ego if this had been a real date.''

''Maybe you could write a book on the subject. After all, you have the experience.''

He grinned. ''Too many women would want to be mentioned in the dedication. There wouldn't be room for actual text.''

''I see.'' Beth smiled at him. ''You're much nicer than I thought you would be. I like that in a man. So, have you ever been married?''

Her question, on the heels of her compliment, left him fumbling for words. Normally he knew exactly what a woman was going to say at any given moment, yet Beth caught him off guard on a regular basis.

''Not even once,'' he told her. ''My parents have made marrying, divorcing and then marrying again something of a second business. I've lost track of their combined number of marriages, but as of three or four years ago I'd had about thirty-six step- or half siblings. I keep in touch with a few of them, but not many. There are some I can't even remember.''

''Wow. The rich really are different.'' Beth tilted her

head. "I can't relate to that, except maybe from watching *Dynasty* on television. Do you remember that show?"

He shook his head. He loved how the afternoon light filtered in through the window and caught her hair. The dark red brightened like fire coming to life. He noticed she had tiny lines by her eyes. They crinkled when she smiled and he wanted to trace them.

"The Carringtons were this really rich family. Several of them and their friends got married a lot. It was interesting but nothing like my life." She took another sip of tea. "I met Darren—my husband—in high school. Both of our families were completely boring. No second or third marriages. Darren was a couple of years older than me and we got married when I was nineteen. I worked to help put him through his last year of college and then through graduate school."

She continued talking about Darren's job as a geochemical engineer for a Houston-based oil company. Todd realized that her life sounded as strange to him as his had been to her. He'd never known a woman who worked to put her husband through college. He thought that only happened in the movies. What would have made her do that? Love? Did it really exist? He had his doubts.

"Tell me about your children," he said when she paused.

She straightened and her whole face took on a glow. "They're wonderful. They've been terrific since they lost their dad. Jodi is sixteen, and a junior in high school. She's brilliant and beautiful." Beth fingered her bangs. "She has my red hair. Matt is fourteen and he takes after his dad. Brown hair, brown eyes and glasses. He's my little man."

Her mouth turned up in a smile. "When I got home early on Friday, Matt wanted to know if something bad had happened. There he was, all long legs and too-big feet, ready to defend my honor. I love them both. They've been a blessing to me. I don't think I would have survived Darren's death without them. They gave me a reason to keep on living.''

Todd didn't know what to do with the information she'd given him. He was used to being the object of adoration in any relationship. Women wanted and he gave. From the looks of things, Beth didn't need anything he had to offer. Not that he was interested in having a relationship with her. The contrasts were intriguing, but not significant.

She glanced at her watch. ''It's nearly four o'clock. I'm sure I'm keeping you from important work.''

''Just a meeting. I walked out without saying where I was going. I'm sure everyone is in a panic right about now.''

''You sound happy.''

''It keeps them on their toes. Sometimes I'm too predictable.''

She shook her head. ''I can think of several words with which to describe you, but 'predictable' isn't one of them.''

That pleased him. He finished his iced tea.

''Would you like some more?'' she asked. ''I also have some cookies. Peanut butter, and chocolate chip.''

''Homemade?''

She filled his glass with ice, then poured in more tea. ''Of course. They taste better and they're cheaper.''

That got his attention. She was a widow with two children. Was money a problem? He remembered her concern about prices at the restaurant on Saturday, then he glanced around the room and wished he knew enough about residential real estate to be able to estimate the value of the house. He could price commercial buildings in the loop to within a penny per square foot, but this market was beyond him.

Had Darren left her a decent insurance policy? He wanted to ask, but it wasn't his business.

Beth set a plate of cookies in front of him. He took one of each and ate them. "Perfect," he announced.

"Jodi made the peanut butter ones, and I did the chocolate chip. I'm not expecting you to claim a favorite."

"Definitely the chocolate chip."

"Liar." But she was smiling as she made her charge. Smiling in a way that made him want to sit at her table for a long time, just listening to her talk about her life. There was something to be said for simple pleasures shared with a woman close to his age. Why hadn't he ever dated someone like her?

"We should finish our date," he said impulsively. "You barely tasted your drink and we didn't have dinner. Let's go out some night. I promise to do a better job of picking a restaurant. There won't be any bone marrow flan in sight."

She was still standing and took a step back as he made his request. She folded her arms over her chest in a protective gesture. "It's really nice of you to ask, but I don't think it's a good idea. I'm not ready to get involved. I mean, to go out. I don't think you'd want to get involved with me. Why would you? Actually, we don't have anything in common. I know that. You're being kind and I appreciate it. But the two different worlds thing…my kids, your busy schedule. It just isn't a good idea."

She was babbling. Todd told himself she didn't know what she was saying and that he shouldn't take any of it personally, even though it was damn hard not to.

They stared at each other for a full minute while Todd tried to think of some way to respond to her assorted statements. Beth jumped in to fill the silence.

"It's me," she said. "I'm not your type. I'm too old,

almost forty and not attractive enough. I mean, I think I'm fine compared with, well, you know, regular women. But you date model types. They're so skinny and young and I've had children. Two.''

She took another step back, bumped into the wet bar and came to a stop. "To be honest, I'm busy that night."

This time there was no way to tell himself not to take it personally. She'd been doing fine...right up to her fatal mistake. "I didn't suggest a specific night."

Beth could feel the heat flaring on her face. Her skin felt like it was on fire. She could only imagine what incredibly bright color of red stained her cheeks. Talk about putting her foot in her mouth. The worst part was she hadn't meant to be insulting or rude or whatever else Todd was thinking of her. She just couldn't figure out why he was being so nice. He wasn't really interested in her, so she was simply trying to give him a polite out. What was that old saying? No Good Deed Goes Unpunished.

None of this made sense. She didn't know why he'd shown up at her house or why he was asking her out again. Everything she'd told him was the truth. Especially the part about them having nothing in common. Although, if she was honest with herself, she sort of wished they did. Todd looked really great sitting in her kitchen. Just being close to him made her heart act as if she was in the high-intensity portion of a step aerobics class at the gym.

It wasn't just that he was good-looking, although that was certainly true. It was that she liked being with him. He was a nice guy. She hadn't spent much time in the company of men in the past eighteen months and she'd missed that. Since Darren had died, Todd was the first single man to actually have a conversation with her.

Speaking of which, she owed him *another* apology. "I didn't mean anything bad by what I said. I don't understand why you're asking me out. I wish I did. You're a great guy and it's not that I don't like being with you—I do.''

"So what's the problem?" he asked.

A reasonable question, to which she had no reasonable answer. If only she didn't feel so quivery around him. "While you make me incredibly nervous, I also feel really comfortable around you. I think I can say anything and you'll understand. Do you know how much trouble that means? As you've already noticed, I have a great talent for saying the wrong thing. I would spend all my time apologizing. That would get old."

"Not for me," Todd said. "You are the least boring woman I've ever met."

She beamed. "Thank you." While she would have preferred he said she was stunningly beautiful and incredibly sexy, she would settle for least boring, even if the compliment sounded a little too close to "best of breed" at a dog show.

He rose to his feet. He was a couple of inches taller than Darren, maybe six feet or six one. As he moved toward her, the kitchen started shrinking. Her throat tightened. Unfamiliar heat rose in her body and she didn't know whether to bolt or strip.

"You owe me, Beth," he said when he was a scant foot away from her. "You ran out on me and now you owe me a date. I'm the kind of man who collects what's due him, so don't think you're going to get out of this one."

He was so...demanding and manly. She was embarrassed to find herself shivering, and not in horror. And to think she'd never liked the he-man type. Still, there was something to be said for masterful.

"But I—"

He held up his hand to stop her in midsentence. "This

Saturday night you and I are going out. I won't take no for an answer.''

"I can't," she said. "I have too much to do."

He raised his eyebrows in disbelief. "Try a different line. That one's not working."

"It's not a line. I have to plant flowers in the morning, help with concessions at Matt's baseball game in the middle of the day. At four o'clock is a pool party for several of his friends. By seven in the evening, I'll be little more than a tired, sweaty puddle. I don't think you'd be very interested in taking me out then."

His gaze narrowed.

"I'm not lying," she insisted, mostly because she wasn't. Some Saturdays were brutal.

"I'm out of town on Friday," he said, "So we can't do it then. It has to be Saturday."

It didn't have to be anything at all, Beth thought, but she found she sort of liked the idea of Todd insisting on taking her out. It was very romantic. "Tell you what. You come with me for the day. If you can get through all of that and still want to go out to dinner, I'll put on my best dress, even though you've already seen it, and we'll head out to the restaurant of your choice. But I'm willing to bet money you'll be too exhausted to think about dates or dinners."

"You're on," he said and held out his hand.

She slipped her palm next to his. His skin was warm and tempting and she found herself sort of leaning toward him. Todd Graham was a very tempting man. It was like being by the tiger exhibit at the zoo. The cats were so beautiful you wanted to be in the cage with them, even though you knew that they would simply see you as lunch. Todd was dangerous. She had no business letting him into her life. Still, it was too late to back out now. And it was only for one day.

He glanced at his watch. "I need to get back to my office," he said.

She led him to the front door.

"Saturday," he told her. "What time should I be here?"

"Eight in the morning."

"Fine."

He stared at her. His gaze dipped to her mouth and she had the sudden thought he was going to kiss her. She held in the squeak that formed at the back of her throat, thought about praying but didn't know what to pray for, so she settled on waiting. When he opened the front door and stalked out without saying a word, she didn't know whether to be relieved or disappointed. The only thing she knew for sure was that Saturday was going to be one interesting day.

Chapter Five

"I want details," Cindy said when Beth opened the front door to let her in. "I want you to start at the beginning of the date and tell me everything that happened. Don't leave out a single word."

Beth smiled at her friend. "When did you and Mike get back in town?"

Cindy glanced at her watch. "Oh, about ten minutes ago. I left him to unpack and put the kids in bed. After all, I do have my priorities."

"I'm thrilled that I rank so highly on your list."

Beth led the way into her family room. She'd known that Cindy would want to hear what happened on her date with Todd Graham. The fact that her friend had been out of town for a long weekend had only meant a postponement of the inevitable.

"At least Mike didn't come with you," Beth said.

"I promised him I would give him the abridged version

when I got back." Cindy plopped on the sofa and patted the cushion next to her. "Come on. Have a seat and start talking. I'm not leaving until you spill your guts."

Beth glanced toward the stairs. At least both her kids were upstairs studying in their rooms. She wouldn't have to bear the humiliation of them hearing about her date in more detail than she'd given them before. She settled on the sofa and thought about protesting that this was private and something she didn't want to share. Unfortunately she'd teased Cindy as much or more when her friend had been single, and she'd wanted to know what was happening as Cindy and Mike had started getting involved. It was what she'd told Todd yesterday—payback.

"There's not much to tell," Beth began.

"I can't tell you how much I don't believe that," Cindy said. "Come on. Spill it."

Beth touched on the highlights from her aborted date with Todd. She described the limo drive into the city, the awkward conversation, the expensive restaurant.

Cindy nodded sympathetically. "I would have hated being in a place that fancy. Did you feel really out of place?"

"Yes. The food on the menu was strange, the other customers were wearing designer clothes. I didn't know what to do."

"But you survived the experience."

Beth felt a faint heat on her cheeks. "Um, not exactly."

"What do you mean? Of course you survived. You're sitting in front of me, looking completely normal."

"It's not that simple." Beth folded her hands together in her lap. "I left him there. After we ordered drinks I realized the whole situation was crazy. Todd and I have nothing in common, I didn't want to be there and...well, it seemed like a good idea at the time. I went into the rest room, wrote him a note and took a cab home."

She was afraid to look at her friend, but when she finally did, she saw Cindy staring at her with a stunned expression on her face. Then she burst out laughing. "You stood him up?"

"It wasn't exactly like that."

"Oh, what was it like?" Cindy chuckled. "Mike is going to love this."

Beth thought about asking her friend not to share the information, but she doubted it would do any good. "I'm not proud of what I did. I know it was rude and thoughtless. I just panicked. The dating thing is too hard. I'm too old to be going out with men. Todd was actually pretty nice, and when we were in the car, it wasn't that difficult to talk to him, but in the restaurant I felt like everyone was staring at me."

Cindy's smile faded. "I'm sorry for laughing. You're right. Starting over isn't easy. I wish your first experience had been a little nicer, but at least you got started. The next time won't be so bad."

"I don't think I should have a next time. I never learned the rules in high school, so I still don't know them now. Besides, I'm not someone a man would be interested in."

"Oh, please!" Cindy glared at her. "You're intelligent, you have a great sense of humor, you're attractive. What's not to like?"

Her friend's compliments made Beth feel a little better. "You're kind to say so, but the fact is I'm nearly forty. That's too old to be dating."

"Why?"

"Todd only dates women in their twenties."

Cindy's gaze turned speculative. "How interesting."

"What do you mean?"

"I was talking about dating in general, but you were talking specifically about Todd. You liked him."

It wasn't a question. "No. He was fine. Very nice." And very nice looking. "But not my type."

"As you informed me when I was freshly divorced, you have to actually be dating to have a type."

"Fine. If I had a type it wouldn't be Todd."

"He's not the only single guy around."

"I know." But he was the only one who had caught Beth's attention. She reminded herself he was also the only one she'd ever been out with, too, which meant that she would probably be attracted to other men...assuming she ever met one and he asked her out.

Cindy leaned toward her. "So if you ducked out on him, I guess I don't have to ask about a good-night kiss."

Beth swallowed. She hadn't even thought about the possibility of kissing. If she had, she would never have been able to get into the limo in the first place. She wouldn't know what to do if a man tried anything like that. Just the thought of it made her want to curl up and die. Having it actually happen would be worse.

"No kissing, no significant touching," she said.

"How about insignificant touching."

Beth glared at her friend. "Leave me alone. Nothing happened. I abandoned the poor man in a restaurant. It was not my finest hour and I just want to put the situation behind me."

"Okay. You've made your point." Cindy held up her hands in a gesture of surrender. "I take it you're not going to see him again."

Beth paused. "I am, but it's not what you think."

Cindy's hazel-green eyes widened slightly. "I'm not thinking anything."

"Yes, you are. You're thinking that he likes me or something, but he doesn't. I sent him flowers to apologize for what I did. He came here yesterday because he wanted to hear me grovel in person. Then he suggested we go out and finish our date. I told him it was impossible. My life is full. I'm not interested in having a man.''

''But if you're seeing him again, you *did* say yes to the date.''

''No. I told him I was busy next Saturday. I've got to do the planting, then there's Matt's baseball game followed by the swim party. After all that I'll be way too exhausted to go out with anyone. When Todd didn't believe me, I invited him to participate in all I have to do. If he has enough energy after that to go out, I said I would.'' She shrugged. ''He won't want to. It's going to be a long day.''

''Beth has a boyfriend,'' Cindy sang under her breath.

More heat flared on Beth's cheeks. ''I do not. He doesn't like me. It's not like that.''

''Oh, honey, it's so exactly like that. He does like you. Why else would he bother?''

The question had kept Beth up most of the night. She picked at the hem of her shorts. ''I'm all wrong for him. He likes perky young women. I'm a widowed mother of two. It doesn't make sense.''

''Maybe he wants a change.''

''Maybe this is Be Kind To Widows And Orphans Month.''

''Does it matter?''

Beth looked at her friend's face. She wanted to say that it didn't matter, but if she was going to be honest with herself, she knew that it did. She didn't want to be a mercy date for Todd. Being around him was exciting. For the first time in many months, she'd awakened early, with a sense of expectation. But she was afraid, too. She didn't want to start anything with a man. She wasn't ready, and even if she could get ready, she didn't know how to play the game. The last thing she wanted was to make a fool of herself.

"It's too strange," she said at last.

"You could see him naked," Cindy told her. "When I was single, isn't that what you always told me? That you wanted to see a man other than Darren naked?"

"I must remember to be more careful about what I say," Beth muttered. "Everything seems to be coming back to haunt me." She drew in a breath. "Okay, I did mention that I wanted to see another man naked. I'd only ever been with Darren and I was curious. But that was before. I was making a joke from the safety of a happy marriage. I didn't really want to do it, I wanted to talk about it."

"Now you can have both."

"Do it and talk about it?" Beth shuddered. "Not in this lifetime. I can't have sex with a strange man."

Cindy grinned. "If you do the wild thing together, he won't be a stranger."

"I couldn't do that. I'm willing to admit seeing another man naked would be interesting, and I guess I don't actually object to the sex part, but I don't want to take my clothes off."

She tried to imagine the moment and couldn't. "I hate to harp on the age thing, but it's true. I've had two kids. There are lumps and bumps and stretch marks. Do you realize that I'm about sixteen years older than the last woman Todd saw naked?"

Cindy looked at her. She didn't say anything, she didn't have to. Beth closed her eyes for a moment and groaned. Once again Cindy had been talking generalities and Beth had been talking about Todd.

"You like him," Cindy said. "You don't have to admit, but we both know it's true. That's okay. It's nice that you like him. If he wants to see you again, he obviously likes you, too. Go with that. Have fun."

"I absolutely cannot have a relationship."

Cindy tucked her hair behind her ears. "I want to ask why, but you have that stubborn look on your face and I'm afraid you'll snap at me."

"I don't mean to be difficult."

"I know. Maybe it would help to think of all of this as a chance to learn those rules you never understood before. A practice class, like Lamaze when you were pregnant. Instead of learning about childbirth, you'll be learning about dating."

It could work…in theory. "Lamaze training was nothing like having a baby. It's a lot easier to do the breathing when you're not having labor pains. I doubt a practice relationship is anything like a real one."

"It gives you a place to start. Or you could just call him up and cancel."

Beth opened her mouth, then closed it. She didn't want to cancel on Todd and she didn't want to go out with him. Great. She was going to have to phone her mother and find out if mental illness ran in her family.

"Maybe the practice thing isn't such a bad idea," she said slowly. "I know he's not really interested. I'm not, either. I guess." She wasn't sure she would know what being interested in a man felt like.

"Then tell him to forget it."

"I can't do that."

"Why not?" Cindy's expression was bland.

"Because."

Cindy raised her eyebrows.

Beth glared at her. "Because I don't want to. Okay? Isn't that what you wanted me to say? I want to see him again. There. I've admitted it. Are you happy?"

Cindy smiled. "Very."

Saturday morning Beth pulled on a T-shirt, tucked it into her shorts, then stared at herself in the mirror. Due to an extra ten minutes of fluffing, she was having a good hair day. She'd put on mascara, a little eye shadow and lipstick. She'd even slid on a pair of gold hoop earrings. Considering her to-do list for the day, she was dressed up. Every other person at the plant store, then at the baseball game would be casually dressed. On any other Saturday, she wouldn't have given her clothes another thought.

But this wasn't a regular Saturday. Todd was due in a few minutes and despite telling herself that this wasn't a date and that he didn't matter, in her heart of hearts she wanted to impress him. Even though after a half hour in the chaos that was her world, he would want to run screaming in the opposite direction.

She heard footsteps upstairs and smiled. Talk about a miracle. It was a Saturday morning and her kids were up before eight. Of course last night she'd explained that Todd would be spending the day with her, which could have something to do with their desire to get up earlier than usual.

What would Todd think of her children? What would they think of him? During the discussion the previous evening Jodi had been intrigued by the concept of her mother dating, even though Beth had taken great pains to explain it wasn't a date. Matt had just looked worried. No doubt Todd threatened his memories of his father. Beth told herself that if she ever starting dating for real she was going to have to sit with Matt and discuss his concerns.

She touched the waistband of her shorts, reminded herself that a party dress and pumps would be inappropriate for her plans that day and left the room. If Todd was interested in glamorous, he was going to have to start seeing a fashion model. She was doing the best she could with what she had.

Once in the kitchen, she made coffee then wondered if Todd would eat before he came over. Should she start breakfast? The thought of serving pancakes or waffles made her shudder. It was too much like a movie scene, one symbolizing the morning after. As they hadn't had a night before, doing the morning-after thing seemed premature.

Footsteps thumped on the stairs. She glanced up as her kids walked into the kitchen. "We're here to check out the man in your life," Jodi said cheerfully.

Beth's sixteen-year-old daughter was radiant as always. Her bright red hair had been pulled back into a ponytail. Her skin was clear, and between her youthful metabolism and her running around, she was all of a size four. Todd would probably take one look at Jodi and fall for her instead, Beth thought grimly.

"While he is a man," Beth said, "he's not really in my life."

"Then why's he coming here?" Matt asked, as he pushed up his glasses.

Her youngest had pulled on shorts and a T-shirt. His feet were bare and his hair stood up in spikes from his night's sleep.

The sound of a car engine saved Beth from coming up with an answer. Which was a good thing because she didn't have a clue as to what to say to Matt. She wasn't sure why Todd wanted to hang out with her for the day, although Cindy had proved her point by making Beth admit she was happy about it. Life was so confusing.

The front doorbell rang. She hurried to answer it. Through the glass panels in the door, she could see Todd standing on the front porch. He held a large plastic-covered tray and several brown bags.

"Good morning," she said as she pulled open the door.

"Hi, Beth. I hope you haven't eaten. I brought breakfast."

She was vaguely aware of him stepping into the house and handing her a couple of the bags. She must have led the way into the kitchen because they were suddenly there and he was putting down the tray. But she couldn't remember any of it. Instead, all she could do was tell herself to breathe.

He was taller than she recalled. His seemingly genuine smile and pleased expression were difficult enough for her to deal with. Both made her toes curl inside her athletic shoes. Then her gaze moved down to the T-shirt he'd tucked into tight-fitting jeans. She wore a T-shirt, as did Matt, but their articles of clothing had nothing in common with Todd's garment. On him, the thick navy cotton clung to his broad shoulders, emphasizing a chest that had been hidden by his suit jacket or the loose-fitting dress shirt on their previous encounters. The color brought out the blue in his eyes. His arms were tanned and muscled. She didn't dare drop her gaze lower to his jeans. What if he was just as wonderful down there?

"I stopped by a deli in my neighborhood," he was saying. "There's bagels, different kinds of cream cheese and lox." He pointed at the tray. "Fresh fruit. I got some of everything because I didn't know what you liked."

There was enough food for the neighborhood, Beth thought, still stunned by the physical reality of Todd Graham in her kitchen.

"Thank you," she managed, then realized he was looking at her children and they were looking back. Shock number two. How did one introduce a strange man to one's children?

"Todd, this is my daughter, Jodi, and my son, Matt." She turned to her kids. "This is Todd Graham."

"Nice to meet you, Mr. Graham," Jodi said, and gave him a wide smile. "Thanks for bringing the food."

"My pleasure. Please call me Todd." Todd angled toward her son. "Matt." He held out his hand.

Matt hesitated, then shook the older man's hand.

Beth saw the potential for an awkward disaster so she put Matt to work getting out plates, knives and forks, while she had Jodi unpack the food.

"Do you want coffee?" Beth asked as she motioned for Todd to take a seat at the table.

"That would be great. Just black."

She opened the cupboard with the mugs and searched until she found a plain green one. Until that moment she hadn't realized she had a collection of cartoon character mugs, mugs celebrating various openings at banks, and mugs from several Mother's Days and Father's days. She doubted Todd would want to drink out of something that told him he was "the world's greatest mom."

"What is this?" Jodi asked.

Beth set Todd's drink in front of him, then turned to the island counter. Jodi stared down at a small container filled with thinly cut smoked salmon. "It's called lox. Some people eat them with bagels and cream cheese."

Jodi wrinkled her perfectly pert little nose. "Fish for breakfast?"

"It's no worse than when you have pizza in the morning."

Jodi laughed. "Yeah, it is. But I'll try it."

Matt put the plates on the table, added napkins, then walked over to get silverware. Beth took a step back and they bumped. She apologized, as did Matt. Jodi had moved on to the fruit assortment.

"There's mango and something that looks like mango, but isn't," she said.

"Probably papaya," Todd told her. "It's delicious."

"Okay." Jodi ducked around her brother and set the fruit in the center of the table.

Beth leaned against the counter and tried to relax.

The picture was all wrong, she realized. It had been over eighteen months since a man had sat at the table with them for breakfast. Having Todd join them now was strange. Beth found herself missing her husband with a fierceness she hadn't felt in a long time. She wanted the ritual of preparing the meal to be what it had been before. She wanted her children to move in a familiar dance as each performed his or her chores. She wanted to be comfortable, to not have to worry about saying the wrong thing or acting foolish. She wanted her past back.

"I set the table, Mom."

She blinked and saw Matt standing in front of her. Confusion darkened his brown eyes. He looked so much like his father that he sometimes made her heart hurt. This was difficult for him. He was trying to be the man of the family and some male had just strolled into his territory. He was only fourteen—how was she supposed to explain this to him when she didn't understand it herself?

"Would you like to take your breakfast into the family room and watch TV?" she asked quietly.

Matt nodded. He knew that she didn't usually allow them to eat meals in front of the television. She knew he needed a temporary escape.

"Thanks, Mom."

Both her kids filled plates with food, then disappeared. Beth sat across from Todd. "Thanks for bringing all this."

He looked at the open containers, most of which were still full. "I guess I brought too much. I didn't know how much teenagers would eat."

"Don't worry about it. While bagels and fruit aren't a

traditional pool party snack, I promise they'll eat everything this afternoon. Individually, fourteen-year-old boys are fairly normal about food, but when you get them in a group, they turn into locusts.''

Todd smiled at her. "I'm excited about today. I'm glad we're going to be spending so much time together.''

She blinked. Dear Lord, how was she supposed to respond to that? "Um, yeah, me, too,'' she mumbled at last.

She spread some veggie cream cheese onto an egg bagel and took a bite. Conversation. She needed to come up with something witty. Unfortunately, by the time she'd finished chewing and swallowing, all she could think of was the truth.

"It's very strange to have you here,'' she said. "Oh. I mean that in a good way.''

Todd sipped his coffee. "How is it good?''

"I don't mean it in a *bad* way. It's just this is so different from my usual life. Having a man here and all. If a male person were to come calling, I would have expected him to be interested in Jodi.'' She replayed the last sentence in her head and cringed. "Not that you're calling on me. I know you're just, um, visiting,'' she finished, feeling both lame and confused. She really didn't know what Todd was doing here.

He leaned toward her. The round table had always seemed plenty big until she had a handsome man invading her personal space. She resisted the urge to shift her chair backward.

"Let's get a couple of things straight,'' he said, his voice low and smooth. A shiver rippled down her spine.

"I'm listening.'' *Her* voice was practically a squeak.

"I think your daughter is very lovely and very young. You seem conscious of the age of the women I usually go out with, and I don't want you worrying that I see Jodi as anything other than a very nice *girl*." He emphasized the last word.

She remembered her questions from her first date and all the things she said about the age of his companions. "I never thought you'd—" She waved her hand toward the family room. "I wasn't worried about that at all."

"Good. I just wanted to make myself clear. Item two. If your definition of a man coming calling means that he wants to spend time with a woman because he's intrigued by her, then that's exactly why I'm here." His blue-gray eyes seemed to stare into her soul. "I like you, Beth. You're different from anyone I've ever met before and I want to get to know you better."

She coughed. It felt like something had gotten stuck in her throat, only she wasn't eating at that particular moment. Her chest tightened, her heart pounded loud enough for the neighbors to hear and she knew she was going to die right then. How could he say that? How could he come right out and tell her that he liked her? This was so much worse than high school, she thought. At least then the boys kept their feelings to themselves.

"I've shocked you," he said.

"'Shocked' is a strong term," she told him. "I'm a little out of my depth with all of this. Just keep on talking and I'll catch up eventually."

"I could change the subject to something a little easier for you."

"Good idea."

"Okay. Why don't you tell me what we're going to be doing today?"

That sounded like a nice, safe topic. "As I mentioned before, I need to go to get some plants. This is just for around the trees in the front yard. I want to put in something hardier to survive the summer. Matt's baseball game starts at eleven-thirty. I have to help with refreshments. The parents all take turns and this is my week.''

''Will I be helping with that, too?''

''If you don't mind.'' Although she was going to make sure they were in separate booths. She didn't think she would survive close quarters with him for two or three hours. Better to just gaze at him from afar.

''From four to seven is a pool party here, then the boys all go over to one of Matt's friends for a barbecue and sleep-over. Jodi is studying with a friend this morning, then baby-sitting from three until around midnight.''

''I brought a suit with me,'' Todd told her. ''You said if I still wanted to go out with you tonight, you'd come.''

Beth grinned. ''Why don't you remind me about your fancy clothes at about six-thirty tonight? I'll bet you'll be more than happy to cancel.'' She glanced at the clock. It was close to nine. ''If you're finished, we need to get going.''

''I'm ready.''

They stood up. Beth called out to her children and told them they would be back in less than an hour. She led the way to the back door.

''We can take my car,'' Todd said.

She thought about the sleek vehicle parked in front of her house, then shook her head. ''We're going to buying plants. They're packed in dirt and generally very messy.'' She unlocked the garage side door, reached inside and pushed the button to open the main door.

She looked at Todd who was staring blankly at her sports utility vehicle. ''It's a Durango,'' she said helpfully.

''It's big.''

''I know. Isn't that great? To quote my son, 'It's the best set of wheels I've ever had.''' She laughed. ''Welcome to the suburbs, Mr. Graham. Why don't you climb on board?''

Chapter Six

Todd stood in the center of the garden section of Home Depot and glanced around in amazement. This must be gardener heaven, he thought as he took in the rows and rows of plants, trees and flowers. He hadn't known this many different kinds of things grew in the Houston area.

Beth had left him in charge of the shopping cart, an oversize affair without a child seat, while she picked flats of plants. He watched her walk up and down the long aisle, going to the end and returning halfway before bending over to pick up a flat. Todd hurried to her side.

"I'll get that," he told her.

He could see the protest forming on her lips, then she stepped back. "Thanks," she said.

In the ten-minute drive from her house to the store she'd alternated between nervous chatter and shy silence. Even if she hadn't told him about her solitary life since the death of her husband, Todd would have guessed she didn't get out with men much. For reasons he didn't completely understand, being around him made her nervous. He was used to women wanting to impress him, but he couldn't remember reducing one to a stammering blush before. He found he liked that he upset her equilibrium.

"I think that's everything," she said as she looked at the four containers sitting at the bottom of the cart. They headed toward the cashier.

The store was crowded, with couples and families filling the aisles. He heard parts of conversations. Sentences about retiling bathrooms and installing play areas in backyards. This was an unfamiliar world for him. If his penthouse condo needed painting, his secretary arranged it. When he wanted different furniture, he called in a decorator.

"Do you plant these yourself?" he asked.

"Matt will help, but yes. I've thought about getting a gardener and I'm sure I will when both kids are off at college, but for now we can keep up with the yard."

He wondered again if it was a matter of finances. Was money tight for Beth and her children?

They reached the front of the store. About half of the two dozen checkout stands were open. He and Beth walked along until they found one that had a short line. Todd automatically reached for his wallet.

"What are you doing?" Beth asked as she put her hand on his forearm to stop him. "These are my plants and I'll pay for them." She softened her words with a smile.

She was about five-five or five-six, shorter than his six-one, not to mention the tall, leggy model types he dated. If he were to pull her close, he could probably rest his chin on her head. For some unknown reason, the thought made him want to protect her, as if her size made her vulnerable.

"Morning, Beth," a female voice said from behind them. "I see you're out taking care of the front yard."

He turned around and saw a dark-haired woman pushing a cart filled with cans of paint. She smiled. "We're redoing the downstairs half bath. Jack thinks it will take all of an afternoon. I've tried to explain this is a two-day project, but you know how they get about this kind of thing."

"Rita," Beth said. "Hi. Nice to see you." She put her hand on the cart. "I'm buying plants, like you said."

Rita's gaze never left him. There was an awkward pause. Finally Todd leaned toward her and held out his hand. "Hi, I'm Todd Graham."

"Oh." Beth shifted uncomfortably and looked as if she wished she were anywhere but here. "Um, Todd is a friend of the family. He's helping out today, with the planting, then later at Matt's baseball game."

The cashier announced the total. Beth handed the woman a credit card. "It was nice to see you, Rita. Say hi to Jack for me."

She scribbled her signature on the offered receipt, then hurried out of the store. Todd pushed the cart after her. When he caught up with her by the Durango, she was leaning against the vehicle and breathing heavily.

"That was so horrible," she moaned. "I'm sorry. I should have realized we'd run into people I know. She was staring. She's going to tell everyone." At last she looked at him. "I hope you don't mind I said you were a friend of the family. I didn't know what else to tell her."

"It's fine," he said easily, even as he wondered why she didn't just say they were dating. Except they weren't dating. He liked her and all but he certainly wasn't interested in dating her; at least he didn't think he was. He didn't date widows, with or without teenagers. Of course, if they weren't going out, then what the hell was he doing loading plants into the back of her truck? He'd told her he wanted to get to know her better...which was true. But that was somehow different from dating. At least that's what he told himself.

As he slid into the passenger seat next to her, he stroked his index finger against her cheek. "We're both confused about what we're doing," he said. "We'll just wing it."

"Sounds good."

Her voice was breathy, which was fine with him because touching her cheek had sent an electric shock clear down to his groin. What was going on? Was he attracted to Beth? He stared straight ahead and tried to ignore her long, bare legs. She was a little more curvy than he was used to, but he liked the idea of something other than narrow bones digging into his body. She was the kind of woman who made a man think about comforting hugs as well as making love.

Just forget about it, he told himself. He would finish out his day with her, take her to dinner, then get back to his side of town. That was where he belonged. He didn't want to risk getting in too deep.

When they pulled into the driveway, Matt came out to help them unload the plants.

"Todd said he would help me plant," Beth told her son. "So you don't have to if you have something else you would rather be doing."

"I don't mind," Matt said. He pushed his glasses up higher on his nose, grabbed a flat and headed for the front of the house.

"We have to leave at eleven," Beth called after him. "Be sure to stop in time so that you can get ready for the game."

She walked into the garage and came out with an assortment of garden tools. "I have gloves if you don't want to get your hands dirty."

"I think I can handle it."

"We'll see."

He picked up a flat and followed her to the front yard. Matt had started digging up the flowers already planted in the mulched circle under the large tree to the left of the walkway.

"Pansies don't make it through the Houston summer," Beth explained. "So we take them out and put in something else. It's a relatively simple procedure—take out what's already there and put a new one in its place."

Todd knelt down on the cool ground. In his world plants and flowers came in delivery trucks. At the office all the foliage was rotated monthly by a service. He didn't think he'd ever worked in a garden before, but it didn't look difficult. Maybe he would like it and buy a plant for his balcony.

The soil was moist and the pansies came out easily. He set the flowers aside, watching Matt as he peeled back the plastic container of the new greenery. The boy set the plant into the hole and tapped down on the earth. Todd followed suit.

"I didn't think we'd get this finished before we had to leave for the game," Beth said, "But with Todd's help it's going to go fast."

They worked in silence. Todd became aware of the noises of the neighborhood. Up and down the street car engines started as families prepared for Saturday outings. A few lawn mowers roared to life. This world was so different from his childhood. He couldn't remember his family doing anything as a group, with the exception of attending the latest wedding.

Inside the house, the phone rang. "Has Jodi already left?" Beth asked her son even as she rose to her feet.

"Yeah, after you did."

"I'll be right back," she said, and hurried inside.

Todd sensed Matt's attention on him. The kid had something on his mind, but Todd wasn't going to rush him. Matt would get it out when he was ready. They continued to work together, finishing with the first tree, then moving to the second. There were two on the left side on the lawn and one on the right.

"My dad is dead."

Todd stiffened in surprised. He hadn't expected that to be Matt's opening salvo. "Your mom told me. I'm sorry. That's got to be rough."

Matt shrugged. His hair was barely to the bottom of his collar, but it was all one length and it hung forward, covering his face as he worked. "He was great. He worked for an oil company. They'd sent him out of town on business and he died in a car crash. The other guy was drunk."

"I'm sorry," Todd repeated, feeling inadequate. He wished Beth would come back so he didn't have to deal with this conversation. He didn't know squat about talking with kids.

"My parents met in high school. I don't think they ever dated anyone else, but each other. It's kinda weird, but nice." Matt sat back on his heels and stared at Todd. "They loved each other. It was really hard on her…afterward. She cried a lot. Mostly at night after we were in bed. I don't think she wanted us to know, but we did."

Todd didn't like hearing all this, especially not from a fourteen-year-old boy. "That situation would be difficult for anyone. Your mother seems to have handled it well."

Matt shrugged. "She doesn't get out much. You know, dating and stuff." Color flooded his face, but he didn't back down and he didn't turn away. "I don't know who you are but from what my mom's friend Cindy's husband said, you're this rich guy and you date a lot. I know I'm just a kid, but I'm not gonna let you hurt her. She's funny but she's real serious, too. She has a lot of responsibilities. She doesn't need some jerk messing her up.''

He paused and swallowed. "I'm not saying you're a jerk. I don't know. I'm just telling you that I'm going to make sure she's okay.''

Todd waited for the anger or at least a hint of irritation, but all he felt was admiration for the kid's guts and envy that Matt was so close to his mother. This family lived an emotional life that was foreign to him. The only feeling his parents generated in their children was the sense that they were unwelcome and in the way. His mother had remembered him when she wanted to use him as leverage against his father, or her latest husband.

Todd looked Matt straight in the eye, as if they were equals. Perhaps in this they were. "I appreciate your honesty,'' he said. "That's a good quality in a man.''

Matt straightened at the words. His shoulders went back and his chest swelled. "Yeah, well, I wanted you to know.''

"I'm going to be just as honest with you. I don't want to hurt your mother. I know that she's still dealing with her loss. But I like her. She's very unique and I'd like to get to know her and you and your sister a little better.''

"So you're dating?''

Todd wanted to say yes, but he wasn't sure. "It's more like special friends.''

Matt thought that over. "She needs more friends in her life. She still misses my dad.'' He glanced behind him as if checking to make sure they were still alone. "Sometimes, at night, she still cries. She thinks Jodi and I don't know, but we do.''

Todd found himself wishing Matt hadn't told him that piece of information. He didn't want to know that Beth still mourned her late husband. He was left with a feeling of disquiet. He'd never known anyone like her before—someone who actually cared for another human being in a genuine way. He could accept parents loving children. He'd seen it demonstrated many times even if he'd never experienced it firsthand. But he didn't know that adults could love each other completely. He didn't even believe romantic love existed.

But why else would Beth miss her husband so much? They must have had a kind of connection he didn't know about.

He started to ask Matt about their marriage, but the front door open and Beth reappeared. "Sorry," she said as she joined them. "It was the magazine."

"What magazine?" Todd asked.

Beth knelt down between him and Matt. "I work part-time for a local magazine. I write some articles, do editing, just to get me out of the house a few times a week. They were checking on some work that's due in a couple of weeks. One of the feature articles fell through and they wanted to know if I could fill the empty space."

"Can you?"

Her smile hit him in the gut like a sucker punch. If he hadn't already been on the ground, he might have gone down on one knee. "Of course."

He ignored his reaction to her smile and focused on what she'd said. If she worked part-time to, as she'd put it, "get out of the house" then money wasn't a big problem for her. Relief settled over him. He'd been trying to think of ways to help her financially and hadn't come up with a single scenario that didn't end with her calling him names and showing him the door.

"I gotta get ready for the game," Matt said, and stood up.

Todd looked at him. "I'm looking forward to seeing you play," he told the kid.

Matt gave him an appraising gaze, then nodded. "I'm glad you're going to be there."

With that he was gone.

Todd felt as if he'd been handed the key to the city. Matt had warned him about his mother and he'd responded in a way that let the young man trust him.

"So, what did you two talk about while I was gone?" Beth asked. "I could see you from the window and it looked very intense."

"Guy stuff."

"Could you be more specific?"

Todd winked. "Sorry, no can do. If I were to tell you, I'd be sharing male secrets. There are two possible punishments for that. Either I'd have to kill you, or I'd be thrown out of all male society. No more sporting events, no more beer in front of the television, no more swimsuit calendars. It's a fate worse than death."

"I can tell. So you'd be forced to kill me."

"Exactly."

"You wouldn't like prison."

He shuddered. "I don't think I'd make many friends there. So I'm going to keep my mouth shut instead."

"Probably the best idea."

Beth continued to look at him. Todd knew he was going to have to tell her something.

"It really was just guy stuff," he said. "He's a good kid. I like him."

"He has a lot of his father in him."

Todd didn't like hearing that, either, but there was no way to tell her. If Matt was like Darren, then he—Todd—would have probably liked Darren, as well. More unsettling news. Who could have predicted that a couple of hours in the suburbs would rattle his nearly perfect world?

"Good luck," Beth called as her son gathered his gear and ran off to join his teammates.

Todd glanced around at the crowd. "There are a lot of people here."

Beth nodded glumly. "The baseball games are very popular. Todd's a freshman at Clements High School. This is Texas and we take all high school sports very seriously. You should see the crowd at football games."

Todd said something else, but she wasn't listening to him. As she stepped onto the ground and reached back for her purse, she wondered, for the thousandth time, what on earth she'd been thinking when she invited Todd to share her world for a day. Especially here!

She knew practically all the parents of Matt's teammates. She had brought a strange man to what was considered a family event. It wasn't just that she would be fielding dozens of questions today, it was that come Monday morning, her phone would be ringing off the hook. Word was going to spread like kudzu and she didn't have a clue as to what she was going to say to anyone.

"You said something about concessions," Todd said as he came around the rear of the vehicle to join her.

"The coordinator is right over there." She pointed to her right and started in that direction.

She thought about giving Todd an out. If she worked and he simply went up in the stands to watch the game, no one would know whom he was with. But she doubted he would agree to that, and she wasn't about to explain why it was a great idea. He wouldn't understand, she would look foolish and—why on earth hadn't she thought this through?

It was a warm, sunny day. The temperature would hit the high eighties, with humidity to match. She fingered her hair and knew that by the middle of the afternoon, it would be completely flat. She would get flushed in the heat, her

T-shirt would droop in a most unattractive way. If nothing else, she would probably scare Todd into abandoning her.

A small child ran between them, followed by her mother. Beth sidestepped to let them past. Todd glanced at them over his shoulder.

"This is a dangerous place," he said. "I don't want to lose you." With that, he took her hand in his.

He might have continued talking. Beth wasn't sure. She was too busy screaming inside her head. *Ohmigosh! Another man is holding my hand!*

Another man was really touching her hand. She could feel Todd's warm flesh against hers, the way his fingers cupped her hand, the feel of his palm. She could feel herself hyperventilating as heat spread through her body. Embarrassment heat, not oh-I-love-what-you're-doing heat. They were walking through the parking lot, holding hands.

She couldn't do this. In some circles, the whole dating-hand holding thing was no big deal. But this wasn't those circles, this was her very small life. She'd only ever held hands with Darren. After nearly twenty years with his fingers lacing with hers, this felt too strange. It was too sudden, and what if someone noticed?

"Are those the concession stands?" Todd asked.

Beth could only nod mutely. She wished she could die. She wished she could run back to her car and never be seen in public again. She wished—

The change in heat caught her attention first and broke through her thoughts. Heat that climbed from that hand up her arm. Heat as in, maybe this wasn't so bad. She wouldn't go so far as to say she *liked* it, but the contact wasn't hideous. She ignored the faint sense of being disloyal and focused on the warmth, the way Todd's arm brushed against hers. A part of her was pleased to be half of a couple again, if only for a few minutes.

When they reached the main concession stand, Todd released her. Instead of relief, Beth felt a sense of loss. She wanted him to touch her again. She'd been so caught up in the shock of what was happening that she felt as if she'd lost the opportunity to absorb the good stuff.

"Hi, Sharon," she said, and smiled at the harried-looking blonde setting up the popcorn machine.

"Beth, you're early. Thank you for being so diligent. I'm desperate. The Morrisons' got called out of town so I'm short a couple of bodies."

"It just so happens I brought an extra one with me. Todd, this is Sharon. She's the head of the concession committee."

Sharon glanced up briefly, got an eyeful of Todd, then abandoned the popcorn machine to give him her full attention. "Hi. You must be…"

Todd held out his hand. "A friend of the family. Nice to meet you."

Sharon shot Beth a look that warned her she would be getting a phone call next week. "The cotton candy machine takes a little getting used to so I'm going to need Beth to handle that for me. I can give you a choice between hot dogs and ices."

"Ices sound fun."

Beth thought about warning him that ices came in various flavors, which meant working with syrups that were not only sticky but that stained hands. Then she decided he would figure it out himself, like the other parents had.

Sharon gave them trays with singles and coins for making change, then sent them to their respective booths.

"I'll see you in a couple of hours," he said, making it sound like he was really going to miss her. Boy, was he ever good.

"Have fun. I'll be right across from you, so yell if you need anything."

Beth walked over to the small cart she would be manning. The father there gave her a grateful smile. From the wisps of spun sugar clinging to everything, this was his first time.

"The trick," Beth told him, "is to not let it get away from you. Keep turning it at a steady pace."

The man grinned. "The trick is to take hot dogs next time, or be out of town."

Beth laughed. She glanced up and saw Todd watching her. He wiggled his eyebrows at her. Maybe this wasn't going to be so bad, she told herself. At least the view was terrific.

An hour later, she knew her first instincts had been right. Bringing Todd to the game had been a terrible error in judgment.

"How's it going?"

Beth finished making change with a family she'd just served, then turned and found Cindy leaning against a corner of the cart.

"If this thing had a wall, I'd be beating my head against it," Beth told her.

"A lot of questions?"

"People I barely know are coming up and asking about Todd. I feel like I'm on display at the zoo. 'Come see the newest exhibit. A widowed mother of two and a single man.'"

Cindy smiled. "Now you know what I went through when Mike was first staying with me. You're just dating. I had a wounded bodyguard living in my house."

Beth thought about that time in Cindy's life and winced as she remembered her own teasing comments. "Did I ever apologize for some of the things I said?" she asked.

"Nope."

"Is it too late to do that now?"

"Absolutely. I don't want an apology, I want my pound of flesh. I plan to torment you at least twice as much."

"Great."

Cindy touched her arm. "Don't take it so hard. Todd looks like he's having a good time."

Beth followed her gaze and saw the man in question chatting with some older boys. They were probably on the varsity team and wouldn't play until later. As if he felt her attention, he glanced up and gave her a quick smile. It wasn't as shocking as when he'd held her hand, but it still sent heat through her...all the way down to her knees, which threatened to knock together.

"He's too good-looking," she said. "This entire situation would be easier if he was ugly."

"I'm sure he'll be thrilled to hear that."

Beth shook her head. "I'm not kidding. Look at him. He's got those ruggedly handsome good looks. He's tall, with an amazing body."

"All the better to see him naked."

Beth grimaced. "Perish the thought. I couldn't take my clothes off in front of him. If I ever have sex again I want it to be with a nearsighted sailor from the merchant marines, or maybe a guy in a submarine. Some male who hasn't been close to a woman in three or four years. That way he'll be so grateful, he won't care what I look like."

"Wouldn't it be easier to work on your self-esteem?" Cindy asked.

"It took me thirty-eight years to get this messed up. You think I can fix it in time to interest Todd?"

"Are you going to let him get away because you're afraid to flash your stretch marks?"

"If you're going to be logical, I'm not going to be your friend."

Cindy leaned toward her. "I'm pointing out that we don't always get to pick who we fall in love with."

"Love?" Beth took a step back. "I don't even know if I like the man. We're not dating. He's just in my world for a day. Then he'll be gone."

"And if he isn't?"

Beth didn't have an answer for that. Todd had to leave. She couldn't exist in his world and she wasn't prepared to have him in hers.

"I'm not ready to start dating," she said.

"Too late. You already are."

Chapter Seven

Todd stretched back on the lounge chair and took a deep breath. "I hate to admit it, but you're right."

Beth sat on a matching chair to his right. Light spilled out from the kitchen and family room windows and there were a few floodlights in the plants surrounding the pool, but most of the area was in semidarkness. He thought about looking at his watch to check the time, but that would involve raising his wrist and he was way too tired. He guessed it was around seven-thirty in the evening.

"About dinner?" she asked.

"About everything. I've had a great time today, but I'm worn-out."

"Gee, and here I'd had my heart set on dancing."

He looked at her. "I didn't know you still wanted to go out. I brought a suit. I can be ready in about ten minutes."

She waved a hand at him. "Down, soldier, I was kidding. I'm as tired as you are. Right now I just want to lay here and relax. If only I had servants. One of them could come rub my feet.''

"I don't mind doing that for you.''

He'd known the comment would embarrass her, but he couldn't resist making it. Beth was an odd combination of a grown-up his own age and an innocent young woman. She had wit and intelligence, but he could make her blush without any effort.

"Yes, well, isn't that nice of you to offer." She cleared her throat. "Maybe next time.''

"I'll remember that.''

He heard a faint, strangled sound and smiled in the darkness. Another direct hit, although the best one had been when he'd taken her hand earlier that day. His action had been instinctive, but Beth had reacted as if he'd suddenly stripped off all his clothes and danced around naked. She'd tried to hide her shock, but her wide-eyed gaze and blushing cheeks had given her away. Her insecurities only made him like her more. He wanted to stay close enough to protect her from the dangerous men out there. Unfortunately, most people would say he then had to protect her from himself.

"I don't think you'd enjoy being seen with me tonight,'' he said, returning to a safer topic of conversation. "What with me turning into a Smurf and all." He glanced down at his stained fingers. So far, three thorough washings hadn't made the color fade in the least.

She laughed. "I thought about warning you that the ice flavors stained, but I didn't.''

"Thanks. So my choices were the hot dog stand and sweating in the heat, or blue hands.''

"They look cute.''

"I'm sure my entire staff will share your opinion, and they won't bother to keep it to themselves.''

"Do you want another drink?" she asked.

"No thanks. I'm fine."

He was, too. The day had left him pleasantly tired. "I had a good time," he told her. "The gardening was interesting. I might have to get a couple of plants for my patio. I enjoyed the baseball game, but next time I want to watch Matt play more."

He'd been relieved for a couple of innings, long enough to see Matt hit in the winning run. Despite his short acquaintance with the boy, he'd felt a swell of pride, as if he'd had something to do with the kid's success.

"The pool party was a shock," Beth said.

"It was loud," he admitted. Matt and his friends had yelled and shouted as they dive-bombed each other in the cool water. "Next time I'll bring a suit so I can join them."

"Oh, you should."

He glanced to his right. Beth's voice had sounded a little strange. "You all right?"

"Oh, fine. Perfectly fine." She cleared her throat. "I could order take-out. There's pizza or Chinese. They both deliver."

He sat up and faced her. After leaning forward, he grabbed her lounge chair and tugged until it was close to his, then he stretched out again. He slipped his hand down next to hers and laced their fingers together. "Better," he said. "Now what was your question?"

"T-take-out," she stuttered.

He grinned. "I'm not hungry. I ate too many bagels while the guys were swimming. But we can order something for you if you'd like."

"No, I'm fine."

She didn't sound fine. She sounded incredibly nervous. Todd liked that he got to her. He also knew he was walking a very narrow line. While he was confident that Beth liked him and found him attractive, he also knew she felt completely out of her league with him. He made her nervous. She'd survived without a man in her life for nearly two years and from what he would tell, she wasn't interested in having one around now. If he pushed her too far or too fast, she would simple run away.

He didn't want to lose her. Insanity perhaps, but the truth.

"Tell me about your marriage," he said, surprising both her and himself with the request.

"What do you want to know?"

What did he want to know? A list of Darren's flaws would be nice. Maybe a hint that he'd been a smuggler or had laundered money in the back room. "Tell me how you met."

"In high school," she said, confirming what her son had already told him. "He was a couple of years older than me. I was a lowly sophomore while he was a senior. I'd never really been out on a date or anything. I knew who he was and I liked him, but I didn't know how to meet him. Then I found out he tutored other students. Darren was always kind of nerdy."

He heard the smile in her voice. She was lost in a past he could neither share nor understand. He wanted to call her back, to remind her that she was with him, not her husband, but he'd been the one to pick the topic of conversation. Besides, for reasons he didn't understand, he really wanted to know.

"I told my parents I was having trouble in algebra and asked for a couple of tutoring sessions. As I'd always been a good student, they were happy to help. I felt terribly guilty about the whole thing and ended up confessing the truth to Darren during our first study session."

"What did he do?"

She laughed. "He stared at me for a long time, then asked me to the Homecoming Dance. We were together from then on. When he went away to college, I still had two years of high school left. He was on scholarship and had to keep up his grades, but we saw each other as much as we could. I joined him at his college after I graduated. We were married the following summer. I was nineteen and he was twenty-one."

She sighed. "Being married wasn't the fairy tale I thought it would be, but we muddled along. When I think about how young we both were, it's amazing we made it work at all. After he graduated from college, he wanted to go on to get his master's degree. But he didn't have a scholarship for that. We took out some student loans and I went to work."

"You didn't finish college?"

"No. I always meant to go back, but then Darren got a great job and we decided to start our family. I thought there would be time later. Now it doesn't seem to matter anymore." She chuckled. "If you repeat that last statement to either of my children, I'll deny it. I keep telling them how important a college education is. If we hadn't practically paid off this house and had a great life insurance policy on Darren, I would have needed that degree to help me get a decent job."

"I won't say a word," he promised, relieved to have the question of her finances answered.

"Am I boring you?" she asked. "I don't know how to tell you about Darren without chronicling our past. If you're interested in what he was like as a person, that's different. He was a good man. Kind. He loved the kids. He never got over being a nerd, but I always thought that was kind of charming."

"You've answered my question," he said, wishing she

would stop with the praising. Inadequacy was an unfamiliar sensation. "I can't relate to anything you've said," he admitted. "It's like hearing a story, not someone's life."

"I guess it is different from what you're used it. Hearing about your life would be as strange for me. Everyone I know has a somewhat similar history. People fall in love, get married, have children. When part of that disappears, it leaves everything out of focus."

Her hand still pressed against his. She was close to him, physically, but he sensed she had, in her heart, left him behind. She was caught up in a past he couldn't understand.

"You still miss him very much." It wasn't a question.

"Yes. Every day. I loved him. I've always believed there was one great love for each of us, and mine was Darren. Oh, we fought and irritated each other, but none of that mattered. We had the same view of life and we wanted the same things. I can't imagine loving anyone else."

Todd stared up at the sky. Her belief in one great love for each person was one more love than he was willing to believe in.

"Tell me about your family," he said.

She laughed. "It's even more boring than my life with Darren. I have two sisters. One lives in Ohio near my folks. My other sister moved to Alaska with her husband. We talk on the phone, exchange cards at holidays, but we don't see each other very much. My parents are still married to each other. Dad worked for the postal service and Mom was a schoolteacher. What about you?"

"My family is nothing like yours," he told her. "I'm technically an only child, but all that means is that while my mother and father were married to each other, they didn't give birth to any other children. However they each had many children with other partners."

"How many times were they married?"

"I've lost count. Dad's pushing eight or nine and I think my mother hit six with her last marriage, but I'm not sure."

Beth's hand tightened around his. "I'm sorry."

"You don't have to be. It's all I know. One of the reasons I never wanted to get married was because I didn't want to get started playing that game."

"You don't believe it can be forever?"

"I've never seen a relationship that lasted more than five or six years."

"Except for a couple of friends who had their husbands walk out on them, I've never seen one fail. If Darren hadn't died, he and I would still be together."

The thought was disquieting to say the least, Todd thought. If Beth's husband hadn't died, then he wouldn't be with her tonight. He would never had met her at all.

They were silent for a while, then Beth asked, "What did you think of your day in the suburbs?"

"I liked it."

"What would you have done today if you hadn't come here? If we'd never met. "

He looked at her. She'd turned in her chair so she was facing him. The light spilling out of the house caught the side of her cheek and illuminated her pale skin. He wanted to touch her there, trace the curve, then slide his fingers through her hair. He had a feeling that if he did, she would run screaming for cover. With Beth he was going to have to take things slowly. A startling revelation, he thought. It implied they were going to have a relationship. Is that what he wanted?

"I would have worked in the morning, played golf in the afternoon, then probably gone out on date tonight."

"With one of your blondes?" she teased.

"Of course. Although I happen to be between women right now."

"How convenient." She wrinkled her nose. "Do you cruise the community colleges? I mean they are the right age there and you do like young, pretty women."

"I suppose I should be grateful you didn't say it the other way. 'Pretty young women.'"

"But that's what I meant."

"I know. You're not very subtle."

"I can be."

He chuckled. "When?"

"I just can if I want to."

"I don't believe you."

They were flirting and he had a feeling she didn't have a clue as to what was happening between them. He recognized the attraction. It was fueled by her uniqueness and the fact that he sensed he could talk to her about anything.

"Why so young?" she asked. "Wrinkles aren't contagious."

"It's not about looks."

"Oh, please, of course it is."

"No, it's about…" He frowned. "I don't know why I date women in their early twenties. One of my theories is that while I've gotten older, the women I see have stayed the same age."

"There's also the whole issue of winning," Beth said. "You're a rich, powerful man. You can flaunt that by attracting a beautiful younger woman."

He didn't like the direction this conversation was going. "You've been reading those women's magazines, haven't you? They always get guys into trouble."

"I think men get into trouble just fine on their own. They don't need any help." She tucked her free hand under her cheek. "I think you should consider going out with women your own age. You might like it."

If she was anyone but herself, he would have thought

the comment was a come-on. But she was Beth and that wouldn't have occurred to her. "You could be right."

He stared into her eyes. In the darkness, they were a dark, indeterminate color. He wanted to move closer and lose himself inside of her. Not just sexually, although he had a feeling that was going to be very nice, too, but emotionally. He who never trusted anyone, least of all a woman, thought he might be able to trust this one.

The thought scared the hell out of him.

"It's getting late," he said, releasing her hand and sitting up. "I should head back to the city."

"Okay. I'll walk you out."

The words fell out of Beth's mouth before she could call them back. That voice in her head started shrieking again. She couldn't walk Todd out. They were alone, it was nighttime, he might think this was a real date. She couldn't deal with that. Or any of it.

She stood up and led the way through the house, thinking that when the brochure came in August for adult classes at the local community college and high school, she was going to have to bypass things like cooking and decorating and concentrate on the male-female stuff. Maybe there was a class on how to date the second time around. Or maybe she should just return to her quietly fulfilling life and pretend she didn't mind being lonely.

"This has been really great," she said as they approached the front door. "Thanks for all your help with the planting and at the game. It was nice. Great weather, too. It's tough when it's this hot and it's only going to get worse."

"Beth?"

"The pool party went well, too, don't you think?" she went on, ignoring him. "Matt always has a good time with his friends and—"

"Beth!"

His voice sounded insistent this time so she pressed her lips together to stop the flow of words. "I'm babbling," she said. "It happens."

"Only when you're nervous."

She wanted to protest, but it was the truth. "How did you know that?"

"I know a lot about you."

If he was trying to make her feel better, he was failing. They'd reached the front door. She stopped and stared at the oak and glass. All she had to do was open the door and he would leave. It was so simple. She reached for the handle. He grabbed her hand and pulled her around until she was facing him. She didn't dare look at his face so she fixed her gaze on his throat. He had a very nice throat.

"Not so fast," he told her.

Oh, God.

He placed his hands on her shoulders. "I'm going to kiss you and you're going to like it."

He paused as if expecting her to speak. She couldn't speak. She was lucky to be breathing. Kissing? She was not ready for kissing. She didn't think she wanted to kiss anyone but Darren, although she liked Todd and he was very good-looking and it might not be too hideous, but she was bound to mess up, and then what would he think of her and—

"Stop!" he said. "You're thinking too much. Just relax."

"Relaxing is not possible," she told him.

"It's just a kiss. I'm not going to dismember you."

"I think that would be easier to deal with."

"Fine, then close your eyes and keep breathing."

Her heart was pounding so hard, she thought it might leave bruises on the inside of her chest. Her hands curled into fists, she tightened her stomach, then slowly closed her eyes.

She wanted to scream that he couldn't do this to her. Then she wanted to scream that he'd better do it fast because she was going to throw up. Then he kissed her.

She felt a soft brush against her lips. Not too quick, not too slow, just a gentle contact that was over before she'd actually registered what was going on.

Her eyes popped open. He was smiling at her. "How was that?" he asked.

"Not horrible," she said, pleased that it hadn't been gross. "I didn't really feel anything. I'm sort of shut down physically. I saw a family counselor after Darren died. Actually the kids and I went for a few months. Anyway, she said it would be hard to start dating and that sexually I would be sort of backward for a while. Not really connecting with my body."

He looked as if he was in pain. Beth replayed what she'd just blurted out. She felt yet another blush climbing her cheeks. "More than you wanted to know, huh? I'm sorry."

"No, it's fine. But maybe you could not think so much."

Not think? How was she supposed to do that? Still she nodded her agreement and waited. Were they done?

"You want to try that again?" he asked.

No. Yes. She waved vaguely with one hand.

"Just as I thought," he said, and bent toward her.

Beth closed her eyes again. This time, the kiss wasn't so brief, although it was as gentle. His mouth pressed against hers. She could feel the warmth of his skin, the firm smoothness. One of his arms slipped around her back and he drew her closer to him. She allowed herself to relax enough to move into him, even as the analytical part of brain cataloged his every action.

There was the scent of his body—masculine and pleasing. The heat he generated, the breadth of his chest and how he was much taller. Tentatively she rested one of her hands on his shoulder. He was strong. She could feel the muscles bunching there.

His mouth moved back and forth. With sudden clarity she knew that what happened next was up to her. Todd was a gentleman and based on what he knew about her history, or lack thereof, he wouldn't push her. If she stopped things now, he would accept that. However, if she didn't...

A faint tingle tickled at the base of her spine. If she didn't stop him, he would go on kissing her. Would she like it? She sort of liked it now, although she couldn't really feel what he was doing. Oh, all the tactile sensations were there, but none of the sensuousness. A part of her had gone into hibernation when Darren had died and she hadn't experienced springtime yet. Part of her body was still sleeping. Looks like it was going to take more than one kiss to wake her up.

"Wow," he said when he pulled back. "You kiss great."

She wanted to return the compliment. She wanted to feel enough to be able to say "Wow" back to him. "Thanks" was the best she could do.

His gaze turned knowing. "Don't give up on us, Beth. We're just at the beginning."

He cupped her face in his strong hands and kissed her again. This time his tongue teased at her lower lip. She definitely felt that tingling again. It moved up her spine and drifted through her chest. Involuntarily her mouth opened. He slipped inside.

Her breath caught. Another man's tongue was in her mouth. He stroked her slowly, gently, circling. She felt more tingles and a prickling sensation. This was starting to get interesting. Tentatively she kissed him back.

Something tightened low in her belly. She felt a jolt of heat, then the dam burst. Sensation and need and fire raced through her, consuming her. She lost the ability to think and breathe. All she could do was hang on as he kissed her deeply.

She wanted.

After so many months of being dead, she was alive again. When he hauled her closer, she went willingly, raising herself on tiptoe, desperate to be next to him.

The kiss went on until the rest of the world disappeared. Until all she could do was be with him. Hunger filled her. Hunger and desperation.

One of his hands cupped her rear. Instinctively she arched toward him and felt the ridge of his desire pressing against her. He was hard and she liked it. She wanted…

More. And that realization terrified her.

Beth pushed on his chest and took a step back at the same time. The sound of their heavy breathing filled the quiet of the night. What had just happened? How had she gotten so turned on? She could feel the dampness of her panties, not to mention the ache in her breasts. The passion was as unexpected as it was unfamiliar. She'd always enjoyed making love with Darren. Their sex life had been great. While he'd initiated their intimacy enough that she rarely found herself in a position of wanting him, there had been a few times when she'd been in the mood.

But she'd never once been on fire before. The hot, animal need frightened her. If she hadn't gotten scared and pulled back when she did, who knows what might have happened. Even thinking about him on top of her, inside of her, made her want to run for cover…and rip off her clothes. What was wrong with her?

"You okay?" Todd asked.

She nodded. "Fine. I guess I wasn't prepared for that."

"It was nice."

Nice? How about life changing? How about incredible? How about terrifying? "Sure. Nice."

"Next weekend is my turn," he said.

That got her attention. She blinked at him. "What are you talking about?"

"You showed me your world, now I want to show you mine."

She wasn't interested in his world. She wasn't interested in him. She flinched, half expecting to be struck by lightning. Okay, maybe she was a little interested, but she couldn't do this. Not with him. If she ever started dating, she wanted it to be with an average guy who was a little boring. Someone she wouldn't care about too much. Someone safe. Not a handsome hunk who made her go up in flames.

"Why do you want to see me again?" she asked, hoping she didn't sound as scared and confused as she felt. "We're not going to date."

"Why not?"

She stared at him. "I'm not your type."

"My type just took a turn for the better. We like each other, we have fun together. There's plenty of passion." He grinned. "Why wouldn't I want to go out with you?"

"I'm too old."

"You're the perfect age."

"I can't do this."

Instead of answering, he moved close and kissed her again. Her body responded with a speed that left her hungry and breathless. She was shivering with need when he pulled away.

"I *will* see you again," he promised.

"No, I—"

He cut her off with another hard, fast kiss, then he was gone…leaving her alone and panting.

"Let me see if I understand this," Cindy said the next afternoon as she measured dressing for the potato salad. "You're not going to see Todd again because you like him and his kisses make you hot."

"Exactly."

Beth had spent the last thirty minutes bringing her friend up-to-date on all that had happened the previous day. The two women were working together in Cindy's kitchen. She and Mike were hosting a barbecue for a dozen or so close friends. Beth glanced at the clock. Company was due to start arriving any minute.

"Beth, you're crazy."

"No, I'm not. Todd is too risky for me."

"Because you like him?"

"Yes. I can't take the thought of falling for him. Besides, it's wrong."

"Why is going out with him wrong?"

Beth couldn't believe she had to explain this. "It's so obvious. I'm married."

Cindy groaned in exasperation. "You're widowed. You're allowed to date. I think it would be healthy for you to have a personal life that didn't involve your children."

Beth didn't want logic or good advice, she wanted sympathy. "He's too different."

"That's not a bad thing. If they aren't much alike, you won't get the two men confused in your mind."

"There's nothing to be confused about. I'm not getting involved with Todd. I'll admit that this experience has shown me that maybe it's time to start thinking about dating. So I will think about it."

"For years."

Beth shook her head. "I need a couple of months to get used to the idea, then I'll do something. I promise. Just not with Todd."

Cindy stared at her. "You must have it bad if you're running so scared."

"I should hate the way you can read me, but I suppose it's one of the reasons we're such good friends." Beth finished slicing the tomatoes and moved on to the cucumbers. "I had my chance at love and I don't get to do that again. I believe that everyone gets one shot. I've had mine and I was really happy. There's no point in trying to make something work that's doomed from the start."

"That is ridiculous," Cindy said. "There are many chances at love in life, but I'm not going to argue that point with you. Let's say your ideas are correct and there is only one great love for each person. For you, that was Darren, right?"

Beth nodded.

"So you can't fall in love with Todd?"

Beth hesitated. According to her own theory, that was right. So why was the question difficult to answer? "No," she said at last. "I can't love him."

"Then what's the problem? If you're not going to fall in love, then you're not at risk. You can go out with him, get the experience you need, then move on."

"You make it sound so simple."

"It is."

Beth leaned her elbows on the counter. "Today I picked up one of Jodi's teen magazines and took the quiz. According to my score, I have a major crush on Todd. Therefore I'm vulnerable. I don't want to start something I'm not ready for, and I don't want to get hurt. Why would a man like him want me? I'm nearly twice the age of the women he dates, I have two teenage children. We travel in completely different circles."

"Seems to me you've thought of everything," Cindy said. She smiled. "With all that stacked against you, I doubt he'll pursue you."

"That's what I think," Beth said, then wondered why the thought didn't make her happy. "And it's unlikely we'll run into each other anywhere."

"Right." Cindy's smile broadened. "Beth? You might want to turn around."

Beth did so. She kept turning until she was facing Cindy's backyard. Several guests had arrived. Mike was getting them drinks. A lone man stood by the pool. He looked very familiar. He looked very much like Todd.

"I guess I forgot to mention the fact that he called Mike earlier today," Cindy said smugly. "When he heard about the barbecue, he invited himself."

Chapter Eight

Even from across the patio, Todd could see the look of surprise and dismay on Beth's face. Maybe this hadn't been a good idea. Maybe he'd been wrong in his assumption that she would have been thinking about him as much as he'd been thinking about her. In the past twenty-plus hours, he hadn't been able to get her out of his head. He kept thinking about things she'd said, how she'd looked, how he'd felt when he'd kissed her.

He'd called Mike Blackburne to find out more about Beth. The man hadn't wanted to discuss his wife's best friend until Todd had admitted his personal interest. Then Mike had mentioned the barbecue and Todd had asked to be included. Had that been a mistake?

It couldn't be, he told himself. Yesterday had been one of the best times he'd had in years. He'd actually kissed a woman to the point of desperately wanting her, then he'd walked away. Had he ever done that before in his life? Yet with Beth, the restraint had felt right. He'd enjoyed wanting her, even though it had kept him up half the night. She wasn't the kind of woman a man slept with on the first date. He was going to have to earn her. He found himself looking forward to the challenge...and his inevitable victory.

Beth left the house and headed toward him. He met her by the pool and grinned. "You turn up in the strangest places," he said. Her expression was two parts welcoming, one part cautious. He liked the odds.

"I could say the same thing about you. This is hardly your style."

"Maybe I'm changing."

"I don't think so." She studied him. "So what *are* you doing here?"

"Hanging out with friends."

"Except for me, and possibly Mike, you don't know anyone here."

"Aren't you my friend?"

She paused. She wore shorts and a T-shirt, as she had the day before. Today her top and bottoms were both white. She looked pretty with her wide blue eyes and short red hair. Her mouth turned up at the corners. "You sound like Mr. Rogers. 'Will you be my friend?'"

"In a heartbeat," he said, leaning close and lowering his voice. "I'm not here to invade your world or to make you uncomfortable. I just wanted to see you again. I can't stop thinking about you, about what happened yesterday."

A visible tremor swept through her. Until that moment, he hadn't really been thinking about their hot kisses at her front door, but with them obviously on her mind, he found himself reliving them, too.

"I actually meant spending time together. The talking

and laughing, but now that you mention it, the kissing was also great.''

She swallowed. ''I didn't mention the kissing.''

''You didn't have to. You were thinking about it.''

''How did you know that?''

There were several other couples around them. They were on the Blackburnes' patio in full view of invited guests and neighbors. Yet he couldn't help moving closer and touching her cheek. ''I know,'' he said. ''I watch, I listen, I pay attention. You matter to me.''

She shivered again. ''Why me?''

''Why not you?''

''We've been over this. I'm not anyone you would want.''

''You couldn't be more wrong.''

He read the confusion in her face. It was time to pull back. He'd already figured out that if he pushed her too far, too fast, he would lose her. Better to go slow. Beth had been in mourning for so long, she'd forgotten how to live any other way. He could afford to give her space and time because there wasn't any direct competition. Just her fear of him and of the situation.

''Do you want something to drink?'' he asked.

She looked surprised at the sudden topic change, then nodded. ''A beer, please.''

He collected two bottles, then returned to her side. She still looked dazed by all that had happened, so he led her to a couple of plastic chairs in the corner and sat her down. Some neighbors of Cindy and Mike's joined them. Introductions were made. Todd explained his presence as a ''friend of the family'' then went out of his way to be charming and friendly. He was determined to show Beth that he could fit into her happy world.

If a voice in his head occasionally asked why he was

bothering with this particular woman, he pushed the question away. He didn't have an answer yet. All he knew was that when he was with her, he felt as if he'd finally found a place in which he could belong. With Beth he was home.

"That was very nice," Beth said a couple of hours later when they left the barbecue together. At least she thought it had been nice. Much of the evening had passed in a blur for her, as if she were watching events through a layer of glass and water. She could hear everything said and respond appropriately, but she didn't feel as if she was actually there.

It was all Todd's fault. He'd invaded her life and she didn't know how to make him go away. Worse, she wasn't sure she wanted to. Nothing made sense to her. She believed that she had a crush on the man, which was scary and left her feeling exposed. She didn't for a moment fool herself into thinking she was more than a passing amusement for him. Any second now he would get tired of her company and disappear. She wanted him gone—he wasn't right for her. But the thought of him leaving made her anxious.

She couldn't remember ever being so confused. She wanted him around and she didn't want him around. Maybe she was just too old to be starting over in the dating game.

They walked across the street and paused in front of her house. All night Todd had been at her side, bringing her food, chatting with her friends, and generally being a wonderful companion. She knew that he was winning her over. What she didn't know was what he expected now.

Were they going to kiss? She was embarrassed to admit that she wanted them to. She wanted to feel his arms around her, pulling her close. She wanted his mouth on hers and his hands everywhere and the fire tearing through her as they—

"Beth?"

"Huh?" She blinked several times to bring him back into focus. "What?"

"We're just standing on the sidewalk. Is something wrong?"

She glanced up at her house. "No. Everything is fine. But it's Sunday evening and my kids are home." She wasn't sure if she was warning him away or offering him an excuse to leave.

"Great." He looked at his watch. "It's still early. Will they be up?"

"Yes."

"Then let's go inside. I want to get to know your children better."

He led the way up the driveway, toward the rear of the house. She trailed after him. "I thought men were supposed to be afraid of women with children, especially teenagers. I know my kids are great, but you don't."

"Sure I do," he said as he opened the back door and motioned for her to enter first. "I had a nice talk with Matt yesterday. I'm sure your daughter is as terrific."

Maybe he was from another planet, she thought, knowing that there had to be some explanation for his behavior and comments. No man was this good. At least not in her limited experience. And even if he was being completely honest, she wasn't ever this lucky. She had a good life, but she'd had to work for it. Some times had been hard. So what exactly was going on with Todd?

"It's me," Beth called as she stepped into the house. Both her kids were in the kitchen, about to make popcorn. "Todd was at the barbecue, too. I brought him back for a little bit."

"Hi," he said as he stopped next to her. "Matt, Jodi. Good to see you again."

Her children greeted him, then looked at her with surprised expressions. She didn't know what to tell them. One minute they'd been at Cindy and Mike's house, the next they were here.

Her sixteen-year-old daughter must have decided Todd's presence was a good thing. She smiled at him. "We're going to watch a movie and we're having the usual discussion on caramel versus regular popcorn. Do you want to have a vote?"

"How about making both and mixing them together."

Jodi looked at Matt who gave her a thumbs-up.

"Okay with you, Mom?" Jodi asked.

"Sure. Did you two eat?"

Matt kept glancing at Todd. "Yeah. The chicken pasta salad you made this afternoon. It was good. Did anybody bring their kids?"

Beth had invited her children along to the barbecue, but both had declined. They knew from experience that these kind of events rarely included anyone their age.

"No. You were right." As Matt came around the counter and walked past her, she ruffled his hair. "As usual."

He grinned at her. "I'm a guy. I'm used to it."

Todd winked. "Enjoy that feeling, Matt. As you get older you'll realize that women are right a lot more often than any of us would like to admit."

"No way," Matt said with all the confidence of a fourteen-year-old.

"Way," Todd promised. "You're in for a rude awakening, my man."

Some of the wariness Beth had noticed in her son the previous day seemed to have faded. "Do you like science fiction?" he asked. "We rented a movie called *Stargate.*

It's a really cool story about this device that lets you travel across the galaxy to another planet in about thirty seconds. It's kinda Egyptian there and there's this weird-looking bad guy who looks a little like a girl, but isn't.''

Beth left them talking and walked into the kitchen. Jodi had already put the regular bag of popcorn into the microwave and was reading the directions for the caramel corn.

"You didn't say Todd was going to be over at Cindy's,'' Jodi said, her voice low.

"I didn't know,'' Beth admitted. "Apparently he heard about the party and asked to be included.''

Jodi sighed. "It's very romantic.''

Beth found it more terrifying than romantic, but she didn't say that to her daughter. Teenagers needed their illusions. Sort of like Matt's firm belief that he would always be more right than any woman in his life.

"What would you two like to drink?'' she called into the family room.

"Soda's fine,'' Todd answered.

"Same for me,'' Matt told her.

She collected glasses and filled them with ice, then loaded cans of soda onto the tray and carried everything into the family room. As usual, Matt was sprawled out on the floor. Jodi's books spilled out of the green wing chair in the corner, which left only the sofa. Todd had settled there, not quite in the middle, but certainly not all the way to one side. Which meant she was going to have to sit next to him.

"Thanks, Mom,'' Matt said when she handed him his drink.

"Ditto,'' Todd said as he took a glass. "Not the Mom part, though. My feelings are not the least bit maternal.''

Light flashed in his blue-gray eyes. Light and desire and a thousand promises she didn't have the courage to believe.

She could feel the heat beginning inside of her. It started at her toes and worked its way to her feminine place, then up to her breasts and then to her face until she felt flushed all over. She hoped her children were too interested in Todd to notice her physical reaction to the situation...and his nearness.

When the drinks were served, she had no choice but to settle on the sofa. She sat a little more toward her side than in the center. Not that he was going to try anything with both her children in the room. Not that she even wanted him to, although it would be kind of nice to be close for a while.

"Hurry up, Jo," Matt called. He started the tape, fast-forwarded through the previews, then paused at the beginning of the movie.

"I'm coming."

She walked into the family room carrying three bowls of popcorn. She handed one to her brother, placed a second between Beth and Todd and carried the third to her wing chair.

Over the opening music, Beth leaned close. "You don't have to stay if you don't want to," she whispered.

"I want to be here," he told her. "Is that a problem?"

"No." Her voice was small and shaky. She hoped he didn't notice that or her nervousness. For once she couldn't dig into the popcorn, although the mixture looked tasty. She couldn't concentrate on the plot or the characters, either. All she could think about was Todd sitting next to her.

After he'd crunched his way through about half the bowl of popcorn, he moved it to the coffee table in front of them. As he sat back, he shifted a little closer and rested his hand on top of hers.

Beth resisted the urge to scream. She didn't look at him, didn't acknowledge the contact in any way. She did try to keep breathing and to pretend to be calm. Then she glanced at each of her children. They were both engrossed in the story and didn't seem to notice the amazing thing happening right in front of them.

The heat inside of her intensified. She recognized the flames of desire, flames that until yesterday she'd only read about in books. With Darren the sexual wanting had been different. More quiet and steady. It was the difference between dependable heat and an out-of-control, raging fire. She'd never spent much time wanting Darren in her bed. She hadn't imagined them making love, him touching her or holding her.

Unfortunately, in the past twenty-four hours, she hadn't been able to get that image—and Todd—out of her mind. She wanted him. She wanted them to be together. Which was completely insane. She was not going to have sex with him.

Maybe all this heat was just a hot flash, she told herself. Maybe she was starting the change early. But the thought died as quickly as it had come to her. She knew the truth. It was definitely biology, but not that kind. It wasn't about age, it was about the man sitting next to her.

He turned her hand until her palm faced up, then he laced their fingers together. Beth wanted to moan. This was so much worse than high school when her parents had been in the next room. She had to make him stop, or ask him to leave or something.

Before she could open her mouth, Matt made a comment about the movie. Todd responded and they were off and running, comparing different science-fiction worlds and stories, arguing about which was more "real."

When Beth was close to exploding, she jumped to her feet. "Who wants more to drink?" she asked.

"I'm fine," Matt said.

"Me, too," echoed her daughter.

Beth looked at Jodi in time to see the teenager smiling at her. Great, now she was entertaining her children with her dating practices.

When she resumed her seat, Todd again took her hand. She told herself she hated it, that she didn't want him touching her. It wasn't much of a lie and she didn't bother spending any time paying attention to it.

She suffered in silence until finally the movie was over. Todd rose to his feet and stretched. "That was great," he said. "Thanks for including me." Before Beth could stand, he leaned down and kissed her cheek. "I know they have school tomorrow, so I don't want to stay too long. I'll show myself out."

"But..." She got up and trailed after him. "You're leaving?"

"I'll be in touch," he promised.

But she'd planned on walking him to his car. Weren't they going to kiss again, like last night?

"Bye," he said, and was gone.

Beth stared after him, more confused than ever. Wasn't she the one who didn't want a relationship with anyone, least of all him? Shouldn't she be happy that he was behaving so sensibly?

"I'm going up to bed," Matt said as he came over and gave her a hug. "See you in the morning."

"Night, sweetie."

Matt turned to leave, then paused. "He's not so bad."

Beth stared at her son. He was giving her his approval. Not that she needed it, but the gesture was very nice. She should probably tell him there was nothing to worry about. Todd was not going to be a part of her life. Instead she found herself saying, "I'm glad you think so."

Then she listened to the sound of Todd's car starting and

the silence after he'd driven off. She stood there for a long time and wondered why she suddenly felt so alone.

"Beth, you owe me," Todd said, his voice low and seductive and fifteen miles away.

Beth shook her head as she paced in her bedroom, the cordless telephone against her left ear. "I don't."

"I spent the whole day in your world. I have the blue hands to prove it. Now come see what I do. If the thought of that is too much, then let's just go out to dinner. You can even pick the restaurant."

"We can't date," she said, even as she wished they could. This was his third phone call in as many days and she was starting to look forward to talking to him. She'd never been the object of anyone's desire before. Or, if that was a little strong, then the subject of male interest.

"Why are you making this so complicated?" he asked.

"Because it is."

"I'm attracted to you, you're attracted to me. Don't bother trying to deny it, either, because your kisses gave you away."

She wouldn't dare fight him on that one, she thought. If Todd knew anything, it was women. She wished she had the backbone to simply order him out of her life. But the truth was, she *did* want to see him again. She liked him. She liked being with him. She liked how he made her feel. But he also terrified her for a lot of reasons she didn't want to think about.

"I'm not ready," she said. It was a lie. She was more ready than she'd realized, she just couldn't handle someone in Todd's league. He would date her until he got bored, then he would dump her. It was the dumping she didn't think she could handle. Okay, that and the attraction.

"You're being difficult."

"I'm…" She'd been about to say she was being honest, but that wasn't true. "I'm doing the best I can, Todd. You confuse me. I don't understand what you want."

"You."

She sank onto the bed. "That's clear enough."

"Not just in bed," he added, "although that would be nice. I want to get to know you better. I want to spend time with you. I like you, Beth. Is that so horrible?"

How was she supposed to answer that? "I have to go," she said.

"Beth, wait."

"No. Goodbye, Todd."

She hung up.

She was still sitting on her bed when Jodi walked in the room. "Mom, have you seen my—" She stared at her mother. "What's wrong?"

Beth shook her head. "Nothing. Everything." She drew in a deep breath. "It's just Todd. He keeps calling and asking me out."

"Gee, how terrible. What are you going to do about it?"

She looked at her daughter's smiling face. "You're not being sympathetic."

"I don't see the problem."

"I can't figure out why he wants to go out with me." She held up her hand. "I know, I know, I have a lot of wonderful qualities. I just wish I knew what it was he wanted."

Jodi plopped down next to her on the bed. "Maybe you're a challenge. You know how guys get. They don't want something until they can't have it, then they'll die if they don't get it."

Beth stared at her daughter. Was it as simple as that? "You could be right. When this all started, the first thing I did was walk out on him at the restaurant. That had to be a huge blow to his ego. Maybe this isn't about me at all. Maybe I'm just a symbol or something.''

She ignored the disappointed voice inside that whispered she *wanted* it to be all about her. In fact, she *needed* it to be about her and not some male thing he had to prove. But wanting and needing didn't make a thing so. Darren's death had taught her that.

"The best way to get rid of him is to give him what he wants,'' Jodi said. "If you're not a challenge, he won't have anything to prove.''

"So I should go out with him.''

"Absolutely. He's a nice enough guy, so it will be easy to like him. Once he thinks he has you, he'll be finished.''

And she would be left holding a slightly battered self, she thought grimly. "It could work,'' she said. "Although I have to tell you, it's very humiliating to be taking advice from my sixteen-year-old daughter.''

Jodi laughed. "Anytime, Mom. Oh, I do have warn you about one thing.''

"What's that?''

"If this isn't about him reacting to a challenge, then all you're doing is encouraging a man who already likes you. In which case, you're going to be stuck with him.''

I can live with that, Beth thought, thinking there could be worse fates in life than having Todd fall for her.

Chapter Nine

Todd found himself glancing at his watch and wishing the meeting would speed along a little faster. Then he realized it was barely after three in the afternoon so it didn't matter if things went slowly, he still wasn't going to see Beth until early that evening. But he *was* going to see her, and that was good news. After nearly a week of him calling her every day, she'd finally agreed to go out with him.

Todd tried to listen to the presentation on retail lease space availability projections for the next quarter. This was his business and he should be interested. After all, the less there was available, the higher the price on the remaining properties. This year was going to even better than last. But all he could think about was seeing Beth.

He'd missed her these past few days. Usually he saw his female friends on weekends and for an occasional midweek dinner. Work was his prime interest. If Beth had let him, he would have seen her every night this week. Despite their daily phone conversations, he missed her. He wanted to be in the same room with her and see her face. He wanted to talk to her and hold her. Hell, he even wanted to see her kids.

He couldn't remember the last time he'd had it this bad for someone.

The irony of the situation was that she didn't seem that interested in him. She'd refused several of his invitations. Even though she'd accepted this one, she'd insisted on dinner only, not agreeing to his request to come spend the day in his world. He suspected his disappointment at that was more about his desire to show off his "stuff," be it the condo or his cars or his boat. He told himself there would be time for that later. For now it was enough that he was going to see her again.

The projection analyst finished her remarks and looked at Todd. He glanced at the pad in front of him…the one that was usually covered with questions. It was blank.

"Good job, Teresa. You're expecting a record-breaking quarter."

The petite brunette nodded, but her gaze turned quizzical. "Yes, Mr. Graham. I have a further breakdown, if you would like to see it."

"Drop it by my office later."

"You don't want to see it now?"

"Not really."

There was no point in his trying to work his way through her information when he wasn't in the mood to pay attention. He rose. "Let's pick this up on Monday," he said.

There was a moment of stunned silence. "Are you sure?" Teresa asked.

"It's Friday," he told her. "A beautiful spring afternoon. Why don't you let everyone go a little early today?"

Her brown eyes widened. Todd understood her confusion. He often worked until eight or nine at night and he expected his senior staff to put in an equal number of long hours.

He leaned toward her. "Just this once," he murmured. "I won't tell the boss."

Her mouth twisted as she tried to decide if he was serious or not. Todd walked into the hallway and figured they would all get it soon enough.

He paused by his secretary's desk. Mrs. Alberts had been with him for nearly ten years. She was a few years older than him, with three children, the oldest of whom had graduated from college the previous year.

She handed him a slip of paper. "Here's the list of restaurants. I can vouch for all but the last two. Those names came from several people in Personnel."

Her thick brown hair was cut in a wedge. She wore tailored suits and expensive jewelry and had an assistant of her own to help with his schedule and work correspondence. She delegated, bullied, protected and generally did an amazing job of taking care of him. He frequently told her that her husband of twenty-plus years was a lucky man. She usually agreed.

"While these are all very nice," she said, "They're not your usual style."

"I know," he told her. "I want something different. Good food, but understated." He hadn't forgotten Beth's horror at the last restaurant he'd taken her to. This time he wanted prices on the menus, easily recognizable food and an atmosphere designed to make her feel comfortable.

He scanned the list. There were a couple of Italian places, a steak house and two restaurants specializing in "American cuisine." "Whatever that is," he said under his breath.

"I took the liberty of making reservations at the first one

on the list," Mrs. Alberts said. "It's quiet and they have booths, which are very private. The menu covers a wide range of Italian foods, their wine list is impressive, and while most people would consider it on the expensive side, I'm sure you'll think it's quite modest."

He shot her a look and she grinned at him. One of Mrs. Alberts's best features was that she wasn't frightened of him. She had no trouble expressing her opinion, regardless of how it might conflict with his. He frequently used her as a sounding board before large meetings.

"Sounds great," he said, and tucked the list into his shirt pocket. "What florist do you use when you order for me?"

"Occasions," she said. "They do lovely work. Shall I order something for your young lady?"

He wondered how shocked Mrs. Alberts would be if she knew his newest "young" lady was in her late thirties. "I'd rather pick them out myself," he said. "Just give me the address and I'll go down there."

"Of course," Mrs. Alberts said as she scrawled an address on a piece of paper.

He heard her questions as clearly as if she'd spoken them out loud. What was different this time? Why was he acting so strangely, picking out his own flowers, worrying about the right restaurant?

Because this time it matters, Todd thought, and knew he wouldn't share that private information with someone who worked for him. While he and his secretary had an excellent business relationship, they never spoke of their personal lives, except in the most general of ways.

He took the paper. "Tell you what. Let's both go home early today. It's a Friday and we've been working hard all week."

She looked as shocked as Teresa had at the meeting. "It's not even three-thirty."

"I know." He grinned. "Isn't that great?"

"But Mr. Graham, you like to work late. Even on Friday."

"Sometimes it pays to be the boss."

"What about the phone?" she asked, the phone that at that moment started to ring.

He put his hand on the receiver to prevent her from answering it and shook his head. "Let it go to voice mail. I promise I'll check in the morning. What could happen between now and then?"

She looked at the still-ringing phone. Finally it was silent. "Are you sure?"

"Absolutely." He headed for his office to collect his sports coat and car keys. "See you on Monday," he called over his shoulder.

He went by his condo to shower and change, then found the florist and picked out a large spray of flowers for Beth. He wasn't supposed to pick her up until six-thirty and it was barely four-thirty. Even so, he headed for Sugar Land. Instead of driving to Beth's house, he stopped at the local mall and killed some time wandering around.

The mall was filled with teenagers and young families out for their Friday-night entertainment. He watched fathers helping their toddlers try on shoes, and a young couple window shopping for diamond engagement rings. As far as he could tell, he was the only man there alone.

These people lived in a world that was unfamiliar to him, yet commonplace for most people. This was Beth's world. Her children shopped here, as she did. He could picture her walking purposefully while she worked her way through her list of errands. The image was oddly appealing, but nearly everything about Beth appealed to him.

Why? What was it about her that made him leave work early, then hang out at a mall just to kill time so he wouldn't show up two hours before she expected him? Why couldn't he stop thinking about her? She was a mature woman, a widow with two teenage children. She was attractive enough, but not a beauty. She was bright and funny, but so were hundreds and thousands of other women. Why her? Why did thoughts of her fill his head, making it difficult for him to sleep at night? Why did he want her more than he'd ever wanted anyone else in his life?

He didn't have the answers to those questions. All he knew was that when he was with Beth, he felt as if he belonged somewhere…probably for the first time ever. She made him want to believe in things he'd never believed in before.

He walked around for another few minutes, then figured Beth would have to put up with him being early. He pulled into her driveway a few minutes after six. If she wasn't dressed, he could always talk with her kids. He liked both Matt and Jodi and wouldn't mind getting to know them better.

After collecting the large bouquet of flowers, he made his way to her front door and knocked. There was no answer. He rang the bell. And waited. Still no answer. He was about to return to his car so he could leave a message on her machine, when he heard a noise from inside. The front door opened.

Beth stood in the foyer. Her face was pale, her hair mussed. She wore a stained T-shirt and shorts. Her feet were bare. She looked tired and worried, and not the least bit happy to see him.

Disappointment filled him. He felt like a kid who'd been promised a remote toy car for Christmas only to find the box empty when he finally got to open it. He shifted the flowers from one arm to the other. "Hi," he said when it became apparent she wasn't going to speak first. "I thought our date was for tonight."

She motioned for him to come in. "It was. I'm sorry. I'm exhausted," she said as he stepped inside. "I should have gotten in touch with you sooner, but I haven't had the time. When I tried calling you at work late this afternoon to cancel our date, no one answered your phone."

"You want to cancel?" He was stunned. "You can't."

She couldn't. He'd been looking forward to this all week. Didn't she know how much he wanted to see her? Didn't she want to see him?

"It's Matt," she said. "He's sick and I can't leave him."

Beth watched Todd's expression tighten, then close her out. He didn't believe her. The last bit of her strength faded away. All she wanted to do was sit on the floor and cry.

"I'm disappointed, too," she said. "I've been looking forward to tonight."

"Sure," he said curtly. "I could tell by how eagerly you accepted all my invitations."

She'd hurt him. Although that didn't seem possible, it was true. Ironically she *had* been looking forward to their date. She had a new dress, she'd read the newspaper every morning all week so she would be current on what was going on in the world and be able to make intelligent small talk. She'd wanted to impress him even though she suspected he was only going out with her to get her out of his system.

She looked at the tall, handsome man standing in her foyer. He held an outrageously large bouquet of flowers in his arms. His suit was tailored to fit and emphasize his lean body and male strength. His dark blond hair was recently trimmed and his jaw looked freshly shaved. He'd done all that for her. Her thank you was to greet him while looking like a refugee from the home for the badly dressed and cancel their night together.

She took a deep breath. "I wanted to see you tonight," she said. "You can believe me or not, but it's the truth. But it's not going to work. Matt has the stomach flu. It hit him about one in the morning and neither of us got much sleep after that. I'd already worked until midnight because I wanted to get my editing done early, so I wouldn't have to do it today. I had planned to get my hair done, have a pedicure and generally pamper myself in anticipation of our evening together."

Frustration welled up inside of her. Reciting all that had gone wrong wasn't making her feel any better.

"I ended up canceling my appointments because I needed to take my work into the office, then hurry back to be with Matt. Jodi only had a half day at school. She hasn't finished driver's training yet, so she doesn't have a license. I had to run her around this afternoon, then take her over to her baby-sitting job at five. Matt is still throwing up. I've been washing sheets and towels all day and now the washing machine is making a funny noise. The pantry is bare, which wouldn't be a big deal except I'm out of soup and juice, and just about anything else he might be able to keep down. I did try to call you late this afternoon. The only number I have is the one I got out of the phone book for your office and no one answered."

She could feel herself getting more and more upset. Tears burned at her eyes, but she refused to give in to them. At least not in front of Todd.

"I see," he said, but she couldn't tell if he did or not. She didn't know what he was thinking.

"I'm sorry," she repeated.

"You don't have to be." He handed her the flowers and gave her a quick smile. "I guess the last thing you need is some guy hanging around all upset because you had to cancel a date, right?''

She nodded because that was what he expected, but in her heart she didn't want him to go. Despite his engineering degree, Darren hadn't been much use around the house. But at least he would have gone to the grocery store for her. If only Todd would offer to do the same.

''I'll see you later,'' Todd said, and left.

Beth closed the door behind him. A single tear rolled down her cheek. He'd left. Just like that. She cradled the flowers to her chest and admitted that in her heart of hearts she'd been hoping for more. Maybe a white knight to come rescue her. But that wasn't Todd's style. It probably wasn't any man's style. Every now and then life took great pleasure in reminding her that she was well and truly alone.

Foolishly she'd allowed herself to think it might be different this time. As much as she'd told herself that Todd wasn't really interested in a woman like her, that they had nothing in common and that she didn't know why he was courting her, in some corner of her heart she'd allowed herself to wish it was all real. She'd wanted him to sweep her off her feet and carry her away...figuratively if not literally.

But fantasy men were just that...fantasies. It was wrong of her to expect him to be something or someone who didn't exist. He was a nice man who had made a sincere effort. The fact that he didn't want to spend the evening with a scruffy mother and her sick kid shouldn't count against him.

She promised herself that if he called and asked her out again, she would go. She would accept him for what he was and stop wishing he had traits that weren't realistic. Then she put the flowers on the kitchen table and went upstairs to check on her son.

* * *

Forty-five minutes later, after Matt had finished throwing up again and Beth had helped him back to his bed, the front doorbell rang. Beth nearly decided to ignore it, but the sound of insistent knocking drove her downstairs.

As she crossed the foyer, she could see a shadowy figure through the glass in the door. Todd? Was he back?

Fierce gladness made her hurry toward him. She turned the lock and jerked open the door. It *was* him!

"Bet you thought I was gone for good," he said, as he stepped inside. His arms were full of bags, two of which he handed to her. "Yeah, well, I thought about it. I told myself I didn't need this kind of hassle. Sick kids, canceled dates. What a mess. I nearly made it back to the freeway when I realized I didn't care if we stayed in tonight. I don't want to go out, Beth, I was to see you. There's a difference. So here I am."

"I don't know what to say." Mostly because she couldn't believe he'd come back.

His blue-gray gaze searched her face. "Are you happy to see me?"

If they both hadn't been holding grocery bags, she would have wrapped her arms around him and wept with relief. Instead she nodded. "More than I can say."

"Good. Let's take this stuff into the kitchen."

"What is it?" she asked.

"Mostly food. I went to the grocery store and bought soup, bread and sparkling water. The kind of stuff I thought a sick kid would like. I rented a couple of science-fiction videos, in case he's bored but can't sleep. There's even some take-out Chinese for us."

Her head was spinning. Had he really done all that for her?

He set his packages on the counter, then took hers and

set them down, as well. Then he placed his hands on her shoulders. "Here's the deal," he told her. "My car comes with a built-in toolbox in the trunk. While you fix some dinner for Matt, I'll take a look at the washing machine. I don't make any promises, but I'm a pretty handy guy to have around. Then I'll sit with the kid while you go relax for a few minutes. Just to wind down."

She fingered her hair and remembered she wasn't wearing a speck of makeup. "I'd love a shower."

He groaned. "Don't say stuff like that. I already spend too much of my day thinking about you naked. When you're ready, we'll heat the take-out, flop down on the sofa in here and veg out with the movie of your choice. Even one of those romantic comedy chick flicks. How does that sound?"

She tried to speak but couldn't. Her mind whirled with all that he'd told her. That he'd cared enough to go to the store and bring back food for Matt, not to mention movies. That he would actually risk getting his beautiful suit dirty simply so he could check out her washer. That he thought about her naked and it didn't make him run into the night screaming.

"Beth?" He sounded worried. "Your face is getting all scrunchy. Did I do a bad thing?"

She sniffed. The tears were back and this time she wasn't going to be able to hold them at bay.

"N-no," she managed, then flung herself at him. "E-everything is perfect."

He wrapped his arms around her. "I would believe you a whole lot more if you weren't crying."

"These are good tears," she told him.

He smelled so clean and masculine as he held her close. His suit jacket was smooth against her cheek. She never wanted to let go.

"I want to help," he said. "If you'll tell me what you need, I'm happy to take care of it."

Don't go away, she thought, but that was the one wish she didn't get to make. Todd would go away. Even if he wanted to settle down, it wouldn't be with her. Still, for tonight, he was definitely white-knight material.

"Just hold me," she said.

He tightened his arms and rested his cheek against hers. "Easy enough. I can do this all night. Of course, eventually we'll get leg cramps and fall to the floor, but it would be worth it."

She giggled. "I really appreciate all of this."

"I'm happy to do it."

She still believed that there was only one love for each person, and that she'd already experienced hers. She still knew that Todd would, in time, get tired of her and return to his usual type of female. But none of that mattered anymore. She *didn't* know what combination of events had brought him into her life, but she was going to stop questioning her good luck. For now he was here. She was going to do her best to enjoy that…and him…for as long as he let her.

Three and a half hours later, life had returned to something close to normal. Beth pushed the mute button on the television as the closing scene of the movie they'd watched began.

Todd stared at her. "That can't be the end," he protested. "Did they win the gold medal?"

Beth grinned. "Of course, but that's not the point." She picked up the video cover for *The Cutting Edge* and pointed to the close-up of the actors on the front. "It's a romance. The medal is incidental. What's important is that they were willing to admit they were in love."

"I'll never understand women," he said, shaking his head. "It was a sports movie. Kind of interesting even if it was about ice skating. But the whole movie was about winning a gold medal. I want to see the scores. I want to know for sure."

"You are such a guy," she said. "Fine, in the theater version, they showed them winning and even had a couple of clips from the ceremony. There. Are you happy?"

"Yes, and I don't care that you're lying."

Todd picked up the remote and turned off the television and the VCR. He angled toward Beth, then placed his arm along the back of the sofa. "This has been really nice. Thanks for asking me to stay."

Her feeling of relaxation went spinning down the drain and she was left with a dry throat, shaking hands and a boulder sitting on the bottom of her stomach. Dear Lord, it was late and they were practically alone. Matt had finally kept soup down and as of the last time she'd checked on him, a mere twenty minutes ago, was sleeping fine. The couple who had employed Jodi for the evening had come home early and Jodi had gone off to spend the night at a girlfriend's house. So there weren't going to be any distractions...or excuses...or easy escapes.

"Yes, well, it's the least I could do," she said nervously. "You got the food, then you fixed my washer. Did I thank you for that? I do appreciate it. I hate it when the washer breaks. I remember once, we were all about to go on vacation. I'd been really busy with work so I hadn't been keeping up with the laundry. It was sitting around in these huge piles and then the machine just stopped working. I didn't know what to do and I—"

"Beth?" Todd interrupted.

She tried to swallow but couldn't. "What?"

"You're babbling."

"No, I'm sharing my life with you. There's a difference. I think it's important for friends to talk to each other, and we are friends, aren't we? I'm sure, compared to what you're used to in a day, my life is very boring, but sometimes I go exciting places. Once I even—''

He touched his index finger to her mouth. Which was an interesting way to silence her. And effective, she thought, as her remaining words died a quick death.

He shifted toward her. "I'm going to kiss you now," he said as he put one arm around her. "I don't want you to worry. I'm very aware of the fact that we're sitting in your family room. You have a sick kid upstairs, so you're going to be wondering if he's okay or even if he might come downstairs. I'm going to listen for him so you don't have to."

"Okay," she breathed. "I can handle a kiss."

He smiled a slow, confident male smile that made her melt against him. "It's not going to be just one kiss."

The anticipation was sweet, she thought hazily as he drew her closer and pressed his mouth to hers. But not as sweet as the taste of him.

She was a little more prepared than she'd been the last time they'd kissed. Her nerves weren't quite as jumpy and she didn't worry that she was going to throw up or anything equally humiliating. But when his hand cupped her face and his tongue touched her bottom lip, urging her to open for him, she was still overwhelmed by the explosion between them.

As soon as he deepened the kiss, her body went up in flames. She wrapped her arms around his neck and had to resist the need to crawl all over him. She wanted to feel him press against her. She wanted to touch him and have him touch her. She wanted to know if he was as aroused as she was, and if it had happened as quickly.

His tongue was hot and bold. He invaded her, teased her, taunted her until she had to chase him back and do all that to him. He stroked her shoulders and spine, his large hands sure and strong and warm through the thin layer of her T-shirt.

They were angled toward each other, knees bumping. She wanted more. She wanted to be pressing against him but she couldn't figure out a way to make that happen on the sofa…not unless one of them was lying down. And she knew she wasn't ready for that.

She took his face in her hands and felt the smoothness of his jaw. She ran her fingers through his short hair, then traced his ears. When he broke their kiss, she wanted to protest, right up until he bent down and nibbled on the side of her neck. The fire in her doubled in size. Heat consumed her. She felt her muscles begin to tremble as every cell in her body responded to his touch.

There was too much passion, she thought as her breathing grew more rapid. His mouth slipped to her throat, then down to the vee of her shirt. She could feel his lips, his tongue, his breath. Her breasts ached, her thighs tingled. She couldn't remember ever being this turned-on before.

"Beth," Todd said hoarsely. "Come here."

He put his hands on her waist and urged her to straddle him. She went willingly, hoping he didn't notice her awkwardness. She didn't quite get her left leg over his lap and came down too hard. Embarrassment heated her face. But Todd didn't say anything. Instead, he wrapped his arms around her and pulled her next to him until they were pressing together intimately.

Her breasts flattened against his chest, her feminine place nestled against a substantial bulge in his trousers. He kissed her long and slow, making her ache with wanting him.

His hands dropped to her bare legs. He ran them up and

down, from her knees to the hem of her shorts. She found herself wishing he would rub her down *there* on that small spot that was so sensitive. The idea of it stunned and aroused her in equal measures. It was wrong of her to think that. It was also incredibly delicious.

His hands moved up to her hips, where he cupped her, then urged her to rock against him. Tension built as they pressed together. Her breath caught. She hadn't thought she would ever feel sexual again, and it scared her to want him so much. She told herself to stop, that this was crazy, but the need couldn't be denied.

She didn't notice that he'd shifted attention again until she felt his fingers stroking the undersides of her breasts. Her nipples were hard and tight. He circled around them, then took the full curves in his hands. She gasped against his mouth. When he teased her nipples, she thought she was going to die.

It was too wonderful, too amazing. His tongue in her mouth, his hands on her breasts and the feel of his arousal pressing and rubbing against her most private place. If the seam of her shorts had been a quarter of a inch to one side or the other, she would have had direct pressure on that one special spot and she would have exploded. Beth could feel herself collecting toward the moment.

It had been so long. The thought of release was blissful. But she couldn't do it. Not like this. Not with him. Not yet.

She pulled back, physically getting to her feet. She felt disheveled and foolish and incredibly out of her league.

To his credit, Todd didn't scold her or complain. He simple asked if she was all right.

"I'm great," she lied. "But look at the time. I sure didn't mean to keep you out this late."

He glanced at his watch. "You're right. It's nearly eleven. Whatever were we thinking?"

Tears threatened again, but for the life of her she couldn't say why. ''Todd, don't,'' she whispered. She couldn't face the teasing, however gentle. Not after what they'd just done.

''Okay.'' He rose to his feet, then kissed her forehead. ''I'll leave. But I'll be thinking about you.''

''Me, too,'' she whispered.

Then he was gone and she was left wishing he was still there. He was the one she feared and needed to get out of her life, yet now, in an hour of confusion and pain, he was the one she wanted to hold her tight.

Chapter Ten

Beth sat in the tufted chair by her bedroom window and watched the sun rising over the rooftops. The sky was clear now, but the weather was expected to turn rainy later, with a springtime afternoon storm forecast. Dark skies and a little lightning would suit her mood perfectly, she thought.

She leaned back in her chair and told herself everything was going to be fine. The problem was she didn't believe it. Not anymore...not after last night.

As it had since the moment Todd has left, guilt swarmed through her. She ducked her head until her chin rested on her chest and she felt the familiar ache inside her heart. How could she have let things go so far? How could she have allowed herself to get carried away? What about Darren? Didn't their love mean anything to her?

She wanted to cry, to find some solace in the release of emotion, but there weren't any tears left. She looked down at the framed photograph on her lap. It had been taken about five years before, one of those family portraits sold door-to-door. Darren, like most men, hated the thought of getting all dressed up on a Saturday just to pose for a picture, but Beth had insisted. She looked at the faces of her children, then at the familiar features of the man who had been the most important part of her life for nearly twenty years.

She'd never dated anyone but him, she'd never kissed anyone but him, she'd never needed anyone but him. Oh, when he'd been alive, she'd joked about wanting to see another man naked. She'd complained, as all wives do, about his inability to understand what she was thinking, his reluctance to participate in heart-to-heart conversations. But none of that really mattered. They had a meaningful and shared past.

They'd grown up together. She'd learned to think before she spoke, to try to figure out what was bothering her instead of simply giving him a two-hour emotional dump that rambled and circled around itself. He'd learned how important it was to help around the house, and that spontaneous gifts of flowers, small trinkets, anything that said "I was thinking about you today" brought him untold rewards.

They had discovered, that for them at least, the old adage of never going to bed angry didn't work. When they were tired they said things they regretted later. As they'd had children and worked together to be good parents they'd learned that sometimes marriages need a time-out, too.

She traced his familiar face, the slightly too-big nose, the glasses, the happy smile. She thought about the fights, when they'd come so close to saying they wanted to break up, only to realize that their love lived on, despite being battered by day-to-day living. She recalled the ebb and flow of their passion, how after twelve or thirteen years of marriage, they'd rediscovered a love that was as intense and fresh as it had been when they'd first married. In the last couple of years of their lives together, there had been talk of the kids' college plans and what they would do when they retired. A small place on the water. Maybe they would buy a boat.

Beth clutched the photograph to her chest and rocked back and forth. Darren had been a wonderful man—decent, kind, loving. No matter how bad things had been, he'd never once strayed. They'd survived so much together and they were still in love. How many couples could say that?

She swallowed against her hurt as she remembered the dark days after his death. The children had saved her. Their needs had continued, forcing her to get up each morning and get on with her life. Eventually the sharp pain that had made it nearly impossible to breathe had faded to a dull ache. The ache had slowly lessened, but the sense of having lost something important had remained…until Todd Graham had walked into her life.

Beth glanced at the open boxes on the floor around her. Pieces of her life with Darren. Souvenirs from plays, amusement parks and vacations. Several photo albums including the one from their large wedding. She'd kept his favorite tie, the letters he'd written when his work had taken him away for nearly a year when Jodi had barely been a toddler and she'd been pregnant with Matt.

She'd dug out all these things last night when she hadn't been able to sleep. She'd gone through them, read the letters, looked at the pictures, and none of it had helped. No matter how she tried, she couldn't bring Darren back. Her midnight visit to her past had left her feeling more alone than ever.

She'd not only betrayed him, she'd lost him. That's what hurt the most. He was gone forever. For a while, right after his death, she'd still felt connected with him. Sometimes, when the pain was unbearable, she'd talked to him, telling him how she was feeling, imagining what he would say back to her. The odd ritual had provided some comfort, often just enough to get her through.

She couldn't talk to him now. Not only did she feel apart from him, the subject matter was hardly fair. What was she going to say? *Hi, honey, I nearly had sex with a man last night. What do you think about that?*

"Oh, Darren," she breathed. "I'm so sorry. I never meant to betray you."

She closed her eyes. She knew some people would tell her the guilt didn't make sense. Darren had been gone over eighteen months. She was relatively young and no one expected her to give up her life and remain true to a memory. Nice words, but her remorse over what had happened with Todd told her she wasn't sure she believed them.

Everything was too confusing. In her head she knew that Darren wouldn't have expected her to build a shrine to him and spend her days worshiping at the altar. If she had been the one killed in a car accident, she would have wanted him to marry, as long as the woman was willing to love her children and shepherd them through their last few years of growing up. Why would Darren be any less caring and concerned about her?

A voice whispered in her head. She'd been ignoring it for most of the night, but now, with daylight spilling across her bedroom, she found herself forced to listen.

Maybe this isn't about Darren at all. Maybe it's about you and Todd.

Maybe it was, she agreed at last. Maybe her guilt was more about fear and wanting to run back to something safe than because she worried about betraying her late husband's memory.

Could that be possible? Was she hiding behind her past in order to avoid her future?

"Too many questions," she said softly. "Besides, it's a nonissue. Todd will never be more than a crush. I've already fallen in love once. That's all I get."

But for the first time, the familiar words didn't ring true. She found herself swept up in a distant memory. She was maybe four or five and her mother was reading her a story about a sleeping princess awakened by the kiss of a handsome prince.

"And they lived happily ever after," her mother had read.

Beth remembered being worried. "How do you know?" she'd asked. "How do you know they lived happily ever after?"

"Because her prince is her one true love. Every girl gets one."

"But what if I want ten?"

Her mother had smiled. "Sorry, munchkin, you just get the one."

Beth had believed her because at four or five, it never occurred to her that her mother might make something up to satisfy a child's curiosity. She'd carried the knowledge with her, making it part of her inner truth. She remembered having fights with Darren early in their marriage. He'd been frustrated, she'd been angry. They'd often ended up speechless, not sure what to do next. She'd usually shrugged and said, "We'd better find a way to get over it. We're each other's true love and we're stuck together forever."

"I want to believe," Beth said now in the quiet of her bedroom. "I want it to still be true."

But she knew too many people who had gone on to love someone else. She was hiding behind that childhood story because it was easier than risking herself again. Falling in love as a teenager was painful and seemed earth-shattering, but the truth was, there wasn't much to lose. But now, approaching forty, she had an entire life at stake. She couldn't afford to make a mistake. She had to get it right or not do it at all.

It was so much easier to take herself out of the game by saying she'd already had her turn.

Beth stared out the window. She needed to make a decision. If not today, then soon. If she didn't want to get involved because she was afraid, that was fine. If she wanted to start dating because she didn't want to be lonely anymore, that was okay, too. But she had to stop lying to herself. She had to stop hiding behind her past and her dreams. She had to accept that Darren was never coming back, that she was a grown-up and responsible for her own life.

"Moments of clarity are never easy," she whispered. "All this introspection, pain and tears because some handsome guy reminded me that I was alive and still had physical needs."

What an odd catalyst, she thought, remembering the horror she'd felt after Todd had left the previous night. She'd been sick with a sense of having betrayed Darren. Now, with a little more thought, she recognized her fear. Todd terrified her because she was attracted to him. He was successful, funny, seemed to like her kids, seemed to like *her*. They talked, they laughed, he made her body go up in flames... Why wouldn't she want to be around him?

Darren had been easier. She'd understood what he saw in her. They'd been a lot alike. Same background, same goals, same life-style. With Todd, she couldn't see her appeal. Why did he want to be with her? Why was he so nice about everything? Was she a temporary diversion from his usual kind of woman?

She didn't mind if it was the latter. She could use the experience as practice, just as Cindy had suggested. Then, when it was over, she would do better with a man who made more sense for her. For now, she could simply attend the Todd Graham School of Dating.

There was only one small flaw in her plan. That was the issue of her feelings. What if she fell in love with him? She didn't want to love anyone but Darren.

Her first instinct was to run and hide. She didn't need this complication in her life. Everything was much easier when it was just her and the kids. But she had a bad feeling that now that she'd been reminded about what it was like to have someone who cared hanging around, she was going to find it difficult to return to her solitary existence.

She wasn't ready to date, but she was ready to start thinking about dating. The question was: Did she risk staying involved with Todd, or did she wait for someone safer?

"Bravery is highly overrated," she said as she rose to her feet. She put the family picture on her bed, then headed for the bathroom. "The most logical and sensible thing would be to tell Todd I can't see him anymore. Why risk it?"

Except the thought of never seeing him again made her sad. It wasn't just because he set her on fire when he touched her. It was also because he'd come back with soup for Matt, take-out for them, then he fixed her washer. Flowers were easy. How was she supposed to resist someone thoughtful? The handsome face and great body didn't hurt, either.

She turned on the water in her shower. So what was it going to be?

Jodi was dropped off from her friend's house around ten-thirty that morning. She banged in through the back door, dumped her book bag and overnight duffel by the family room sofa, then stole two still-warm cookies from the cooling rack.

"I was going to put icing on those," Beth said, glancing at the sugar cookies in her daughter's hand.

"That will give me an excuse to eat some more later," Jodi teased. "Just to make sure you have the icing recipe correct."

"Oh, thanks so much for your concern. Amazing how I've managed all these years whenever I baked while you were in school."

Her oldest poured herself a glass of milk, then leaned against the counter and took a sip. "How's Matt feeling? What can I do to help?"

"He's better, and thanks for the offer, but everything is under control. He's been keeping food down and he slept though most of the night. Right now he's in my room, watching videos on my TV."

Jodi raised her eyebrows. "And...how was your date?"

Beth had known the question was as inevitable as the earth's rotation. She'd wanted to be prepared to act casual. Despite the faint heat on her cheeks, she kept her voice low and calm. "Not what either of us expected, but still very nice. He brought over take-out Chinese. The leftovers are in the refrigerator. I thought you'd want them for lunch today."

"Oh, great. Thanks. So, go on. What happened?"

"Nothing very exciting," Beth said, telling herself it was a small lie and barely counted. "He fixed the washer, we ate dinner, then watched a movie. He was out of here by eleven."

Jodi finished her milk. "Did you have fun?"

Beth wiped her hands on a dish towel. "Yes, I did. Does that bother you?"

Jodi's long hair was pulled back into a ponytail. Her face was so incredibly beautiful, and so young. "Todd seems nice," Jodi admitted. "Not a jerk like some of my friends' moms' boyfriends. But it's weird, you know?"

"Yes, I do know," Beth said wryly. "I'm having a little trouble with the whole situation."

"I know you loved Dad. He knew it, too. But he's gone and he's not coming back." She bit her lower lip. "I want you to be happy. Matt's already in high school and I only have one more year until college. I don't want you to be alone."

"You're just afraid I'll start collecting cats and be one of those old ladies who talks to themselves."

Jodi giggled. "Then I'd be scared to come home for a visit."

"I don't want that," Beth said. She let her smile fade. "Just because I'm going out doesn't mean I've decided to remarry. I might find I prefer being on my own. I have to figure what's right for me. I'm very happy right now. But things change. I just want to make sure you and Matt know that you'll always come first in my life."

"We know."

Jodi moved close and gave her a hug. Beth held on tight and wished she didn't have to ever let go.

"So you don't mind me seeing Todd?" she asked.

Jodi stepped back. "No. He's pretty cool. Besides, he doesn't have kids of his own, so he's going to spoil us."

Interesting logic, Beth thought. "How do you figure?"

"He'll want to impress you with how well we all get along. He doesn't know how to do the dad stuff, so he'll try buying us. Matt and I have talked about that. He's really rich, so maybe you could start hinting that I'd like a car."

Beth put her hands on her hips. "That's terrible."

"Oh, please, like you wouldn't try for one if you were in my position."

Beth opened her mouth, then closed it. At sixteen she would have done exactly the same thing. "There will be no car hinting. As for the gift buying, you might be right, but I'll be watching, so don't get your hopes up."

"I won't." Jodi took another cookie and broke it in two. "Seriously, Mom, he seems okay. Matt likes him, too. It's going to be strange, because we miss Dad and nobody can take his place. But we trust you." She glanced at the clock on the microwave and frowned. "I have tons more homework to do, so I'd better get started. I'll check on Matt when I go upstairs."

Her daughter disappeared with a flick of her red ponytail. Beth stared after her. No matter what else happened in her life, something had gone very, very right with her children, and she was grateful.

Todd pulled up in front of the baseball field and got out of his car. It was Wednesday afternoon and he was supposed to be at a marketing meeting, but he'd postponed it so that he could attend Matt's baseball game.

He'd expected to arrive sooner, but he'd changed his mind about coming and had twice turned around.

Why did he care about some fourteen-year-old kid's baseball game? Why was he even involved with a woman who had kids? Did he plan to be a surrogate father?

Yeah, right, he thought grimly. All he knew about fathers was that they were never around. A lot of help he would be. He was in over his head. He couldn't make anything about this relationship work. Except...

Except he liked being around Beth and he liked being around her kids. He liked how she made him feel. He liked the differences and the similarities between them. Maybe he was heading for trouble, but he wasn't ready to walk away. Not until he figured out where they were headed.

He crossed the half-full parking lot, then walked over to stand by the dugout. Matt's team was in the outfield, but Todd turned his attention to the bench. Beth had mentioned that while the boy was back in school and that he would suit up for the game, he was still too weak to play.

Matt spotted him and gave an enthusiastic wave. "Hi," he said, trotting over to stand by the fence.

Despite his concerns, Todd couldn't help grinning at the kid. "How's the game going?"

Matt frowned, scrunching up his nose until his wire-rimmed glasses bounced with the movement. "Terrible. We're behind by three and it's only the fourth inning."

"It's because you're not playing. I remember how well you did when I saw you a couple of weeks ago. You hit a double, a sacrifice RBI and a home run. Not bad."

Matt glowed. Todd remembered his own sports history and how he'd felt when no one had bothered to come to his football games or ask how they went.

"Mom told me you might stop by," Matt said, "but I don't think she believed you."

"Is she here?"

"Yeah. Up in the stands. She's trying not to stare, but she looked real shocked when you walked up."

"Sometimes it's important to keep women guessing. Otherwise they get to thinking they're in charge."

Matt nodded, as if he appreciated being told something man-to-man. "I think she likes you," he said. "You've got her nervous, but she says real nice things when she talks about you."

"Thanks for telling me." Todd was pleased by the boy's acceptance. "I remember what we talked about before. I don't want to hurt her. I think she's very special."

"I'm glad."

Matt's coach called his name. "I gotta go," he said.

"I hope to see you soon," Todd told him. "I'm going to visit with your mom for a while. Maybe ask her out."

Matt grinned. "Good luck."

Todd headed for the stands. Beth saw him and stood up, then walked down to meet him on the dirt pathway.

"I didn't think you were serious about driving out to Matt's game," she said when she reached him. "He's not even playing today."

"I wanted to make sure that he was feeling better. And I wanted to see you."

She was in her uniform of a T-shirt and shorts. Most of the other mothers were dressed the same, but he didn't find them nearly as attractive as Beth. Her exposed bare legs made him remember their evening together, how she'd sat on his lap, straddling his hips.

She was an amazing person, and not just because she made him want her in less than thirty seconds of actual face-to-face conversation. He liked how she cared about her kids and the way she looked at him directly, without trying to hide or play games. Not that he objected to her full breasts or pretty face. He glanced up to confirm his theory that she was the most beautiful woman here, when he noticed they were the object of more interest than the baseball game.

Todd took her arm and led her around behind the stands. "How much gossip did I just create?" he asked.

"We won't make the six o'clock news, but tongues will be wagging on street corners."

"I'm sorry," he told her. "I didn't mean to make trouble. I really did just want to say hi to Matt and spend a couple of minutes with you."

"You drove all the way down here for a ten-minute visit?"

"Why are you surprised?"

She shrugged. "I just am."

Mindful of the interested audience not that far away, he lightly touched her cheek. "I want to see you again."

"So you've told me every time you've called."

"You've never said yes."

She smiled. "You've never given me a specific date or time."

Hadn't he? No wonder she hadn't been enthusiastic about going out with him. He was so smitten, he was forgetting all the important stuff. "Saturday morning. I want to show you my world. We'll make it an all-day affair."

"Interesting choice of words. 'Affair.'" She glanced down at her hands, then cleared her throat.

He could tell she was nervous...and he knew exactly how to fix the situation. "I know what you're worried about," he said.

"Oh, I doubt that."

"After what happened the last time we were together, you're afraid I'm going to want to make love with you."

She blanched and took a step back. "Yes, well, maybe you do know what's been on my mind."

He touched her chin until she looked at him. "I want to," he told her. "Very much. But I won't do anything to make you uncomfortable. You matter to me, Beth. I want it to be right. While you tempted me beyond measure the last time we were together, I was concerned that we'd gone too far, too fast. I won't rush you."

"You're saying you'll wait."

"For as long as you need me to."

"Why? You probably don't wait with the other women you've dated."

She wasn't asking a question, he thought, but she didn't have to. She knew him pretty well. "Because they don't usually matter. You do."

"This is guy thing, isn't it? In theory, I'm important so you won't sleep with me. They're not important, so you will? That doesn't make sense."

"It's not a guy thing, it's a Beth thing. I don't want to scare you off, and to be honest, I'm enjoying this slower pace. I want to get to know you. If you and I ever become lovers, I want it to mean something to both of us."

She'd managed to get through almost the entire conversation without blushing. Todd watched her jump when he said the word *lovers*. Color followed instantly.

She didn't look convinced. He didn't know how else to make it clear. He'd told her the truth—she was special and deserved more than a quick affair. He wanted it to be more…which was something he'd never thought he would feel. While he wouldn't admit it to her, he was also willing to wait because he didn't know how *much* more it was going to be. He had a bad feeling that once they became intimate, it would be more difficult, if not impossible, for him to walk away. And isn't that what he always did?

"Is it because I'm old?" she asked.

He groaned. Despite the interested bystanders who were straining to watch them, he pulled her close. "Do you remember the last time I was at your house?" he murmured into her ear. "Do you remember what we did on your sofa?"

She nodded.

"I was so hard, I thought I was going to explode right there with you rubbing against me. Guys can't fake getting hard. That was all because of you."

She looked at him. A smile tugged at the corners of her mouth. "Really?"

"Yeah, really. I want you. But as much as I want you naked, first I want you comfortable with your clothes on."

He drew her earlobe into his mouth and nibbled gently. She shivered.

"Do you believe me," he asked, "or do I have to be more convincing?"

"Oh, I believe you," she said.

He gave her a quick kiss on the mouth. "Saturday morning, bright and early. I'll be there at eight. Dress casual and pack fancy. We'll be going to a party that night."

"Great. It's been a long time since I went to a hoe-down. It'll be fun to see how the other half lives."

"You'll like it," he promised.

She didn't look convinced. "What time should I tell my kids I'll be home?"

"Sunday around noon," he teased.

She put her hands on her hips. "Be serious."

"Not much past midnight. I don't want you turning back into a pumpkin. See you then."

He walked toward his car. Before he could get there, Beth called his name and hurried after him. She caught up with him and wrapped her arms around him. "Thanks for everything," she said.

"I didn't do anything."

She smiled. "You've done more than you know."

Chapter Eleven

"This was a great idea," Beth told Cindy as they wandered through the clothing displayed in the elegant boutique. "I didn't know what I was going to do about a dress for the party Todd wants to take me to on Saturday. Knowing him, it's going to be expensive and exclusive. My budget doesn't allow for designer originals."

Cindy held up a beautiful, beaded black dress. "Sure it does. Just not dresses that are new this season."

Beth nodded her agreement. At Cindy's suggestion they were shopping at a resale shop that specialized in designer clothing. The prices were still high enough to make Beth wince, but probably a quarter of what the clothes had been originally. The location—close to the exclusive upper-crust neighborhood of River Oaks—guaranteed quality as well as a fair-size selection.

"My only fear," she said as she picked up a rust-colored dress with sheer sleeves and a fitted bodice, "is that I'll run into the woman who sold the dress to the shop in the first place.''

Cindy held up a bright pink pantsuit. Beth groaned and shook her head. Cindy laughed. ''Don't worry about that,'' her friend told her. ''No female is going to publicly admit she's been selling her clothes. She wouldn't want people to think her husband couldn't support her.''

''I guess. Of course she could tell all her close friends and they could spend the evening pointing and laughing.''

''That's what I like about you, Beth. You always manage to put such a positive spin on things.''

Beth sighed. ''You're right. I'm being negative. I'm sorry. It's just this whole situation has me nervous.'' She handed the rust dress to the clerk to take to the dressing room. ''I had a long talk with myself the other night and I realized I've been hiding behind my past. I need to move forward in my life. If I want to stay by myself for a few more years, that's a perfectly acceptable decision. If I want to think about dating, that's fine, too.''

Cindy flipped through a round rack, pausing at a couple of dresses, but not showing any to Beth. ''Sounds logical and sensible. So what's the problem?''

''I want to continue believing that there's only one love for each of us,'' Beth said, remembering the long night of soul-searching. ''Then I could dismiss my attraction to Todd and everything else going on. But I know too many people who have learned to love again.''

''I'm glad you're letting that go.''

''I'm not glad,'' Beth said unhappily. ''Now I have to figure out why I'm still terrified. Some of it is getting back into the whole dating thing again. It's harder now than it used to be. I have responsibilities to my children. I'm a grown-up. I don't think I want to fall in love again. It was great as a teenager, but I remember a lot of pain being involved.''

Cindy showed her a black dress. Beth studied the simple lines and nodded her approval. ''Make sure it's a size twelve. There aren't very many. Apparently most of the rich women around here are also tiny, which I really hate. I would promise to go back on my diet and lose a quick twenty, but I don't think I can do that in three days.''

''I know what you mean,'' her friend told her. ''Not about the twenty pounds, but about the rest of it. When I was first getting to know Mike and there was an obvious attraction, I was terrified. I thought all men left, so I wasn't about to commit myself again. Mike didn't help things by being in a profession that forced him to travel constantly. I still remember the shock of learning everything he owned could fit in a couple of duffel bags.''

''So how did you survive?''

''I didn't have a choice. Like you, I had two kids and a job. I had to cope with my feelings for Mike. I fooled myself for a long time. I told myself I didn't really care about him except as a friend. Then I realized I would rather have loved him, even for a short time, than to have let him walk away without taking a chance. Yes, falling in love is sometimes painful, but it's also a glorious way to feel alive.''

Beth thought about what her friend had said. ''I haven't felt alive in a long time,'' she admitted. ''Even before Darren died, there were times when I was just going through the motions.''

She found one more dress, this one in dark cobalt blue, and nodded at the salesclerk. ''I think I'm ready to start trying things on,'' she said.

Cindy followed her toward the rear of the boutique. There were only two dressing rooms, but both were large, with three-way mirrors and soft lighting. Cindy sat down on the gilded chair in the corner and took Beth's handbag.

"I came prepared," Beth said after closing the door. She quickly stepped out of her jeans and shirt. Underneath she wore a black strapless bra and panty hose. "There are a pair of black pumps in that shopping bag." She pointed to the one at Cindy's feet. "Could you get those out? If a dress looks okay, I want to try it on with the shoes."

"Good thinking."

Beth tried on the rust colored dress first. The long sleeves were too short for her and the whole thing didn't hang right. As she pulled down the zipper, she said, "I'm going to do what you suggested. I'm going to go out with Todd for a while and practice on him. It's the only way I can think of to protect myself from getting hurt."

"You could not go out at all," Cindy said softly.

Beth met her gaze in the mirror. "Yes, well, I thought of that, too."

"But you want to keep seeing him."

Beth exhaled slowly, then reached for the short-sleeved black dress. There were shiny jet beads scattered across the front of the crepe fabric. "As much as I hate to admit it, yeah, I do. I like him. He's a decent guy, which surprises me. He's also good-looking and fun to be with." She thought about how great it was when they kissed, but figured she didn't need to discuss that with Cindy.

"So what's the problem?"

"That I might start to care. I don't know how to date someone. I've spent my entire adult life married. There are so many potentially awkward moments." She thought about when she and Todd had been making out on the sofa and he drew her across his lap so she could straddle him. She'd felt like a beached whale—large and lacking in grace.

"With Darren, we'd done everything a hundred times. Every movement was choreographed. For some people that would be boring, but I like the idea of a comfortable relationship. I want to know what to expect."

"You can find that in time."

Beth stepped into the dress and let Cindy zip her up. She stared at the short sleeves, which fell midway between her shoulders and her elbows. "I didn't know it was possible for a sleeve that length to be unflattering, but I was wrong," she said. Something about the cut made her arms look shapeless. "Apparently I don't have a body that works with designer clothing."

"Don't give up," Cindy told her. "You have several more things to try on. You know it's always an effort to find nice stuff."

"I know. Everything good is work." She handed the dress to Cindy to put back on the hanger. "I wish Darren hadn't died. We had a good life together."

"You're just afraid to try again."

Beth looked at her friend. "Weren't you?"

"Of course. I resisted for ages. If Mike hadn't practically fallen into my lap, I would probably still be resisting."

Beth understood the feeling. While she liked Todd and wanted to keep seeing him, a part of her kept whispering that it would be so much easier to return to her regularly scheduled life. This dating thing was highly overrated.

The cobalt blue silk dress slipped against her skin with a cool softness. Beth shivered with delight as she dropped it over her head. "If this one doesn't look good on me, I might buy it to sleep in. The fabric is wonderful."

The tailored column dress had a deep vee in front. Silk skimmed over her breasts and hips, creating an illusion of a trim waist and sensuous curves. The full-length skirt had a slit higher than Beth liked, but the angle was such that as she took a mock step, her exposed leg looked long and lean.

"Wow, it makes me feel like I have decent thighs," she said. "That would be a first."

"You look great," Cindy agreed. "The color does amazing things to your eyes. They're practically glowing."

Beth glanced at the price tag and groaned. Even secondhand, it was over three hundred dollars.

"Which means it was probably over fifteen hundred new," Cindy said. "I know it's a lot of money, but it looks great."

Beth stared at her reflection in the mirror. "I don't think my wedding gown cost this much," she murmured, "but I really like it."

She turned around and glanced over her shoulder to get the rear view. "My butt's not too bad."

Her clothing budget allowed for impulsive purchases, although not usually ones this expensive. But she hadn't bought herself any clothes so far this year and she didn't think she was going to need much more than a couple of pairs of new shorts for the summer.

"I'm rationalizing," she admitted. "I want to buy the dress. Some of it is because I know I'll feel great in it, and some of it is because I want to impress Todd. Dumb, huh?"

Cindy shook her head. "Both ideas make perfect sense. The dress is a classic. You can wear it again when you're invited somewhere fancy."

Beth wanted to ask how often that really happened, but she was already so close to buying it. She faced front again. With her hair fluffed and the right makeup, she would knock Todd's socks off. Especially since the last time he'd seen her, she'd been all hot and sweaty at Matt's baseball game. Before that, she'd been home caring for a sick kid. Neither impression had been very positive.

"This will make him sorry he doesn't want to see me naked," she murmured, then clamped her hand over her mouth. Has she really said that out loud?

Cindy's eyes widened. "Excuse me? What was that?"

"I... That is... Damn!" Beth took a deep breath. "I wasn't going to talk about this."

"Sorry, but you don't get a choice now. I want details. Start at the beginning and talk slowly."

"There isn't much to say." Beth slipped into her high heels and studied her reflection. The shoes made her legs look even better. It was going to be worth suffering through the viselike grip of control-top panty hose and sore feet from high heels.

"Todd told me he wasn't interested in having sex with me."

Cindy shook her head. "Uh-uh. No way I'm going to believe those words passed his lips."

Beth shrugged. "He said that he was willing to wait until I was comfortable with my clothes on. Then we would talk about getting them off. I think it's an excuse. He doesn't want to see me naked. Not that I blame him."

Cindy covered her face with her hands and groaned. "You make me want to kill you. Of course he wants to have sex with you. He's just trying to be a nice guy. Give him credit for that."

Beth shook her head. "I would rather he was overcome by passion. There's way too much thinking going on, which tells me that he's not really interested. Not that I mind. I don't really want to do it with him, either."

Cindy looked at her. "You're insane. You don't want to have sex with him, but you want him to have sex with you?"

"Of course."

"Okay, I actually understand that, but I don't know why

you're upset that he's being nice. Guys are like that. When something matters, they don't want to take any chances. They go slowly so they have less of an opportunity to make a mistake.''

Beth slipped out of the dress and began pulling on her own clothes. ''I want to believe that, but I think it's more that he's afraid to see thirty-eight-year-old breasts.''

''You didn't get your breasts until you were twelve or thirteen, right?'' Cindy asked.

Beth frowned. ''So?''

''Technically your breasts are only in their twenties.''

''Okay, the women he usually dates have breasts that are barely in their double digits. I can't compete with that.''

''Has Todd said there was going to be a contest?''

Beth glared at her. ''If you're going to be logical about this, I'm not going to talk to you anymore.''

Cindy held up her hands in a gesture of surrender. ''All right. I'll abandon logic. So you want him to want you, but you don't want to want him back, right?''

''Yes.''

''You're afraid of what he's going to think when he sees you naked.''

''Yes, again.'' Beth fastened her jeans. ''I look okay in clothes, but I'm not a young woman. In the bright light of day there's no hiding the stretch marks, not to mention the lumps and bumps that are appearing at an alarming rate. There are some weird vein things. In Darren's mind I was still the girl he married, which was a great quality in a man. Todd has only seen me this way.''

''Do you think Todd is worried about you seeing him naked?''

''No, but guys are different. They don't worry about their bodies the same way. They're very accepting and assume that if a woman says she likes him and wants to be intimate, that she's telling the truth.''

"Don't men mean it when they say they want us and think we're beautiful?"

Beth thought about that for a second. "I don't know," she admitted. "That's what I'm still wrestling with." Not that Todd spent a lot of time telling her that she was beautiful. "I'm going to have to think about this some more. But for now I have a dress and that makes me happy."

They left the changing room and walked toward the cashier. "My credit card is going to whimper," Beth said. "So am I when I get the bill. But it will be worth it."

Cindy paused by a display of costume jewelry. "You want to get earrings?" she asked. "Some of these are really pretty."

Beth shook her head. "I have a pair of plain pearl studs. Those will be fine." She looked at her friend. "Thanks for coming with me tonight and for listening to me complain. I know I don't always make sense, but I'm doing the best I can."

"He's going to be dazzled," Cindy promised. "You'll see."

Beth hoped she was right. Because the truth was somewhat sobering. She was a middle-aged, middle-class mother of two, buying a second-hand dress so she could fake her way through a high-society party.

Beth had to smile. It was that or break down and sob. At least, she thought gamely, her life wasn't boring anymore.

Matt and Jodi didn't appreciate being awakened before eight in the morning on a Saturday, but Beth wanted them to see her leave rather than wake up and just find her gone.

In her head she knew that they were old enough to handle being alone for the day, but in her heart she worried.

She glanced at her watch. Two minutes to go. Knowing Todd, he would be on time. Her stomach tightened as she turned her attention to the garment bag draped over the back of the sofa. It made her feel that she was running off to spend the weekend with a strange man instead of just the day.

"I'll be back around midnight," she said for the hundredth time.

Jodi covered a yawn. "Yeah, Mom, we know. We have all the phone numbers we could possibly need. Cindy and Mike are going to be around all day if anything happens. In fact they might drop by just to check on us, not that we're going to be here all that much." The sixteen-year-old smiled. "You've been over this more than once. We're not kids. We'll be fine."

Before Beth could respond, she heard a car in the driveway, followed by the slam of the car door. Todd appeared on their back porch. Matt let him in. "Hey, Todd."

"You're up early."

Matt rolled his eyes as he ushered Todd into the house. "Mom made us. She's really worried about us, which is kinda dumb. We'll be fine."

Todd greeted Jodi, then smiled at Beth. She tried not to notice how nice he looked in khaki slacks and a short-sleeved shirt. Expensive sunglasses hung from his shirt pocket. Gray-blue eyes danced with humor. "So you're torturing the children again? I thought we'd talked about you getting a new hobby."

"I know, I know." She handed Todd her garment bag. "I've told them I'll be home around midnight."

He feigned disappointment. "But you promised to spend the night."

Beth felt herself getting embarrassed. The good news was that being around Todd always got to her. She had a steady supply of blood to her face so her skin should be in fabulous shape. Free facials, she thought, trying to see the humor in the situation.

"Gee, Mom, if you spent the night with Todd, we could have a really cool party here without you," Matt said.

Beth pulled him close and hugged him. "I'd miss you after I dropped you off at the closest orphanage, but the extra room would be nice."

"You'd never get rid of me," Matt said confidently.

"And you'd never throw a party without checking with me first."

"I know." He sighed. "But it's fun to think about."

Beth released him and kissed her daughter. "Tell me again what's going to happen today."

"Mo-om."

Beth didn't say anything, she just waited. Jodi started talking. "I'm studying this morning by myself. Around noon, Sara's mom is coming to get me. We're going to lunch and movie, then we're baby-sitting at the Andersons. The Johnsons are also dropping off their kids. Then I'm going back to Sara's and spending the night. I have Cindy's number memorized. Sara's folks are going to be home all evening. I'll be fine." She turned to her brother. "You're up."

"Baseball," Matt said. "John's family is picking me up, then dropping me off here after the game. I'll take a shower, eat junk food—" He grinned. "Then Zack's dad is going to come get me. We're going to dinner and a movie. Then I'm spending the night with Zack. I have Cindy's number and Sara's number and the Andersons' number. When I have kids I'm never gonna make them go through this."

"Of course you are," Beth said, then looked at Todd. "I'm ready."

"Don't you want to know what I'm going to do with my day and what numbers I've memorized?" he asked.

Despite her worry and her nerves, he made her smile. "No. Surprise me."

She hugged the kids one last time, then let Todd lead her out to his dark, gleaming BMW. "You sure you don't want to take my car?" she teased. "How often to you get to drive a sports utility vehicle?"

"Gee, that sounds so exciting," he said as he placed her garment bag on the back seat. "It would be too much of a thrill for someone my age. We'd better stick to my car."

"If you insist."

She slipped into the car and fastened her seat belt. Todd settled next to her. They both waved at the children, then he backed down the driveway.

When they reached the end of the street, he pulled the car over and looked at her. "Hi," he said, and gave her a quick kiss on the mouth.

Her heart picked up its pace instantly. "Hi, yourself."

"I'm glad you're with me today. It's going to be fun."

"While I'm sure we're going to have a great time, I'm a little curious as to what our plans are. All you said was that it would be casual."

He put the car in gear and headed for Highway 6. "We're going out on my boat for the day, then tonight we'll be attending a hospital fund-raiser. There's going to be great food at both places and a silent auction at the party."

Boats and fund-raisers? She didn't know which sounded more scary—being around a bunch of rich people she didn't know or being on the water. "It's not that I can't swim or anything," she said, wondering if she would get seasick.

"I'm just wondering about the time crunch. It's going to take a while to get to Galveston, which I assume is where you have your boat docked."

He picked up her left hand and pressed his mouth to her palm. The hot, damp kiss sent fire screaming all the way down to her toes. "Trust me."

"I do," she said, and wondered if he could hear the tremor in her voice.

When he reached the freeway, he didn't head north toward the city and the road out of town. Instead, he continued on the highway another half mile to the Sugar Land Airport.

"A boat with wings?" she asked, confused.

He pulled into the parking lot. "Not exactly. We're taking a helicopter to the coast. It'll save us a lot of time."

"Oh, sure," Beth said. "I do that all the time when I have a lot of errands to run. Helicopters are great."

Todd grinned at her. "You're going to be fine."

She nodded because it was too difficult to speak. He asked her if she wanted to take her dress or leave it in the car. Beth made sure the garment bag was lying smooth along the length of the back seat and then grabbed her small purse. Everything else could stay behind.

As they approached the gleaming helicopter, she thought about how much Matt and Jodi would have enjoyed the trip.

"We can bring the kids next time," Todd called over the loud whirling rotor blades.

Beth stared. "You read my mind."

"I'm glad."

His smile was intimate and it made her even more nervous than the thought of flying in a machine obviously designed by a crazy person. It would never get off the ground, and if it did, it wasn't going to stay there. Still,

Beth wasn't about to confess her fears to Todd or to the impossibly young pilot. She took the seat she was offered and tightened her seat belt until it was hard for her to breathe. Then she prayed…and wondered what kind of man hired a helicopter to take himself and his date fifty-plus miles to the coast.

"Ready?" the pilot asked.

Todd gave him an enthusiastic thumbs-up. When the young man looked at her, Beth weakly imitated the gesture. In a matter of seconds they were in the air.

The ground quickly fell away, giving her a clear view of Sugar Land. She could see the mall and the shopping center just north of it. Houston looked even flatter from this high up in the air. The day was warm and clear and she could see all the way to the horizon. The view was spectacular.

Todd took her hand in his. "Isn't this great?" he asked.

His expression was boyishly proud, and amazingly similar to Matt's when he conquered a new video game. It was a guy thing, she thought. Knowing Todd wasn't all that different from regular nonrich types would help keep her nerves at bay. At least that's what she told herself.

The flight was uneventful. A good thing for a flight to be, she told herself as Todd helped her out of the helicopter. A long black limo waited for them and took them swiftly to the marina where a beautiful and huge powerboat sat in the water.

Beth stopped at the end of the dock and stared. "You own this?" she asked.

Todd shrugged. "Sort of. I own it with a couple of friends. None of us has as much time as we would like to use the boat, so we set up a schedule of who gets it when, and we split expenses." He motioned for her to step on board.

A uniformed man in his thirties appeared by the stairs

and held out his hand. "Welcome aboard, ma'am." When she was standing on the gleaming wood deck, he turned his attention to Todd. "Good morning, sir. We're ready to cast off whenever you give the word."

"Thanks, Richard." He shook the man's hand. "This is Beth Davis. She's my special guest today. She's not much of a sailor, so let's keep things quiet for her. We'd like lunch served around twelve and we need to be back at the dock at four. We're ready to leave anytime you'd like."

"Of course," Richard told him. He turned around and called an order to another uniformed crew member.

Beth was stunned. "You have a staff on your boat?"

"There's a crew of three," Todd said. "This lovely lady is sixty feet long. That's a lot of boat for a bunch of weekend sailors. We decided the crew was money well spent."

"Of course," Beth said, wondering how it was she'd gotten involved with a man who lived such a different life from hers. Still, she wasn't about to complain. So far she was really enjoying the visit to his world.

He showed her around the luxury yacht. There was a main salon, with comfortable furniture and great views. There were three large sleeping cabins, a full, albeit small, kitchen and three bathrooms, or heads.

As the crew started the powerful engines and headed the boat out into the gulf, Todd settled her on a sofa and opened the windows and sliding glass doors. An overhead fan circulated the warm air.

"There's air-conditioning," he said, "but I thought you might prefer to smell the ocean air."

"It's great," she said, and meant it. The boat was luxurious, with fitted brass fixtures, expensive furniture, quality art on the walls, and carpeting that made her sink nearly to her ankles. She liked the location, the surroundings and the company. She had nothing to complain about. If she was a little out of place…or even a lot out of place…she wasn't going to mention it to anyone. Oddly enough, she doubted Todd would even agree with her. For reasons she couldn't quite understand, he thought she fit in just fine.

They talked about their weeks, what the real-estate market looked like for the second half of the year. Beth told him about a couple of stories she was working on for the magazine and some of the editing problems she'd encountered.

He got them each tall glasses of fresh lemonade and when he handed her one, he settled next to her on the sofa.

He was a handsome man, she thought, although that was hardly news. She liked looking at him. She liked the strength of his face, his regular features, the way his mouth always curved up in a teasing smile whenever she fretted too much about something he thought was silly.

"What are you thinking?" Todd asked. "You have an interesting look on your face."

"Just enjoying myself," she said, thinking that it wasn't exactly a lie. She had been enjoying herself…while she thought about him.

"Me, too." He took her hand in his. "Next time let's bring the kids," he said, picking up a thread of conversation they'd discussed earlier. "We could make a weekend of it. Maybe head over to Corpus Christi. Or if we have more time, we can go to Mexico. There are some beautiful beaches on the way. When does school get out?"

"Toward the end of May," she said. It was only April. Was he making plans for the future? She thought that guys weren't supposed to do that. Isn't that what all the women's magazines talked about? How before men were married, they refused to give any indication that a relationship was going to last for more than twenty-four hours?

"I'll bring you a copy of my schedule," he said. "I have

the boat certain weeks, although the dates are frequently flexible. We can pick out some times that work for both of us.'' He paused and looked at her. ''If you think you and the kids would like that.''

''I think it's a great idea,'' she said, equally pleased and terrified by his plans. Was she still going to be seeing him in the summer? Were they dating? She'd nearly convinced herself that he was dating her to get her out of his system. What else could it be? Was Todd Graham really interested in *her?*

She wasn't about to ask him if that was true, and without a question to prompt him, he wouldn't know to volunteer an answer. She decided the best bet was to change the subject. She asked him how long he'd had the boat.

Eventually the cabin grew warm and they went out on deck. Conversation flowed easily between them. After eating a light lunch of shrimp salad and a warm French bread, which was so incredible it deserved to be worshiped, they moved under an awning at the rear of the boat and settled next to each other.

Beth stared out at the flat ocean. ''It's not very deep here, is it?'' she asked.

''No. That's one of the reasons the water is so warm. Off the West Coast the ocean bottom drops considerably. The depth means the sun can't heat it as much.''

''So we get hurricanes and they don't.''

Todd smiled at her. ''They get earthquakes in California. Which would you rather have?''

She grinned. ''How about neither?''

His arm was around her. The contact was very nice. Comfortable, although she could feel herself responding to him. She had a feeling that Todd would always incite passion in her. Was that a bad thing?

She looked around at the beautiful craft. ''Darren would

have loved this,'' she said without thinking, then held back a groan. ''Sorry. That was pretty thoughtless.''

''I don't mind if you talk about him,'' Todd said. ''He was your husband for many years and a large part of your life. You can't be expected to forget about him, nor would I want you to.''

She looked at him. ''You're very kind. Thank you.''

''Did Darren like to go boating?'' he asked.

She had a feeling that he'd asked the question to be polite, not because he really wanted to know. But she didn't know how to get out of answering. ''Yes. We'd often talked about getting a boat of some kind. Smaller than this, of course. Maybe something that fit on a trailer. But the timing didn't seem right.''

They'd lost so much, she thought without warning. So many good times put off until it was more convenient, neither of them realizing how little time they would have together. She closed her eyes against the swell of pain from missing the man who had been both her husband and her best friend.

''You still miss him,'' Todd said. It wasn't a question.

Beth didn't know how to reply. ''Not the way I used to,'' she said at last. ''The emptiness has faded a little. I'll always remember him and I suppose in some way I'll always feel something is missing from my life. I guess it would have been different if we'd gotten a divorce. Then I would have fallen out of love with him.''

Todd didn't say anything. Neither his expression nor his body language changed. Yet she felt the tightness inside of him. He withdrew from her as surely as if he'd moved to the other side of the boat.

''I'm sorry,'' she said again. ''I hate being so inept at all of this. If I'd had a little more experience at dating I would know what I should talk about and what subjects I should avoid.''

''I told you. I don't mind you talking about Darren.''

''I've hurt you,'' she said. ''At least that's what I think has happened. You're sitting right here, but inside you've gone away.''

He looked at her. ''How can you know that?''

''I feel it.''

''I'm not hurt. I'm confused,'' he admitted. ''I tell myself that if you were the kind of woman who could be married to the same man for over a dozen years and not care that he died, then I wouldn't be so attracted to you.'' His smile was rueful. ''Telling myself is one thing, but believing it is another.''

He rose to his feet and walked to the railing. The afternoon sun was high in the sky. Beth didn't have a strong sense of direction but she thought they might have already started back to Galveston.

''Do you think about him when I kiss you?'' Todd asked. ''Do you imagine yourself in his arms instead of mine?'' His hands tightened on the railing. ''Dumb questions. You don't have to answer.''

Good thing, she thought, staring at him openmouthed. She couldn't believe what she'd just heard. Todd Graham was actually jealous of Darren!

Chapter Twelve

Beth absorbed the information, turning it over in her head. Todd jealous of Darren? Was it possible?

She wanted to believe it. Who wouldn't? A charming, sophisticated wealthy bachelor like him, a man who dated incredibly beautiful, incredibly young women all the time, worried about being compared with a sweet, somewhat nerdy engineer? In a strange way the revelation made her proud of her late husband, of the man he had been. Yes, Todd had more money, more things and was better looking, but Darren could match him man to man. In the important things in life, Darren was as much a winner, maybe more. After all, he'd been a faithful husband and wonderful father for over a dozen years.

But Todd wouldn't want to hear about any of that. Even now he stood with his back to her, staring out to sea. Once again she wished for more experience at this whole adult dating thing. But this time it wasn't so she wouldn't make a fool out of herself. Instead, she wanted to know how to make Todd feel better.

She rose to her feet and walked over to stand next to him. If she couldn't come up with something wonderful and witty, maybe she would just settle for the truth.

"I don't think about Darren when you kiss me," she said. "Even if I want to think about something, it isn't possible. I'm always too caught off guard by the passion to do more than just hang on so I don't get too swept away."

Todd wanted to believe her. Hell, what man wouldn't? The alternative was knowing that he wasn't going to match up to the man she'd been married to. A living competitor he could handle. He wasn't afraid to face anyone in a fair fight. But he couldn't fight Darren. The man had been her husband for years. He was the father of her children, and now he was gone. He would never get any older, he would never forget her birthday or be short-tempered. Time would add a glow to his memory until she forgot the bad and only remembered the things that had made her fall in love with him.

Not that he cared, Todd reminded himself. He wasn't really interested in Beth for more than... For more than what? Why exactly was he going out with her? Some of it, he admitted, was because of how she made him feel. He liked being with her. She was easy to talk to. They had a lot in common—they had fun together. He liked her kids. He liked *her*. Wasn't that reason enough?

"I don't know what to do about him," Todd admitted. "It's not usually an issue with the other women I've dated."

Beth smiled. "I would guess very few of them have lost husbands, what with so few of them being legally adults." Her blue eyes brightened as she teased him.

"They're several years over eighteen."

"All right, they're adults according to the law, but not according to life. They haven't been around enough."

He touched her cheek. Most of them had travelled far more than Beth, yet he understood what she was talking about. They hadn't lived through life's hardships. They hadn't had their character tested.

"I don't know how to do this," Beth admitted, her smile fading. "I don't know what it's okay to talk about and what is off-limits. I don't want to hurt you and I don't want to say anything wrong. Everything is so confusing."

Her assumption that she would wound him annoyed and pleased him in equal measures. He knew enough about her to realize her concern came from affection, and not because she saw him as weak, which was how he wanted to take it. He liked that she was worried about saying or doing the right thing when they were together. That meant the relationship meant something to her, too.

"I'm tough," he said as he touched her cheek with his index finger. Her hair blew in the slight breeze. It was an impossible color of red, one he would have suspected as being enhanced...if she'd been anyone else. "Say what you're thinking and we'll deal with the consequences as they occur."

"Sometimes I feel really stupid." She pressed her lips together. "I hate that. I want to be brilliant and witty and sexy and sophisticated, but I'm not."

"You're all those things and more."

He'd promised not to start anything with her, yet he couldn't help leaning forward and gently kissing her. At least they were on the rear deck of the boat, in full view of anyone who wanted to watch. That would keep his need for her in check.

She responded by placed her hands on his shoulders and

leaning into his embrace. Her mouth parted slightly. He was tempted to accept her invitation, but he knew where that would lead. The thought of spending the rest of the evening aroused and aching wasn't pleasant.

"I promised," he said, pulling back and resting his forehead against hers. "It's not because I think you're old or that I don't want you. It's because you're not ready."

"What happens when I am?" she whispered.

"Then I'll ask you to make love with me. If you want to, we'll become intimate."

A shiver rippled through her. He felt the tremor his words had invoked and fought against the need to take her right there on the deck.

"How long will you wait?" she asked.

"As long as necessary."

She straightened and shook her head. "I wish that were true, but I don't think so. I'm a curiosity right now, but that kind of interest fades. I'll be too much trouble. I keep bringing up my inexperience at this sort of thing, which is a major error according to every women's magazine article written on the subject, but I know it's an issue. I don't know how to be the kind of woman you're used to. I'm going to mess up. It's just a matter of when."

He absorbed her words. "For someone who is a positive role model for her children, who pretty much has her life where she wants it, you're amazingly pessimistic about your appeal and your abilities to deal with this relationship. Why is that?"

Beth looked uncomfortable. "Just lucky, I guess."

He touched her face again. "Don't you think that I enjoy being with you?"

She cleared her throat. "Maybe."

He waited.

She sucked in a deep breath and folded her arms over her chest. "Okay, yes, you like being with me."

"And I think you're attractive."

"Do you?"

"Beth!" He growled her name.

"Fine. You think I'm attractive."

"If I like being with you and I find you attractive, why wouldn't I be willing to wait?"

"Because," she said insistently, "guys want to do it whenever they can. If one woman isn't available, they move on to another."

"I'm not a sixteen-year-old kid," he reminded her. "Did Darren run around on you while you were in the final months of your pregnancy, or after the kids were born when you two couldn't make love?"

She looked shocked. "Of course not. But I was having his children."

"So it was a matter of gratitude, not character?"

"No, it was just..." Her voice trailed off. "You're trying to trick me, but I don't know why."

"I'm trying to make you see that some things are worth waiting for. Or even not having at all. You may never be ready to make love with me. You may decide I'm not someone you're really interested in." He could feel himself tensing as he said the words. They were some of his greatest fears, but if he kept his tone light, she would never guess. "I'm still standing here."

"Which begs the question—why?"

She was incredibly tough and wildly insecure all at the same time. How was he supposed to resist that? If he didn't take care of her, she would be out there dating other guys...guys would weren't going to be so understanding. It was up to him to protect her from herself and other men.

"Because I like you," he said.

Color flared on her cheeks. She blushed more easily than anyone he'd ever known. It was just one more aspect of her incredible appeal.

"Oh," she said in a tiny voice.

He led her back to the seats at the rear of the deck. They sat quietly for the rest of the return trip, then took the waiting limo to the helicopter.

Once they were headed toward Houston, Todd leaned over and took her hand. She laced her fingers with his and smiled, then turned her attention to the view out the window. Todd found himself equally captivated, but not by the passing scenery. It was the woman next to him who held his interest.

What was he going to do about Beth? So far he'd broken all his rules with her. They were friends rather than lovers, which he never allowed. Women didn't get close to him—he never saw the point. He wasn't interested in long-term relationships and always made that clear from the beginning. He believed in good times, easy sex and fast, relatively painless goodbyes.

With Beth he'd made several references to future events, which meant that he was considering something more than just a couple of weeks of fun. He'd put off sex indefinitely and for some reason, despite his desire for her, was actually enjoying the chase. More out of character than all the rest, he was getting close to her. Without meaning to, he'd become interested in her life and wanted her interested in his.

None of this made sense. Here he was dating a woman fifteen years older than his last dozen girlfriends. A woman who was still in love with her late husband, a middle-class engineer from the suburbs. A woman with two children. She wasn't his type, they should have nothing in common and everything about her circumstances should send him running in the opposite direction.

Instead he found himself in the unusual position of wanting to prove himself to her. He needed her to see that he was just as…what? Worthy? Just as worth the effort? He wasn't sure. He was in competition with a dead man and he had no way of winning. Worse, he had nothing of value to offer Beth. She didn't care about his money. If anything, it made her uncomfortable. She already had a full life and it didn't necessarily include him. Her children were happy and well-adjusted. How was he supposed to win her when she didn't want anything he had?

He stared sightlessly out the window and realized perhaps the more pressing question was why he felt the need to win Beth at all.

Their evening was to be spent at a fund-raiser for a local cancer hospital. Beth stared at the engraved invitation and realized the event she and Todd were about to attend was a far cry from the 5-K walk/run she'd volunteered for over the holidays. While she'd known it was going to be a fancy evening, she hadn't thought it would be the kind of party that generated gossip in the local society pages.

"There's a simple solution," she murmured to herself as she touched up her eye makeup. "I'll lock myself in the bathroom. End of problem."

She glanced around at the luxurious fixtures and vast space of the suite's master bath. After the helicopter had delivered them to downtown Houston where—through logistical maneuverings she didn't want to think about—Todd's car had been waiting, they'd driven to one of the luxury hotels by the Galleria. Todd has whisked her upstairs to a large suite where he'd left her to get changed for the party starting several floors below.

Just the bathroom was a marvel in decorating wonders. Baskets of incredibly thick, white towels sat next to a

Jacuzzi tub that could easily hold four adults. There were candles and bath salts and a gilded stool and a bidet, which she was far too nervous to even try. She'd only caught a glimpse of the master bedroom. Her lone impression had been of a huge four-poster bed and a wall of mirrors that had made her break out in a cold sweat. Was Todd planning to get lucky later?

She pressed her hand flat against her stomach in an effort to calm her shuddering nerves. Todd had promised he wouldn't push her into bed, she reminded herself. So far, he'd been a man of his word. Why wouldn't she believe him?

Maybe because you don't want to, a small voice whispered. Beth closed her eyes and silently admitted the voice was correct. While the rational part of her appreciated Todd's restraint and his understanding of her need to take things slowly, there was a wild and unruly place in her being that wanted to be swept away. She didn't want to have to behave like a rational adult in this situation. She wanted the excuse of no excuse. Not that he would force her, but that he would make it impossible for her to refuse. If he didn't do that…if he was a gentleman and made her choose, she was going to have to deal with her guilt about Darren.

She exhaled and returned her attention to her makeup. She blotted her lipstick, then applied another coat. Speaking her late husband's name aloud earlier had opened the floodgates. Ever since that moment on the boat when she'd mentioned Darren, she'd been drowning in memories. She was smart enough to acknowledge they were her subconscious' way of protecting her from her very confusing life. But knowing the truth didn't make it any easier to deal with.

Maybe she was wrong to be going out with Todd. Maybe she was supposed to devote her life to her children and her husband's memory. Isn't that what really good women did? Wasn't her life supposed to be over?

Except she didn't feel dead and she didn't like feeling guilty. She'd been a good wife to Darren and she was a good mother to his children. Was it all right for her to have a life that didn't include him? Was she allowed to want to be with another man?

A knock on the bathroom door interrupted her thoughts. "Are you close to ready?" Todd called.

Beth took a step back from the wide mirror and stared at herself. The dress looked better than it had in the dressing room, but she assumed that was the flattering light in the bathroom. She'd sprung for the really expensive, silky panty hose, and as promised, they mushed in her bumps and bulges. She wasn't going to be able to eat very much, and a deep breath was out of the question, but feeling attractive always came with a price.

"I'm ready," she said, and opened the bathroom door.

Todd stood in the center of the suite's bedroom. She'd seen him in a suit before, but never in a tailored tuxedo. The rich black fabric skimmed over broad shoulders and emphasized his masculine strength. Blue-gray eyes seemed to see down to her fragile, imperfect heart. He'd shaved and showered and he was good-looking enough to be a romantic lead in a movie. If she hadn't still been holding on to the door handle, she might have stumbled from the impact of his virility.

His eyebrows raised as he smiled. "You look incredible," he said. "I knew you were going to make me the envy of every man there, and I was right." He moved next to her and softly kissed her cheek. "I was going to suggest we order in and skip the party," he murmured. "But now I want to show you off."

She'd been about to tell him that her shoes were going

to start hurting in less than an hour, that her panty hose felt like a vise grip around her waist and that she'd bought the dress at a secondhand store. Instead, Beth offered her thanks and suggested they head out to the party. There were some things, she decided, that a man just didn't need to know.

Fifteen minutes later they were standing in the foyer of the ballroom. Crowds of incredibly beautiful, incredibly well-dressed people stood chatting comfortably. Beth tried to take a deep breath, but couldn't. She was shaking. This was all a big mistake, she thought to herself as her hands curved around in a death grip on the slender strap of her borrowed silver evening bag. Todd had probably been kidding about staying in the room, but the thought of getting naked with him wasn't nearly as terrifying as the potential for embarrassing herself in front of Houston's social elite.

"Don't be nervous," Todd told her as he led her into the main room. He'd given his name at the entrance and had been handed a card with their table assignment. "You look amazing. Everyone is going to want to know who you are."

"That doesn't make me feel better," Beth murmured back as she eyed a diamond necklace that looked expensive enough to feed a Third World country for a month. The dress had been a mistake. "What if she's here?" she asked.

"Who?"

Beth hadn't realized she'd spoken aloud.

Todd looked at her and she was trapped into answering. Between her nervousness at the unfamiliar surroundings and the line dance by the butterflies in her stomach, she wasn't thinking.

"The former owner of the dress." Beth quickly recounted how she'd wanted something spectacular for the evening but the price of designer originals wasn't in her budget this month.

Todd's gaze never left her face which, oddly enough, made her feel better. "If she *is* here, which I doubt, the only thing she's going to think is that you look a hell of a lot better in the dress than she ever did. You're stunning, you're funny, you're smart and I'm incredibly lucky to have you as my date for the evening. You're going to be fine."

When he went all sincere like that and gave her the smile that made her toes curl in her pumps, she couldn't help but feel better. She kept her feeling of confidence all the way through the walk to their table and the introduction to the three other couples with whom they would be dining. Introductions passed in a blur of names she was never going to remember, then Todd had her in his arms and out on the dance floor.

The live combo was fabulous and Todd led her through an intricate set of steps she hadn't realized she'd known. The lighting was soft and flattering, the crowd well mannered and well dressed. She was sure dinner was going to be delicious. What was there not to like?

"Are you having fun?" Todd asked as the band switched to a slow tune and he pulled her close.

"Very much so."

The music surrounded her in a cocoon of sensual pleasure and safety. In Todd's arms, she could do anything.

"Still nervous?" he asked.

She shook her head. She didn't care that her dress was used, that she couldn't breathe very well or that her feet hurt. In fact, she couldn't feel her feet.

"I've never been to one of these before," she said. "Is it just dinner and dancing?"

"Sometimes. Tonight there's a silent auction, as well.

I've bid on a few things, mostly artwork for the office.'' His smile turned wicked. ''If I didn't think you'd slap me, I would have bid on a weekend retreat they're offering. It's at a private island hideaway complete with blue water and white sand.''

''It sounds lovely.'' And romantic.

He leaned close until his breath whispered against her cheek. ''Native custom requires no clothing for the visit. Everyone's naked.''

She laughed. ''You're right. I would have slapped you.''

''I like this,'' he said as he ran his hands up and down her back. ''I like the pace we've set. I like being with you, but don't for a moment forget that I want you.''

His gaze turned intense. Beth found herself battling nerves again. She didn't know that people—men really— were so up-front about what they wanted. His words made her want to run for cover...or toward that big empty suite upstairs. They were playing a dangerous game, one in which he was the expert. Eventually they would reach a point when he would want to claim her or walk away. Beth sensed that right up until that moment, she wouldn't know how she was going to respond.

She found herself smiling as she realized that it was far more exciting to be chased at thirty-eight than it had ever been at sixteen.

An hour later she found herself chatting with Mary Alice whose last name she'd forgotten. They were at their table, between courses. Todd and Mary Alice's husband were discussing business, leaving the women to amuse themselves.

''Todd mentioned this was your first fund-raiser for the cancer center,'' Mary Alice was saying. ''They get bigger each year.''

Beth glanced around at the expensive decorations and

the gleaming chandeliers glimmering overhead. "It's an impressive setting. I hope they do well."

"Even after expenses, the committee will be able to donate close to two million dollars." Mary Alice, a trim forty-something blonde with green eyes and beautiful long nails that made Beth curl her fingers into her palms and hide her hands on her lap, smiled. "When Todd mentioned he was dating someone new, we all groaned. That man is not known for finding ladies who are able to hold up their end of a conversation. But he promised you were different." Her smile broadened. "I'm so pleased he was telling the truth."

Beth didn't know whether to be flattered or insulted. She felt like a new puppy being shown off for company. *Yes, folks, Sparky is even paper trained.*

She made a low noncommittal sound in her throat.

Mary Alice leaned close and touched her arm. "Did that come out wrong? I do put my foot in my mouth. Martin is forever scolding me. I meant that in a nice way. You're very pleasant and I hope that Todd realizes he's found a prize this time."

Now Beth knew she'd been complimented, but again words failed her. "You're too kind," she murmured.

"Not at all." Mary Alice's expression turned confiding. "We all think it's so romantic, the way you two met. What with your friend buying him for you at that bachelor auction. Fate can be very mysterious."

"Yes, it can," Beth agreed, knowing she sounded like a fool but not sure what else to say.

"Todd talks about you all the time," the other woman continued. "He adores your kids, which is saying something. I can't keep him in the same room as mine."

The woman kept talking, but Beth found it difficult to

listen. Todd talked about her? To his friends? What did that mean?

She filed away the question, determined to ask him later. For now it was enough to bask in the glow of Mary Alice's compliments and acknowledge that fate could indeed be very mysterious.

Later that night, while sitting next to Todd on her sofa, in her temporarily kid-free house, Beth told herself that now was the perfect time to ask her questions about him talking about her to his friends. The only problem was that her throat was too tight for her to actually form words. After all, they were alone…and likely to stay that way until morning.

"You're quiet," he said, resting his arm along the back of the sofa and letting his fingers tease the hair at her nape. "Are you wondering if I have ravishment in mind to-night?"

"Me?" Beth looked at him with what she hoped was real innocence. "The thought never crossed my mind."

"You don't lie very well," he told her. "I think that's probably a good thing."

Beth thought about trying to defend herself, but claiming to be a good liar wasn't much to brag about. Besides, Todd was right. She'd never been good at stretching the truth.

"I had a wonderful time today," she said, thinking that a change in subject might help her relax. "The boat, the helicopter ride, the party. Everything was great."

He shifted until he was facing her on the sofa. "You'd been worried about fitting in with everyone there, but it was fine, right?"

She nodded. "The people I met were very polite." She paused. "I take it that Mary Alice and her husband are friends of yours."

"I've known them for years."

He'd taken off his tuxedo jacket and rolled up the sleeves of his shirt to just below the elbow. His skin was dark and tanned. She could see the muscles in his forearms. The man made her want to melt right there on her family room sofa.

"She said you talked about me," Beth blurted out, then clamped her hand over her mouth. "I didn't mean to say that out loud," she mumbled.

Todd frowned. "Why do you look worried? Yes, I've talked about you. That shouldn't be a surprise. We're dating. At least *I* thought we were."

Dating. As in going out together? As in just the two of them?

Beth considered the idea. She supposed that even with her limited experience she might have categorized their relationship that way, but it had never occurred to her that he would think the same.

"Was I wrong?" he asked.

"No." She wasn't about to explain why the word sounded so strange coming from him. Dating. Wow! Then she had another thought. "Um, are you dating anyone else?"

"No. You?"

She thought he was teasing and laughed. But his serious expression didn't change. "I'm not kidding," he told her. "As far as I'm concerned this is an exclusive relationship. Do you feel the same way?"

She could feel her heart pounding harder in her chest. Next he was probably going to ask her to go steady, and she didn't think she would survive that. "I'm only dating you," she said in a small voice. "I can only handle one man at a time."

"Good. I'd like you to keep it that way."

He sounded possessive. There was a flame flickering in

his gaze, one that warned her he wasn't playing around about any of this. "So, um, we're going to keep going out with each other for a while?" she asked.

"I'd like to. I think this relationship has a lot of potential. On the surface our lives are different, but we have a lot in common. We're both intelligent, we find the humor in the same things, I like your kids and I think they like me."

"But I'm nearly your age," Beth said, as if he needed reminding.

"That's not a bad thing."

He was asking her to take a chance. Beth wanted to tell him that she couldn't. That she was too afraid. What if she continued to see Todd? What if she fell for him? It was just a matter of time until he figured out that she was incredibly ordinary and left her for one of his exciting young women.

She had to tell him no. She had to tell him that this was a really bad idea and they should just forget it. But...

She stared at him, at his handsome face and the way he looked at her as if she had the power to make him happy or sad. Did she really matter to him? Could she let him walk away without finding out how wonderful it could have been? He was asking her to trust in him—in them—when she didn't know if she wanted to be a "them." She still half thought of herself as married to Darren.

"Handsome princes don't fall in love with women like me," she said at last. "I'm having trouble believing this is real."

"Why? What are you afraid of?"

"That you'll break my heart."

He shook his head. "If anyone's heart is going to get broken, it's going to be mine when you find out I'm not going to be able to measure up to the memory of your late husband."

She stared at him, not quite able to believe his words. "You're scared, too."

"Yes."

"But you're not going anywhere."

"If I leave, I lose you."

His logic was so incredibly simple. Why hadn't she thought of it like that? "Okay, I can be brave, as well."

He leaned close and kissed her. "If you get scared, just tell me and I'll hold on tight until the fear goes away."

Chapter Thirteen

Beth finished fluffing her hair and set her comb down on the bathroom counter. All the fluffing and moussing and using other hair care products wasn't going to change the fact that she was nervous.

"There's no reason to be," she told herself. After over three months of dating Todd, she was completely used to the fact that he not only made her nervous, but also made her talk to herself.

She double-checked her makeup, then grabbed the small bag resting on the counter and left the room. "I'm fine," she said, repeating the phrase that she thought might get her though the evening. "It's just another date."

A small lie that offered no comfort. If this was a regular date, it would be easier. She'd actually gotten pretty good at the whole dating thing. She and Todd had fallen into a routine that had them seeing each other several times a week. If the kids were home, they all hung out together, going to dinner locally or ordering in. Sometimes Beth cooked, but not often. Todd claimed she worked hard enough without having to prepare dinner for him. On the weekends the two of them usually went out alone. Sometimes they went to see a touring theater company, sometimes it was just dinner and a movie. Once he'd flown her up to Dallas to see a country music concert.

Beth walked downstairs and set her bag next to her purse. Going out with Todd was a lot of fun. As he'd promised, they had more in common than she'd first realized. They laughed a lot, they argued about politics. He'd given her several great ideas for stories for the magazine and was terrific with her children. He'd also kept his word about the physical aspect of their relationship. Every time they parted company, he kissed her, but nothing more. There had been no repeats of the petting they'd indulged in on her sofa so many weeks ago. He was a perfect gentleman…and he was driving her crazy.

Beth sighed. She wanted more from Todd, and she was terrified of getting more. Nothing was how she thought it was going to be. Every week she half expected Todd to disappear from her life and every week he kept calling. She didn't know what drew him to her, and until she understood that, she wouldn't know why he bothered to return. She hated living in constant anticipation of the worst. It was making her crazy.

She also couldn't forget what he'd told her after the hospital fund-raiser nearly three months before—that she would break his heart because he didn't measure up to Darren.

Beth still didn't know what to make of that statement. She'd had a wonderful marriage with her late husband, but she didn't want another one just like it. She wasn't the nineteen-year-old girl Darren had married. She'd changed and her needs had changed. While she would still love Darren if he was alive, she wasn't looking for a clone of him.

So what was she looking for?

In moments when she was brave enough to be honest with herself, she could admit that she wanted Todd. But she wasn't convinced he was available to her, and she didn't want to have to recover from a broken heart, so she held parts of herself back from him. She waited and watched and wondered when he was going to grow tired of her.

And if he didn't?

Beth didn't like to think about that. She just assumed Todd would grow tired of her. If he didn't, well, she might fall in love with him and that thought terrified her.

A knock at the back door interrupted her thoughts. Beth saw Cindy standing on the porch and quickly let her friend in.

"We're back," Cindy said, plopping down in one of the kitchen chairs. "An amusement park in June. What on earth was I thinking?"

"Hot and crowded?"

"Oh, yeah, and rain. But we all had a good time." Her friend grinned. "I think Mike enjoyed it as much as the kids."

While Beth poured them each a glass of iced tea, Cindy recounted the highlights of her one-week vacation. When she was finished, she leaned back in her chair. "So what's new with you and your boyfriend?"

Beth winced. "It's going well. He got Jodi a great job working for a friend of his. She's basically a gofer in an advertising company and she loves it. The hours are long, but it's good pay and not too far from here. She's already talking about wanting to work in that industry." She rubbed her fingers up and down her sweating glass. "Matt's off at baseball camp this week. He gets home tomorrow night."

"Ah, so the two of you have had plenty of time alone."

Beth made a noncommittal noise in her throat.

"Do you still like him?" Cindy asked.

"Of course. He's wonderful. Very thoughtful and fun to be with." Liking him was not the problem. "I keep telling myself that he's a guy and this is courtship and this is as wonderful as it's ever going to be. If we were in a long-term relationship, things would slack off. But considering how good they are, we'd have a long way to go before we got to boring."

"That's great," Cindy said enthusiastically. "So why aren't you bubbling over with happiness?"

"I am."

Cindy raised her eyebrows.

Beth shrugged. "I usually am. I still wonder what he wants from me. I'm still waiting for him to leave, and he keeps staying. That's nice, but it makes me nervous, too. I'm having trouble keeping my feelings in check. I don't want to fall for someone who is going to move on anytime soon. Anyway, it's going great and I *am* happy." She glanced at the clock over the double oven. "He's due here in about a half hour. We're going back to his place. He's going to cook dinner for me. That will be nice. I've never seen his place before. It's a penthouse. I didn't know actual people lived in penthouses. I thought they were just used in the movies. Oh, and he asked me to spend the night and I said yes."

Cindy had been drinking when Beth made her last statement. Cindy swallowed wrong and started to choke. "Are you okay?" Beth asked.

"I should ask you the same question," her friend said

when she'd recovered. "You're going to spend the night with him?"

Beth had been trying not to think about that. "I guess. I said I would." She waved at the small bag next to her purse. "I'm taking clothes."

Cindy's eyes widened. "This will be your first time making love?"

Using a combination of positive thinking and denial, Beth had managed to keep her insecurities at bay during daylight hours. They haunted her at night, though, when she lay alone in her bed and wondered how she was going to handle Todd taking one look at her thirty-eight-year-old body and running screaming from the room.

"I know," Beth said. "I'm trying not to think about it. I don't want to do this." She stopped and shook her head. "I don't know. I do want to, but I'm terrified. I figure it's inevitable and I might as well do it with someone I trust. I trust Todd."

"I'm glad," Cindy said. "And surprised. You don't trust easily."

"I've given him plenty of opportunities to disappear from my life and he hasn't. This despite the fact that he could have nearly any woman on the planet." Which again brought up the question of why he wanted *her*.

"No way!" Cindy said and placed both her hands flat on the table. "I can see what you're thinking. You want to know why, if he could have anyone, he would want you."

Beth looked at her friend. "That comes from having known each other too long. You can read my mind."

"Of course. Probably because in your situation, I would be thinking the same thing. But I have the perfect answer for you."

"Which is what? I could use a little cheering right about now."

Cindy's smile was smug. "Todd is experienced with women, right?"

Beth nodded.

"Then he's been around enough to know what he likes. And what he likes is you."

Beth opened her mouth, then closed it. "I like that logic."

"Then believe it and let go of the fear. Todd seems like a great guy. He obviously adores you and the kids. Sometimes you just get lucky."

"I want to think so," Beth told her. "But I'm afraid, too. I'm afraid of caring about him too much. I don't want to get hurt. I could be content with something superficial." Beth sighed. "Okay, I couldn't really, but it sounds nice in theory. I just wish I could be sure I wasn't making a mistake."

"We never get to know that until after the fact."

Beth knew she was right, but she wanted to know *now*. She was afraid and nervous and in a strange way, excited about spending the night with Todd. If nothing else, she was finally going to see another man naked. If only she didn't have to deal with the issue of taking off her own clothes.

Cindy leaned forward. "So, are you prepared to practice safe sex?"

"Welcome to being single," Beth said. "Yes, I'm prepared. I didn't know what to buy, so I got three different kinds of condoms."

"I wish I could see the look on Todd's face when he finds that little fact out."

"Funny, I wish I *didn't* have to see it."

The two women laughed together. Beth was fiercely glad she had such a good friend to help her through the tough parts of her life. She drew in a deep breath. Tonight was going to fine. She was a grown-up, and the decision was hers. When Todd had asked her to spend the night, she'd said yes, knowing exactly what it meant. She believed in her heart that if she wanted to change her mind and not stay, he would agree. He might not understand, but he wouldn't make her feel uncomfortable about backing out.

As promised, Todd hadn't pushed her. Becoming intimate was the next logical step in their relationship. If only the thought wasn't so terrifying.

"What if my worst fears are true and I've been doing it wrong all these years?" she asked.

"Then you'll find out." Cindy looked at her. "You have two kids, you were married forever. How wrong could you have been doing it?"

Beth wasn't sure, but if there was a way, she would find it. That was how her luck ran. "Were you this nervous before you and Mike did it?"

Cindy nodded. "I thought I was going to die. I'd asked him over for dinner and hoped he would make a pass at me. When he didn't, I had to tell him what was wrong. Not my finest hour."

Beth wasn't worried about Todd not making a pass at her. He would be gentle and not the least bit insistent, but he would get his point across.

Cindy glanced at her watch. "I should be getting home. I just wanted to come over and say hi." She rose and crossed to the back door. "Remember, I'm going to want details when you get back."

"Sure," Beth promised, and waved weakly. She would be happy to provide details, assuming she even survived the ordeal.

Todd stood on Beth's front porch exactly at seven. He was on time. Despite the distance from his city high-rise condo, he was always on time with her and more often early. It was because he was anxious for the evening to get started. He enjoyed spending time with her. She made him laugh and feel good about himself.

Tonight he felt a faint tension in his body. Anticipation, he told himself. He was a little nervous about having Beth over to his place. He'd been avoiding that particular situation because he'd been concerned about what would happen when the two of them were alone with no possibility of interruptions. More precisely, he'd been concerned about what he would want and push for.

Despite his invitation to spend the night and her acceptance, Todd reminded himself that Beth might still not be ready to make love. From all that she'd told him, Darren had been the only man in her life. Giving herself to another man was bound to be a big deal for her. She would want to make sure she was doing the right thing. As did he. Usually sex was the next logical step. But with Beth it had become something more.

Even though he burned for her, Todd hadn't minded waiting and he would continue to wait if that's what she needed. Because he wanted her first time after Darren to be special. He also wanted it to be with him.

He knocked on the door. She opened it and stared at him. She wore a short-sleeved dress that buttoned up the front. There was a deep V in front that more than hinted at the full curves of her breasts. He quickly took in her bare legs and sandals. She dressed to be easily undressed. The thought made him smile.

"Oh, no. You look too happy," Beth said as she invited him in. "You *are* planning to go all the way."

Despite her wide-eyed stare and her obvious nerves, he laughed and pulled her close. "That's my Beth," he said.

"Always saying what you think. It's the part of your charm that I like best. Promise me you'll never change."

"I can't change," she mumbled, her voice muffled against his shoulder as she clung to him. "Old dogs and all that. Or in my case, old women have trouble learning new behavior patterns."

She trembled in his embrace. He would like to think it was from anticipation, but he knew her better than that. She was terrified.

"So you're going to be a brave soldier and march into battle without a thought for personal safety?" he asked, teasing her gently.

She straightened. "No, I've had several thoughts for personal safety. We never talked about that, but I just went ahead and bought condoms. I didn't know what kind you liked so I got several different boxes."

Her expression was earnest, her words sincere. That was what he loved about her. Her honesty. How she was so literal sometimes.

Then his mind froze and he replayed those couple of sentences. Loved. Had he really thought that? No. Not love. He didn't do love ever. He liked, he admired, he even adored. But that was as far as it went.

"I was speaking generally," he told her. "But since you've brought up the condom issue, I'm glad you're prepared to protect yourself. I have some at home, too."

"Oh."

He looked at her frightened face and pulled her close again. "Don't worry. You're completely in charge of what happens or doesn't happen tonight. I'm excited about having you over for dinner. I hope you like what I've cooked. I've promised you good food, good wine and great company. The rest of it is up to you."

"Promise?" she asked, her blue eyes wide with trepidation.

"I swear."

"Thanks, Todd."

She wrapped her arms around him and rested her head on his shoulder. Her acceptance was absolute. She believed him and trusted him. This was, he realized, one of those moments he would remember forever. The whens and whys of their physical relationship weren't all that important when compared with the faith in him Beth offered.

"Dinner was great," Beth said as she grabbed her glass of wine and stood up.

Todd smiled and almost asked her how she knew. After all, she'd barely tasted the salmon he'd grilled and served with a side of penne pasta. Her conversation at the table had been sporadic—long pauses followed by bursts of conversation. He didn't have to know her very well to realize she was nervous nearly to the point of coming undone. He *did* know her well enough to sense that she would do better if he didn't comment on her erratic behavior and he simply left her to wander at will, talking when she was ready, until she seemed calm enough for him to get next to her.

"I'm glad you enjoyed it."

"Do you want help cleaning up?" she asked. She set her wineglass back on the table, and picked up her plate. "Let's at least clear the table."

"Just leave it," he told her. "I'll take care of it later. Why don't we go into the living room? The sun has set and the view is pretty spectacular."

"Okay."

She followed him as he led the way to the large window that made up two walls of the living room. He'd left the vertical blinds open. In the clear night, downtown Houston was visible, the high-rises slender columns of light.

"If your condo faced the other way, I bet you could see down to Sugar Land," she said.

"Probably."

He crossed to the wet bar and poured them each a snifter of brandy. He doubted she would take much more than a sip, but the glass would give her something to hold in her hands.

"The room is lovely," she said when he approached. "You had someone help with the decorating, didn't you?"

He glanced around at the pale walls and overstuffed furniture. The predominate colors were cream and dark green. A long, low sofa curved through the center of the room, offering perfect seating for his view. Glass-and-brass tables held lamps and objets d'art his decorator had chosen. He'd taken charge of the paintings, most of which were oils in bright colors.

"She did most of the work," Todd admitted.

"It's very nice."

"So you've said."

She took the brandy glass he offered, then walked over to the sofa. As he followed, she sat down on one of the fat cushions, perched there less than ten seconds, then popped back up on her feet. She gave him a quick smile and scurried toward the green wing chair opposite.

"This is nice," she said as she sniffed her brandy. She recoiled. "Wow, strong stuff."

"It's very smooth."

"Are you trying to get me drunk?"

She was serious as she asked the question, but he couldn't help smiling. "No, Beth. You don't have to drink any if you don't want to. Just smell it now and again. It's pleasant."

"All right." She took a cautious sip, blinked, then nodded. "I like it."

Slowly she rose to her feet and crossed to the sofa. She sat at the opposite end from him. "Maybe you should," she said.

"What?"

"Try to get me drunk. It will make things easier."

He angled toward her. "What things?"

"You know." She grimaced. "It. Aren't you planning on us doing it tonight?"

He forced his expression to remain serious despite the urge to chuckle. She was adorable. He wanted to pull her close and promise that he would take good care of her, regardless of whether or not they did "it." But she needed room and time, and he was willing to give her both.

"It?" he asked. "Which it might that be?"

She gave him a "Could you be any more dumb?" look that reminded him of Jodi and Matt when they disagreed with each other. "I thought you'd want us to sleep together tonight."

"Oh, I see." He pretended to consider. "I'd hoped we might make love, but to be honest, I didn't have plans for either of us to sleep."

Her mouth opened, then closed. She dropped her chin to her chest and made a moaning noise. "I can't do this. I have no experience. I know I should be sophisticated. After all, I read those women's magazines. But I'm not prepared to deal with contemporary society."

"Lucky for you I'm the only one here tonight." He patted the sofa cushion next to him. "Why don't you move a little closer?"

She studied him, then shifted until she was about half on the cushion. Close enough to touch but not close enough for them to snuggle. For a woman who'd been married and had a couple of kids, she was surprisingly naive about men, women and their relationships. He knew twenty-three-year-olds who had ten times her experience. He found that he liked Beth and her worries much more than he'd ever cared for the young women's sophistication.

Three months ago when he'd found out about his date with a thirty-something woman from the suburbs, he would have been thrilled to find a way to get out of the evening. Now he couldn't imagine being with anyone else. Those young women had been all wrong for him. They needed to be with men their own age, just like he needed to be with a woman close to his age.

"I want to thank you," he said quietly.

She angled toward him, her knee bumping into his thigh. He noticed that the hem of her dress had crept up her thigh a little, but he resisted the need to stroke the exposed skin.

"For what?"

"For letting me be a part of your life," he told her. "I've enjoyed our time together. You've been generous with me and I appreciate that."

She took a sip of brandy, then set the glass on the table. "I haven't really done anything. You won't let me pay whenever we go out. You barely let me cook you dinner."

"This isn't about money, Beth. It's about sharing. You've opened your world to me. You've let me meet you and your children and share your experiences. I never knew families could be good things. I never understood about parents and kids loving each other. My parents were married for less than five years and it was the longest marriage either of them had. I've learned more just listening to you talk about your relationship with Darren than from all the different families I lived with while growing up."

Her eyes darkened. "I get so confused when you talk

about your life as a kid. I don't know how anyone could ignore their children.''

"That's part of your charm. I respect what you've done with yourself and your kids. They know you love them. That belief is as much a part of them as the color of their hair or their height. You've almost made me believe that love is real.''

Her mouth parted slightly. "I did all that?''

Was it his imagination or was her voice a little breathless?

"Yes, you did,'' he said. "Until very recently I didn't believe that love existed.''

"What about all those young girls?''

He smiled. "Could you please call them young women? Otherwise people are going to think I was raiding the middle school.''

Her lips tugged up at the corners. "Sorry. What about all those young women? Didn't you fall for any of them?''

"They weren't for loving.''

She'd shifted a little closer. He wondered if she was even aware of what she was doing. Her eyes were a brilliant shade of blue. He wanted to get lost in her gaze and never be found again. He wanted to touch her everywhere, hold her close, feel her body against his. He wanted to taste her and make her call out his name. He wanted to take her to a place where she had no choice but to care about him.

"How could you be sure?'' she asked. "We don't always get to chose who we fall in love with. Sometimes it just happens.''

"Not to me. I never felt anything for any of them and they all managed to resist my considerable charms.'' He leaned toward her and brushed her mouth with his.

She sighed. "They are considerable. Your charms, I mean. I have trouble resisting you.''

"Why would you want to?"

"Because it's the sensible thing to do."

He cupped the back of her neck. "I don't want you to be sensible. I want you to be swept away."

"Works for me."

He angled his head and deepened the kiss. She parted her mouth to accept him. She tasted sweet, of herself and of the brandy. His wanting was hard and hot and instant, with a sharpness that told him how much he would hurt if they turned back now.

She groaned as he nibbled a damp line down her jaw to her neck. The low-cut dress had been teasing him all evening and he intended to even the score.

She put a hand on his shoulder and pushed a little, until he looked at her. Her face glowed, her lips were damp from their kisses and there was a light of welcome in her beautiful eyes. "Is this the part where we have sex?" she asked.

"No," he told her. "This is the part where we make love."

Chapter Fourteen

Beth followed Todd into the hall. The good news was she didn't have to tell herself to keep breathing, she thought, trying to maintain some sense of the ridiculous. After all, she was incredibly close to hyperventilating. Wouldn't that be attractive…Todd all worried and carrying on while she hunched over, breathing into a paper bag.

Were they really going to do this? Was she going to be able to handle it? Maybe she should tell him that she'd changed her mind. Except she wanted to do it. At least she was pretty sure she did. It was, she realized, worse than her first time. Because now she knew exactly how incredibly awkward it all could be. Not to mention the fact that Darren had been so in love with her, he hadn't been able to see straight. Not to also mention the fact that at nineteen she'd been pretty pleased with how her body looked. Many things had changed since then.

Todd took her hand and led her into his bedroom. As he

entered, he flipped on a light switch by the door. Several floor lamps sprung to life, illuminating the huge room and the even bigger bed sitting in the center of it.

She had a brief impression of an oak dresser and nightstands, but it was the large expanse of mattress that captured her attention. They could sleep a family of six on that thing. She tried to tell herself that the good news was if she wanted to escape him, there was plenty of room in which to maneuver.

"You look like you're about to sacrifice yourself to the local volcano," Todd said ruefully. "We don't have to do this."

She looked at him, at his strong face and his expression of tenderness and desire. "I want to," she said, and realized she did. She wanted her second "first" time to be with him. Even though she was scared and confused and not at all sure what was going to happen between them. She trusted him. She liked him. And...well, because he was Todd.

"I do have a couple of things we need to talk about first," she told him, and glanced around for a sitting area. The large bedroom lacked that particular facility so she motioned to the bed. "Why don't you have a seat? I'm going to need to pace while we talk about these things."

"Okay." He settled himself on the mattress. He looked so relaxed. She really hated that. Why couldn't he be as nervous and worried as she was? Although if he was, they would be in trouble. Somebody had to be alert enough to take charge. She sighed. Nothing about this was going to be easy.

She crossed to the window and stared out at the view. It was as spectacular as the one in the living room. Then she realized the drapes were open and people could see in. She quickly pulled the drapes closed. Bad enough to be doing this, but far worse to have it witnessed.

She walked toward Todd, realized she was too nervous to stand still, and kept going until she reached the tall dresser. "I'm thirty-eight," she said as she stared at the personal belongings sitting on the smooth wooden surface. There was some loose change, a parking stub, tickets to a play he was taking her to the following week, a business card.

"I know how old you are."

"Yes, but thinking you know and really knowing are two different things." She turned to face him. "Have you ever seen a thirty-eight-year-old woman naked? I'm not talking about those perfect goddess types who work out fifteen hours a day. I mean a real woman. Someone kind of normal."

Todd smiled. "I think you're very beautiful. I like how you look and how you feel in my arms. I want to see you and touch you. I'm excited about seeing your body."

She nodded slowly. "So you haven't."

"Haven't what?"

"Seen a thirty-eight-year-old woman naked. While you may be excited about checking me out, I'm not very excited about having that happen, so I'd like to keep the lights off."

"For the first time in my life I'm actually going to say this a second time. We don't have to make love tonight, Beth. We don't have to ever do that."

She shook her head. "It will be fine. With a little planning and some agreement on procedure I'm sure we'll both have a good time."

She was lying. She didn't expect to do much more than lay there, wishing herself somewhere else. But she wasn't going to share that with Todd. She didn't think he would understand or appreciate her thought process, nor would he get that this was about her, not him.

She walked to the window and pushed aside the drapes so she could stare out at the night. If only there was a way to make him understand how insecure she was about all this. But she was embarrassed enough without spilling her guts even more. But in her heart she wanted to tell him that this would be so much easier if she could keep all her clothes on. Although she really wanted to see him without his.

"We've talked about condoms," she said, because that was something she *could* discuss. "I'm not on any birth control."

"I'm happy to take care of protection."

She thought she might have heard a hint of humor in his voice, but she couldn't tell. To be honest, she couldn't blame the man. The situation was insane.

She drew in a deep breath. "I think that's everything, except maybe the fact that I haven't been with anyone since Darren died. Of course you probably knew that, but in case you didn't, I want you to know. And Darren was my only lover, so there's every chance I've been doing it all wrong. I would appreciate it if you would be gentle when you tell me that. I think a burst of uncontrolled laughter at the wrong moment would scar me for life."

"You worry too much," he said, but his voice was way too close.

As Beth turned, she realized Todd was standing right behind her. Before she could say anything else, he took her in his arms and kissed her. Really kissed her. His tongue stroked her lower lip before plunging inside her mouth. He teased and taunted her there while his hands moved up and down her back.

Her reaction to his touch was as instantaneous as ever,

with need heating her blood and making her feel weak. Her breasts flattened against his chest. Their bodies pressed so close, she could feel his arousal jutting toward her. He wanted her. Despite her nerves, her stupid speeches and her awkwardness, he still wanted her. The knowledge filled her with relief.

"I want you," he said, trailing kisses down her neck to the V of her dress. "I've wanted you from the start. Even when you sprayed me with the hose. Even when Matt was sick and you were in tears. No matter what, I've always wanted you."

His words were a sweet, seductive drug that made her lethargic. She melted against him, knowing that whatever this man planned to do was fine with her.

He reached for the first button on her dress, then pulled back and sighed. "As much as I want to see you, I'm willing to abide by your rules."

It took her a moment to figure out he meant that the lights were still on. "I'll get them," she said and crossed to the still-open door.

She shut it, then hit the light switch. Instantly the room plunged into blackness. She waited a couple of seconds and realized her eyes weren't going to adjust. Not enough anyway. She had a vague idea of the direction of the bed but this was a strange room and she didn't want to break the mood by bumping into furniture.

"Could you say something so I can find you?" she asked.

"I'm over here," he said.

She followed the sound of his voice and slammed her shin into the footboard. Pain radiated out from the point of impact.

"Are you all right?" Todd asked.

"Fine," she said, trying to unclench her teeth. She felt

her way around the bed and settled on the mattress, then reached out to touch him. Her fingers stretched along the smooth bedspread. "Where are you?"

"Here."

His voice came from the other side of the bed.

"Oh. I'll move," she said quickly and scooted toward him.

She kept one hand in front of her and encountered something warm and smooth and very naked. Without meaning to, she shrieked. "You took your clothes off?"

"Just my shirt. Do you want me to put it back on?"

She could feel heat on her cheeks. "No, of course not."

This was going to be worse than she'd imagined, Beth realized. And she'd thought it was going to be pretty awful. "I was startled, that's all," she told him. "I'm glad you took your shirt off." Did that sound as stupid as she thought it did?

He touched her hand, then followed that up to her arm. "Stretch out here," he said, guiding her until she lay on the mattress, her head on a pillow. "Just relax."

Relax? Was he kidding? That wasn't going to happen, at least not in this lifetime. Relax? When all she wanted to do was run screaming from the room?

He shifted. She tried to figure out what he was doing, but the darkness was absolute. She raised her head, hoping that would help her see better, then clanked her forehead against the side of his face.

"Ouch," she yelped, and rubbed the injured spot.

Todd didn't say anything, but he had to be hurting— she'd whacked him really hard.

"Sorry," she murmured.

"No problem."

Beth's eyes began to burn, but not from her various bumps and bruises. This wasn't going to work.

"Stay still," he told her. "I'll come to you."

"Okay." Her voice was small.

His hand found her shoulder and followed it up to her face. Seconds later his mouth touched hers in a warm, arousing kiss. He moved slowly, sensuously, kissing her deeply. When he shifted, to half lie against her, she wrapped her arms around him. She liked the feel of him against her, the weight of him, the smoothness of his skin. When she stroked his bare back, his muscles rippled in response. He was still aroused; his hardness bumped against her hip.

She took a deep breath and willed herself to ignore all the screaming questions and worries in her mind and just concentrate on what he was doing. She liked how he traced her face, his fingertips lightly touching her skin. His kiss was as perfect as always. When his hand moved down her throat, toward the buttons of her dress, she told herself this was what she wanted. It was lovely. Exactly right. And she couldn't feel a thing.

A single tear trickled down her temple and got lost in her hair. Beth swallowed the rising tide of disappointment. It wasn't going to work—not her, not their making love, nothing. While she could sense his hand on her body, the heat and weight of his touch, she couldn't feel it inside. There was no connection between what he was doing and whether or not she was aroused. It was as if there was a barrier between the thin layer of her skin and the rest of her being. Whatever passion he'd aroused before had faded until she was left empty and cold.

He finished with the buttons at the front of her dress. His hand slipped inside and closed over her breast. Nothing. She felt nothing. Not even when his fingertip swept over her nipple.

''Beth,'' he breathed against her ear. He kissed her temple.

She squeezed her eyes tightly closed, but that didn't stop the fresh flood of tears. She knew the exact moment he figured out she was crying.

He shifted, then a light clicked on by the bed. Beth blinked against the brightness, but didn't bother turning away. Where exactly could she hide?

He stared at her for a long time, then nodded.

''What are you thinking?'' she asked.

''That you need more time.''

''No, I don't want to wait. Couldn't you just, you know, do it and get it over with?''

''That's not how I want our first time to be. I want you to enjoy it, too. This isn't some duty to be ended as quickly as possible. Making love is a sensual and emotional experience. We both have to participate to make it work.''

Beth nodded. She'd blown it. ''I'm sorry,'' she said.

''You have nothing to apologize for.''

He was being kind, she thought as she sniffed. ''I guess we can call a cab to take me home.''

He glared at her. ''Don't even think about it.'' He stood up and pulled on his shirt. ''Take off your dress,'' he said as he crossed the room and headed for a closed door on the far wall.

Beth stood up slowly and clutched the open front of her dress together. He wanted her to get undressed?

Todd returned with an oversize navy terry-cloth bathrobe. ''Put this on,'' he said. ''You'll be more covered and more comfortable.''

''What are we going to do?'' she asked as she slipped out of her dress and quickly pulled on the robe. She was nervous about being momentarily clad in her underwear, but he didn't embarrass her by looking.

"We're going to forget this whole thing," he said, turning to her once more and shaking his head. "Don't look at me like that. I mean sex, not the relationship. We're going to go out to the living room and watch old movies together. I have a great collection. Then despite what I said earlier, when we're tired we're going to come back here, crawl into bed, snuggle together and fall asleep. I don't mind that we're not going to make love, but I do want to feel you next to me in bed. I want to hold you close and I want to wake up with you in my bed. Agreed?"

Tears threatened again, but these were good tears. A sign of relief and gratitude. She suspected he didn't understand why this was so difficult for her, and he could have gotten angry or frustrated with her lack of response. Instead he was patient and understanding. How was she supposed to resist that and why did she want to try?

She raised herself on tiptoe and kissed him. "Thank you," she said.

He grinned and patted her rear. "Yeah, yeah, enough of that mushy stuff. Let's go pick a movie."

Fifteen minutes later they were curled up next to each other on the sofa. Beth had confessed that she wasn't a brandy person and accepted a glass of white wine instead. The original version of *Sabrina* started. She sipped her wine and savored the feel of Todd's strong arms around her. She wasn't sure why or how she'd gotten lucky enough to meet him, but she was grateful. He was a wonderful man.

She finished her wine and set the empty glass on the coffee table in front of them. Heat filled her belly, which wasn't surprising. She hadn't had more than a mouthful of dinner. The wine would go right to her head. Already the room looked a little fuzzy. She wasn't drunk, exactly, just very relaxed.

As was Todd. She glanced at him. He seemed focused

on the movie. She studied his profile, the straight line of his jaw and the way it curved up slightly by his ear. She could see the exact spot where stubble gave way to smooth skin. Without meaning to, she pressed her mouth there and kissed him.

He gave her a brief smile, then returned his attention to the action on the television. Beth decided to taste his ear, then nibbled on his earlobe. She was hungrier than she'd realized. She tasted his neck, nibbling and licking.

"What are you doing?" he asked.

"Nothing. Go watch your movie."

"You're making it difficult to concentrate."

Maybe it was the wine giving her courage. Or maybe it was the affection she saw in Todd's eyes. "Difficult, not hard?"

"Oh, it's plenty hard."

"Really?"

Not quite able to believe what she was doing, she shifted until she straddled his lap. Her center met the fly of his slacks. Sure enough there was an impressive ridge pressing there.

She kissed him. "Watch the movie," she instructed between licks and nips on his lower lip.

"I can't. You're blocking the screen."

"I can move."

"That's okay. I like this better."

His hands settled on her bare waist. It was only then she realized that the robe had fallen open. They were in the middle of his living room with the television playing and several lamps lighting the room. But for some reason she didn't care.

She kissed his cheeks, his nose, his forehead, then returned her attention to his mouth. He parted for her instantly, and when she swept inside, he met her and they danced. Their kisses mimicked the act of love that was to follow and Beth found herself trembling in anticipation. Whatever barrier had existed before disappeared. This time she felt everything. The heat of him so close to her, his hardness pressing against her feminine place, the way he reached behind her and quickly, easily unfastened her bra.

Then his hands were on her breasts, cupping her, teasing her nipples. She arched into his feathery strokes and groaned his name into his mouth.

"I want you," he ground out between kisses.

"I want you, too." She bit his lower lip and reveled in her body's awareness. She *did* want him. Already she was wet and swollen. She ached for him everywhere.

He tugged at the bra. "Take this off, please."

She hesitated for a second. The robe gave her a feeling of protection, as if she wasn't really all that undressed. So rather than resisting his request, she compromised by sticking her hands up the voluminous sleeves and pulling down the bra straps. Once she was free of them, the undergarment fell away.

He stared at her breasts. "I knew you'd be perfect," he breathed, and drew her close to him.

She knew what her chest looked like. She'd had two kids and breast-fed them both. While she wasn't completely saggy, she was far from perky. Still, as his mouth closed over her left nipple and sucked deeply, she found she didn't care anymore. He wanted her and she wanted him. Her body functioned; it was strong, and right now it gave her incredible pleasure. What else mattered?

She wrapped her arms around his head as he drew the tight peak inside his mouth. Her breathing increased. Each tug raced through her, making her insides quiver and her skin catch fire. He grabbed her rear and squeezed, bringing her closer and making her rub against him. Back and forth, back and forth. Her dampness heated against him, her breasts swelled. She called out his name.

He slipped a hand between them, found her panties and groaned in frustration.

"Stand up," he demanded hoarsely.

She stumbled to her feet. He quickly stripped off her underwear, then pulled her back to him. This time his fingers encountered bare, damp flesh.

She didn't have time to care that she was naked, something she had sworn he would never see. None of that seemed to matter now. Not when he was kissing her so deeply, and his hand was stroking her so perfectly. He moved in a slow circle, ever closer to that most sensitive place, then he found it. She gasped and surged against him. His free hand closed over her breast. He teased her nipple with the same rhythm as his kiss, as his touch against that tiny point of pleasure.

"Too much," she gasped against his mouth as the sensations overwhelmed her. There was too much to think about, too much to feel. His fingertip brushed against her again and again, with exactly the right pressure and speed, and she was getting so close. She moved her hips, flexing against him, barely aware that he allowed her to set the pace, that she guided him with her body, showing him how she wanted it to be.

She forgot to be shy as the heat filled her and she shrugged off the robe. She was a wild creature. Naked and exposed and filled with a passionate pleasure she'd nearly forgotten existed.

At the last possible second, she broke their kiss and stared at him. She stood on the edge of paradise. He stared at her, his irises so dilated, his eyes looked black.

"Yes," he whispered, and rubbed faster.

It was all she needed. The explosion was hard and fast,

rippling through her, pulling her apart, making her cry out and cling to him.

Even as the last drop of pleasure left her, she found herself being lifted, then lowered. She was on her back on the floor, stretched out on the thick robe. Todd loomed over her. She read his happiness and the questions.

"I'm fine," she told him. "That was amazing and I'm fine."

"Good."

She stroked his bare chest. "That was pretty wild for an old lady like me. I can't believe we did it on the sofa."

"Now we're going to do it on the floor."

"I guess so."

He kissed her. She wrapped her arms around him and held him tight. She'd thought she might be embarrassed afterward, but she wasn't. She was content. She'd been right to trust him.

He kissed her, then dipped lower and traced a damp trail down her chest to her breasts. She was still flushed from her release, but her body quickly collected itself as he nipped at her sensitive skin. His hands were everywhere, touching, learning, teasing her back into mindlessness. She had a brief thought of bumps and stretch marks, then quickly dismissed any worry. Everything he did felt too good.

When his mouth moved lower, to her belly, then drifting to her hipbones, then her thighs, before finally coming to rest against her most private place, she didn't know what to think. No one had ever done that to her before. Of course she'd read about it, but she'd never, they'd never... Was he going to kiss her *there?*

Before she could figure out if this was a good thing or a bad thing, he was licking her, circling around the tender point of pleasure. Her arousal was as quick and unexpected as it was intense. Her entire body tensed in anticipation of a release so perfect, she might just die if it didn't happen.

"I can't," she murmured as she clutched the thick robe and tossed her head from side to side. She couldn't. She'd just had her release. It was too soon. But she could and she was. Already the heat filled her, making the bottoms of her feet burn and her face hot. She thrust her hips toward him, urging him to continue, to never stop. Need spiraled inside of her, pushing higher and higher. He moved his tongue against her, then slipped a single finger inside of her waiting dampness.

She practically screamed out her release. She convulsed into shards of pure perfection, pulling back her knees, exposing all of herself to him, losing herself in the moment.

He waited until the last ripple had faded, then stretched out next to her and pulled her close. As he stroked her hair, he murmured that she was fine, that he would keep her safe. It was only then that she realized she was crying. He rocked her against him until the tears faded.

"What's happening?" she asked. "I didn't know it could be like this. I've never, um…" She paused.

He grinned. "You've never climaxed twice or you've never made love that way?"

She had to clear her throat before speaking. "Well, both."

"I'm glad."

His kiss was tender. He drew her head against his shoulder. She rested her arm on his chest and wondered how this had turned out so right.

"Thank you for everything," she said.

"I just wanted to make you happy."

"You did a fine job."

They held each other for a long time, then she decided

enough was enough. She was finally ready to see him naked.

"All right," she said, raising herself up on one elbow. "Strip."

Todd laughed. "Yes, ma'am."

He stood up, took off his shirt, unfastened his belt, then lowered his fly. In one smooth movement, he pushed down his slacks and briefs. His arousal sprang free, long and thick and very male.

He placed his hands on his hips. "How many naked men have you seen before?"

"Counting you?"

"Sure."

"Two."

"Do you like it?"

She reached up and touched his smooth warmth. He was bigger than she'd expected, bigger than she was used to, but she didn't think that was going to be a bad thing.

She touched him tentatively with the tip of her finger, then smoothed her hand down his hard length. "I like it and you very much."

He dropped into a crouch and stared at her. "I want you. I want to make love with you. But if you're too nervous for me to be inside of you, there are other ways of making this work."

His words raised all kinds of interesting questions that she would have to remember to ask him later, she thought as she lay back and held out her arms. "I want you inside of me," she said. "Please."

He reached into his slacks pocket and pulled out a condom. After slipping it over himself, he knelt between her parted thighs. "I want you," he repeated.

"I want you, too," she responded, then smiled. "What

with all the foreplay, we don't have to worry that I'm not ready.''

"I know." His smile was very satisfied.

He moved slowly, filling her, stretching her until she felt long-dormant nerve endings springing to life. His gaze locked with hers as he moved in and out of her body.

They were on the floor of his living room. This was a far cry from the romantic setting she'd imagined when she'd thought about this moment, but everything was exactly right. She touched his face, his arms, his mouth. They continued to stare at each other while they made love. Beth felt pieces of herself connecting with him. Was this bonding? Was she being irrevocably joined with this man?

Before she could answer the question, she felt her body collecting itself.

"It's happening again," she breathed.

"Good."

He moved faster, deeper, plunging into her, taking her with him. She tensed and pressed up against him. The tingling filled her, the tension. Passion grew and tightened, then exploded into a rippling wave that stretched on infinitely, renewing itself with each thrust of Todd's body.

Again and again until he cried out her name and stiffened. Both still looking at each other, both experiencing the ultimate pleasure, she felt her muscles shudder around him, milking him dry and leaving him in no doubt of what he'd done to her.

Chapter Fifteen

Todd awoke just after dawn and parted the drapes a little so that he could watch Beth sleep. She curled up on her side, facing him, one bare arm exposed, the rest of her buried under the covers.

They'd returned to the bedroom a little after midnight where they'd talked for hours, made love again and had finally fallen asleep in a tangle of naked arms and legs. He couldn't have gotten more than a couple of hours' rest, but he wasn't tired. Energy, joy, *something* coursed through him, making him feel more alive than he had in years.

He stared down at her and smiled. Her hair was mussed, but still a beautiful shade of red. Her pale skin looked luminescent in the early-morning light. She'd warned him dozens of times that making love with her was going to be different than making love with young women in their early twenties. She'd been right. Her body had felt different. She had marks from her pregnancies, badges of honor from bringing forth new life. While he, like most men, could appreciate the appeal of youth, he'd found that what he really wanted in his bed was someone he cared about.

For the first time in his life he understood the difference between sex and making love. For the first time he understood that physical intimacy was about connecting the spirit as well as the body. He had felt things with her he'd never experienced before. Not just physical pleasure—although that had been extraordinary—but a touching of hearts. For the first time he wanted to be with someone until he knew everything about her. He wanted their lovemaking to be familiar. He wanted to be inside her so much, releasing himself again and again until her body chemistry changed and she was a part of him, just like he was a part of her.

He needed her. He needed her in his life. He needed to wake up next to her, to know that she was close by. He needed to be a part of her world, offering support wherever he could. He needed to love her. And that thought scared him to death.

Todd returned to the window and stared out at the early-morning dawn. That's what all this came down to—love. He who had never believed before, he who had no life experience to show him love existed, had fallen in love with Beth. He didn't want to, for a number of reasons. For one thing, she'd been married for years to a wonderful man. If Darren was still alive, then she would be with him...not Todd.

He couldn't compete with a ghost, nor did he want to. He'd reached the place he'd thought was impossible—he'd finally met someone with whom he was willing to risk it and...and she wouldn't want him.

There was a second, more important reason that the thought of loving Beth made him break out in a sweat. She had children and responsibilities. What did he know about that? He could keep his business running without any problems, but this was about family, not commerce. He'd lived with stepparents and stepsiblings. He knew all the potentials for disaster. Was he willing to take that on? Not just Beth, but her kids and her life-style?

He wanted to wake her up and talk to her. He wanted her to tell him that it was going to be fine, except she wouldn't. She'd been having doubts from the beginning. Maybe she'd been right to question their relationship. It was one thing to play at being in her life; it was quite another to want to make it real and permanent.

He clutched the back of the chair next to him. There it was—the bottom line he'd been avoiding for as long as he could remember. All those years of superficial relationships, reminding himself that he didn't believe in love because he'd never seen it or experienced it himself. All the times he'd ended relationships before they got serious, telling himself he was simply accepting the inevitable and getting out before things got sticky, when the truth was he'd been afraid. He'd held back because he hadn't believed anyone would ever care about him, and even if they did, he wasn't sure he knew how to get it right.

He had nothing to offer her—nothing of value anyway. She wouldn't care about his money or his financial success. Her life was comfortable and she wasn't looking for much more. If she were seriously considering letting someone share her world, who would she want? A playboy bachelor with a history of short-term relationships and a family that had made getting married and divorced a sport all could play?

He pressed his fingers against the air-conditioner-cooled glass and shook his head. Of course not. Beth would find someone like Darren. Someone with a track record. And even if she was willing to take a chance on him, he wasn't so sure he was willing to take a chance on himself. In the deepest, darkest shadows of his soul, he wasn't sure he was willing to commit that much to both Beth and her kids. Which made him the biggest bastard of all time.

The kindest thing would be to walk away from her and let her get on with her life. Sure, he would have trouble forgetting her. In fact, she might always be a part of him. But his leaving was best for her. He glanced over his shoulder and watched her sleeping in the morning light. She was so beautiful. Smart and funny and caring.

Pain ripped through his chest, an ache that had no physical source, but came from the loss of the one thing he hadn't realized he'd been looking for—a place to belong.

He loved her. How could he let her go?

Knowing what kind of man he was, how could he ask her to stay?

Beth stirred sleepily, then opened her eyes. Light streamed into an unfamiliar bedroom, and it was a couple of minutes before she figured out where she was. About the time she recognized the oversize pieces of furniture, memories surfaced. Memories of an incredible night spent with an incredible man.

She sat up and quickly pulled the covers to her shoulders when she realized she was still naked. When they'd finally returned to his bed, she hadn't been able to think of a way to tell him she would be more comfortable slipping on the nightgown she'd brought with her. Then he'd started touching her again and she hadn't been able to think of anything except how he made her feel. He'd been romantic and incredible and she'd felt a kind of passion she'd never known existed before. Guilt flared inside of her, guilt for allowing another man to be that intimate with her, but she pushed it away. She refused to let her perfect evening be spoiled by a less-than-perfect morning.

She stretched and touched Todd's side of the bed. The sheets were cold—he'd obviously been up for a while. Then she inhaled the smell of coffee and cooking bacon. Her mouth watered. Last night she'd been too nervous to eat, and now she was starved.

She'd been about to reach for the bathrobe lying at the foot of the bed when she heard the sound of footsteps approaching. She looked up and saw Todd standing in the doorway to the bedroom.

He'd pulled on jeans and nothing else. His hair was mussed, his jaw dark with stubble and he was about the most gorgeous male creature she'd ever seen in her life. Then he smiled—a slow, masculine smile that spoke of a woman conquered in the most primitive, delicious way— and her thighs went up in flames.

"Good morning," he said, his voice low and sexy. "How did you sleep?"

"Both hours were great."

"I know. I'm a little tired, too, but it was worth it."

"Oh, I'm not complaining."

He walked over to the bed and set the tray in the center of the mattress, then settled next to it. He'd prepared coffee, scrambled eggs, bacon, toast and juice.

"Impressive," she said, wondering if all his women got such first-class treatment the morning after. She found herself hoping that he didn't usually go to all this trouble. She wanted to believe last night had been special to him.

"I hope you think so," he told her. "I don't cook much, but I can fake my way through breakfast."

Telling herself she was two kinds of fool for asking and inviting heartache, she spoke anyway. "Ah, so the women are the ones who prepare breakfast the next morning."

Blue-gray eyes seemed to see down into her soul. "I don't do breakfast. I generally leave and drive home, even if it's nearly dawn. I don't like waking up in someone else's bed, or having a stranger in mine."

She blinked, then felt her face heating with embarrassment. Her throat went dry and her hands started to shake. "You wanted me to leave," she whispered. "I didn't realize. When you said, 'Spend the night,' I thought you meant just that, but you were referring to sex."

Once again she'd made a fool out of herself. Just when she thought she'd figured out this whole dating thing, she got it wrong. Someone should keep her locked up.

"Stop," Todd told her as he took one of her hands and brought it to his mouth. He slowly and thoroughly kissed her fingertips. "I said I don't like having a stranger in my bed. That was a statement about my life before. Not about you. I want you here. I'm pleased you spent the night."

Between the intensity of his expression and the sensual nibbling of her fingers, she had trouble concentrating, but his words did get through. All the way down to her heart, which had swelled to near bursting. His hair fell over his forehead in disarray. He hadn't showered, he wasn't dressed in one of his expensively tailored suits. This morning he looked like some man who had spent the night making love. Not Todd Graham, sophisticated tycoon, but Todd, the guy who had stolen her heart.

He said something and she responded automatically. He poured coffee and she took the cup, then sipped the steaming liquid. But all without actually knowing what she was doing. Most of her attention focused on that one statement. *The guy who had stolen her heart.*

Was it true? Had he really taken possession of her feelings? She thought about the night before, all the tenderness and touching, the way he'd made her feel. The lovemaking had been incredible, bringing her to a physical place of pleasure she'd never experienced before. They'd held each other and stared into each other's eyes. They'd kissed and—

She swallowed hard, biting back a groan. She understood a little about biology. She was female. As far as her gene pool was concerned, her purpose in life was to continue the species. That meant when she made love with a man, she bonded so that if they had children, there would be an adult pair to raise the young. In her head she could tell herself it was just sex, it didn't really matter, nor did any number of other twentieth-century truths. Biology was way older than modern thought, and without her realizing it, her heart had decided to be old-fashioned.

When she and Todd had made love, she'd connected with him in a way that women had been connecting with men for centuries. She hadn't just given him her body, she'd handed over the essence of her being. She'd fallen in love.

The panic was as cold and icy as it was instant. She had to get out of here. Now! Before she said or did something incredibly stupid. More stupid than falling for a wildly inappropriate guy. What on earth had she been thinking? Then she realized she hadn't been thinking at all. She'd been feeling and reacting. It was finally time to use her head.

"I know what you're thinking," Todd was saying when she resurfaced and could pay attention to a conversation already in progress. "I'm shocked by the whole thing, too." He still held her free hand in his. He stroked her palm in a way that distracted her and made her bones melt. How did the man keep doing that to her?

"I knew it would be special," he told her. "But I didn't realize how special. You're an amazing woman, Beth." He smiled ruefully. "I woke up early this morning and I was terrified."

That got her attention. Her own questions and concerns faded away. "What do you mean?"

"You're a mature woman with two teenagers. You have a life and a life-style. It would never be just the two of us, at least not for several years. The kids would have to come first. I've only dated young women and I think one of the reasons is that I was always the center of their world. You can't promise me that. It wouldn't always be about us."

He shook his head. "But that was just the starting point. The real issue is that I don't know what I *can* promise you. I watched my parents marry and remarry. I've seen what that does to children, I remember what it did to me. I know what you had with Darren and the level of that commitment. I decided I couldn't do that."

Her face froze. Beth tried to make her expression neutral, but her muscles weren't responding. She'd just realized that she'd bonded with him in the most primitive way possible and he was telling her it was over?

"You got sex and now it's 'See you later'?" she managed with a gasp of pain that nearly made her double over. He was still holding her hand. She jerked it free.

She couldn't breathe, she couldn't believe what he was saying. Her heart clenched in her chest. She wanted to run and scream, she wanted to throw things and hit him. "You bastard. You *bastard!*"

"No. Beth, don't." Todd grabbed her arm. She hadn't realized she raised her hand to him. "It's not like that."

She pulled free of him and scrambled out of the bed. "Don't bother telling me what it's like. I don't want to listen."

"You're going to have to," he said, rising and standing in front of her. "I'm telling you all of this because it's important. I had doubts. I wasn't sure I could be the kind of man you needed. I wasn't sure I wanted to take on two kids. I'm not unaware of the pitfalls of the situation. I don't think it's going to be easy. So, for about ten minutes, I balked at the idea. But then I fixed breakfast and brought it in here and saw you in my bed and I realized that's what I want. Us. Together. No matter what."

She raised her hands to cover her ears and she didn't care how stupid she looked. "Leave me alone."

"I won't. I love you. If I'm not the man I need to be to make this work, then I'll grow to be him. I've changed already. You've changed me in the best way possible. I don't want this to end. I know we have a lot to work out. I know I can't be a replacement for Darren and I don't want to be."

Beth realized she was standing there naked…in the daylight…flaws exposed for the world to see. As if the pain ripping through her body wasn't enough. She spotted her clothes in a pile on a chair by the closet. Sometime this morning Todd had folded them neatly for her. She grabbed her panties and bra and slipped them on.

"What are you doing?" he asked.

"I'm leaving. It's late. I need to be home. This isn't…" This isn't what? She realized she didn't know how to complete the sentence. What was she supposed to say to a man who had decided it was all too much work? Okay, now he thought it was fine, but he could change his mind again.

She reached for her dress, but he got it first. He held it away from her. "Would you rather I lied?" he asked. "Should I have kept my doubts to myself? Wouldn't you have wondered about the reality of that situation? Wouldn't you have questioned my ability to *see* reality if I thought everything was going to be perfect?"

"We don't need you. I don't need you. Go back to your young girls and have whatever you want."

"No. Because however difficult this is and however stubborn you're going to be, I still love you." His gaze settled on her face. "You've been questioning our relationship, your feelings and my commitment from the first time we went out. I've listened and reassured you to the best of my ability. But nothing I've said is enough. Day after day, you keep waiting for me to come to my senses and take off. But I was just supposed to put up with that, right?"

She didn't have an answer. Shame joined the pain and made it impossible to speak.

"I looked at the situation realistically," he said. "I looked and wondered if I could do it. What I decided was I could. But that's not good enough, is it? I wasn't ever supposed to question what I wanted. I was supposed to be this perfect guy who always has the answers."

Her stomach lurched. Beth thought she might throw up. "I have to go." She *had* to get out of here before it was too late. She grabbed for her dress and pulled it away from him, then quickly put it on and began fastening the front buttons.

Her fingers were shaking and she could feel her eyes burning. She was not going to cry. Not here, not in front of Todd. Her throat hurt. Her body ached. Something had gone very wrong and she didn't understand why. The fear was overwhelming as was the guilt. Was he right? Was she really that shallow and unfair? How had last night been so wonderful and this morning been so horrible?

She had to get out of here. She had to regroup and figure things out. She had to not hear whatever it was he wanted to tell her.

"Beth, I love you, and if you walk away from this, you're going to regret it for the rest of your life."

The words pierced her like a thousand stinging darts. She bit her lower lip to keep from crying out. "You don't even know what love is. It's not this," she said, pointing to the tangled sheets on the large mattress. "It's about putting in time and being there through all the tough stuff. Have you ever once done that? You tell me I'll regret walking away from you, but you don't know about regret and pain. You don't know about losing the most important person in your life, then having to decide whether to be alone forever, or make do with second best."

The words came out so fast, she didn't know what she'd said until they filled the room. Todd's face tightened until it was unreadable. Horror filled her. Horror at the incredibly cruel things she'd just spoken aloud. She'd found his one point of weakness and she'd attacked, telling him he would never be good enough.

"Todd," she breathed.

"You'd better go."

She stared at him, at his closed expression. She felt his pain and it was worse than her own. He'd pointed out her character flaws in a gentle way, but she hadn't been willing to face the truth. Instead she'd lashed out, wanting to hurt him more. Well, she'd succeeded.

In eighteen years of marriage she'd learned one important thing. That while one could apologize for words spoken in anger, and the apology could be accepted, the words themselves could not be called back.

She lowered her gaze to the floor. "I'm sorry. I know that's completely inadequate, but I don't know what else to say." She hesitated, wondering if she could try to explain, then she repeated, "I'm sorry," and left the room.

Her shoes were in the living room, where she'd left them, as was her purse. She grabbed both and headed for the front door.

She paused there, wondering if he would stop her.

"I'll drive you home," he said quietly. Not "Gee, I understand. We were both angry." Or even, "Let's talk some more." Just that he would drive her home.

She'd blown it completely.

"I'll be fine," she said, and walked toward the elevator.

The doors opened as she approached. Beth stepped inside without saying anything else and pressed the button for the lobby level. As the doors closed, the world went blurry and she realized she was crying. Her facade of calm crumbled until she was sobbing. By the time she reached the ground floor, she felt herself beginning to break into a thousand pieces.

What had just happened up there? Had he really said he loved her and had she not said anything back? Had he confessed to doubts, then said he still wanted to be with her, and had she thrown that back in his face? Has she really said those horrible things to him?

She stood in the lobby for several minutes, trying to get control of herself. She didn't know what to do. Home, she thought at last. She had to go home.

As if conjured by her wish, a cab pulled up in front of the building. Beth stepped outside. The cab driver opened the passenger side window. "Beth Davis, right? Your husband called and ordered you a cab."

She brushed the tears from her cheeks. Of course Todd had called a cab for her. No matter what had happened between them, he wouldn't have left her to find her own way home.

Her wonderful house had become a prison. Beth walked from room to room, searching for a quiet corner in which to sit and recover, but once-familiar decorations and furniture had become strange and unwelcoming. In the four ours that she'd been back, she'd yet to settle anywhere. No seat was comfortable, no window showed a view that she remembered. She didn't want to stay inside, but she didn't want to go out, either.

Beth found herself wishing that her kids were home. At least then she would have a distraction and a way to escape her scattered thoughts. But she'd been so nervous about spending the night with Todd and how it might affect her that she'd arranged for Matt and Jodi to stay away until late Sunday evening. She was completely alone.

She'd been through three bouts of crying followed by numbness, followed by more emotion and tears. She'd tried television, reading and even chocolate. Nothing was working. She couldn't get Todd out of her head.

"It would never have worked," she whispered to herself as she paused in her kitchen and stared out the window over the sink. She noted the roses in the backyard were in bloom and thought vaguely about cutting some flowers to bring inside. The image of pretty flowers in the center of her table wasn't enough to distract her from Todd's words and her own confusion.

Why had she lashed out at him? Because he'd spoken the truth? Because he'd held a mirror up to her face and she hadn't liked what she'd seen there?

She *had* been doubting him from the very beginning. She'd doubted that he would find her attractive or interesting. She didn't think she could compete with the other women in his life. She didn't think she would fit in with his friends. She didn't know how to date.

And then there was the entire issue of Darren. She'd loved her husband most of her life. He'd been so good to her. With Darren there hadn't been doubts. She'd understood the attraction. They'd been so much alike, with similar backgrounds, similar goals. She'd thought he was handsome, he'd considered her pretty. They'd been equals intellectually. They'd both been so young. *She owed him.*

Beth crossed to the kitchen table and sank down onto a chair. She owed Darren her love and respect—she owed him always being first in her life. Not just her first lover, her first love, which no one could take away, but also first place in her heart.

Beth folded her arms on the table and let her head sink onto them. She closed her eyes and fought the tears. It wasn't enough that she had doubts about her attractiveness, her ability to keep Todd's interest and the fact that blending families was inherently difficult. She also had to wrestle with her guilt. Because she was afraid that if she gave in, if she let herself care about Todd, love Todd, that she might just love him more than she'd ever loved Darren. And she couldn't allow that. No matter what it cost her.

Chapter Sixteen

The phone rang late Sunday night. Todd knew who was calling, even before he picked up the receiver. He suspected he knew what she was going to say before she said it.

"Hello," he said, when he picked up on the fourth ring.

"I thought you might not answer."

"I almost didn't."

He heard Beth's soft sigh, and despite the blackness eating at his heart, he almost smiled. He could imagine her curled up on her bed, her legs drawn close to her chest as she leaned back against the pillows. Her hair would be mussed, her face free from makeup. From a distance of fifteen miles and several hours of pain, he still wanted her.

"I messed up," she said. "I'm sorry."

"There's no need to apologize. You told me the truth."

That's what he'd been thinking about all day. That she'd only spoken the truth. He *was* second best. Darren would always come first in her life.

"No, I didn't," she whispered. "At least not in the way I said it and you took it. I was scared and hurt and embarrassed by all that you were saying. You're right, Todd. I didn't want you to have doubts. That was my department. I wanted you to pursue me unconditionally, then I would take my time saying yes or no. I wanted you to put it all on the line while I made up my mind. That's not fair. And I don't like what it says about me. I lashed out because I was covering."

He stared out at the view of the city. There weren't any lights on in his living room and the blinds were open, so he could see clear to the horizon. Heat rose from the ground and made some of the streetlights seem to flicker.

He wanted to believe what she was saying. That her accusation had just been words spoken in anger.

"I'm not interested in being anyone's second choice," he said.

"I know. You told me you loved me and I didn't say anything back. I treated you horribly. I'm ashamed and I'm sorry. And I'm afraid."

He wanted her words to heal him, but was too numb to believe them. "Of what? That I'll leave you? That I'll realize you're nearly forty and I would rather be with a twenty-year-old?"

"Yes, but that's not the big thing."

He sighed. He didn't have any way to reassure her. "What is the big thing?"

"Darren. I'm afraid if I give you my heart, I'll love you more. I can't do that, Todd. I can't betray him that way. I have to love him best, and I don't know if I can."

He understood what she was saying. A part of him was fiercely glad that she thought she could love him so much, but most of him tensed as new pain shot through him. Rather than take the risk of betraying her late husband's memory, Beth would walk away.

"This would be the difficult part of the relationship," he said. "Now I know why I always got out early. It's a hell of a lot easier not to have to go through this."

"I kn-know." Her voice cracked on a sob. "I'm sorry."

"Don't be." There wasn't any point.

"No, I am. Because I've made it tough from the beginning. Because I didn't believe in you and your feelings, so I've used up all your patience. That was really stupid, because I need it more now than ever."

She should be a hundred percent right, he thought grimly. Unfortunately she wasn't. "Is that what you think?" he asked. "That there is a finite amount of trouble I'm willing to put up with and then I'll be gone? I love you, Beth. I meant it when I said it, and I mean it now. Not just for the good parts, but for all of it. I need you in my life, but that's not enough. You have to love me back and need me, too. You have to trust me to be there. You have to give me a chance to get through the hard stuff."

"I haven't let Darren go yet, have I?"

She'd laid him bare a thousand times before, so he should be used to the sharp pain of his soul being torn open. Still, the agony caught him by surprise. Trust Beth to focus on the truth. He didn't want to think about it, or believe it, but she was right.

"No, you haven't."

"I'm sorry." She was crying now. He could hear it in her choked voice. She sniffed. "I have to make peace with this. I know that. I want to be with you, Todd. I love you."

But it wasn't enough. *He* wasn't enough. He might never be all that she needed.

"You told me you weren't ready to date. I guess I should have listened."

"But I don't want to lose you."

"You haven't." That was the hell of it. Even though he knew he should walk away, he couldn't.

"You'll wait?"

"Yes."

She gave a half-strangled laugh. "I want to ask for how long, but I won't. I'll even pretend to believe you."

"You'll have to do more than pretend, Beth, or you're missing the whole point. You have to believe I love you enough to know you're worth waiting for."

They were both silent. "I do love you," she said.

"I heard you the first time."

"Do you believe me?"

"I want to."

"Ouch. I guess now I know what it's been like living in your shoes."

"I'm not trying to hurt you."

She sighed. "I know. You're telling me the truth. I appreciate that."

He cleared his throat. "I'm not going to call you for a few days. I think you need some time. I'll be in touch next Friday or Saturday and we can talk again. All right?"

"Okay. Bye."

She hung up the phone. He did the same, then sat alone in the darkness wondering how the hell he was going to survive without her.

"Am I crazy?" Beth asked.

Cindy took a sip of her iced tea and shrugged. "You don't really want an answer to that," her friend told her.

Beth considered the statement. "I think I do want an answer. I'm confused." She sighed. "And very, very tired."

It was Thursday and she hadn't talked to Todd since the previous Sunday. Monday morning, flowers had arrived with a card that had been signed with nothing but his name. She didn't know what he was thinking, which was fine because she didn't know what she was thinking, either.

"I haven't slept more than a couple of hours a night since Sunday," she said. "I can't think and I can't stop thinking." She looked at Cindy. "Was he right about what he said? Did I want him to be completely sure from the beginning and to live with all my doubts without having any of his own? Am I really that horrible?"

"You're not horrible, you're human. There's a difference."

"Maybe, but not a very big one. I want…" She drew in a deep breath. "I want to believe all of it. I want to believe that he loves me and that he's willing to ride it out through the tough times. But I keep going back to the fact that he's the most wonderful and amazing man, and I'm just a middle-aged woman with two teenage kids and a part-time job. What on earth does he want with me?"

Cindy leaned forward. "You make *me* crazy. Beth, you're a terrific person. You're funny, you're caring, you're attractive. I'm willing to bet that Todd thinks you're great in bed."

"Like he can't get all that in a much younger, much prettier package."

"Maybe he can, but you're the package he wants. You're the one he's interested in, not them. Why can't you just accept the fact that you got very lucky? Because the truth is, Todd got lucky, too. Besides, I don't think he can get what he has with you with someone else. Assuming you come to your senses and marry the man, he's going to be getting a woman who will be devoted to him. I saw how you were with Darren. You give a hundred and fifty percent in your relationships. You're going to make him wonder how he ever survived without you. I'm not talking about cooking and cleaning, because he can hire someone to do that. I'm talking about loving him. You give with your whole heart. From what I've seen, Todd can get just about everything else he wants, but no one has ever taken the time or trouble to love him. Of course he's devoted to you—you're his fantasy.''

"You don't know how much I want to believe you," Beth said, wishing it were that easy. She knew she could love Todd. Perhaps too much. "I want to have faith, but it's hard. I didn't know that starting over would be so difficult."

Cindy reached across the table and touched her hand. "I know what you mean. After my divorce, I was devastated. My ex left me for a much younger woman. I felt abandoned and old, and my entire life was a cliché. I suppose in time I would have started dating, but I didn't have to. Mike just dropped into my lap. Still, it was hard to have enough faith in myself to trust his feelings. So I understand that part of it." She smiled. "Why do we as women have such trouble believing the good stuff?"

"I wish I knew, because then I could start to fix it." Beth knew she didn't have any answers. Currently all she could think of was questions.

"There's more, isn't there?" Cindy asked. "You're not this upset because you're afraid Todd's going to get bored."

Beth didn't ever bother to ask how Cindy knew. They'd been friends long enough to be able to cut to the heart of a matter. "It's Darren. I'm not ready to let him go. I'm so afraid if I love Todd, I'll love him more." She could feel tears burning at her eyes and she blinked them back. "I can't do that to my husband. He always has to be first."

Cindy stared at her for a long time. "So rather than risk what you see as your betrayal of Darren, you won't love Todd at all?"

It sounded wrong when Cindy said it, but Beth nodded anyway.

Her friend reached across the table and squeezed her hand. "You don't ever have to choose. Darren is the father of your children and he was a huge part of your life. He'll always be with you. You know what? You're always going to love him. Anyone who knows you wouldn't expect anything less. But it's also all right to open your heart to someone else. Someone different. Todd isn't going to take Darren's place, he's going to fill the remaining empty spaces in your heart. Just like I told you, you're lucky. You will have been loved by two wonderful men. Instead of panicking, be grateful."

"But what if I love Todd more?"

"You can't. There's no rating system—not a real one. You will love Todd differently. It might feel stronger in some areas and not as strong in others, but he'll never replace Darren. Not in your life or your children's."

Beth leaned back in her chair. "You don't know how much I want you to be telling the truth." She truly did want to feel that it was all right to love both men. "I thought it was supposed to be hard, that I was supposed to suffer and meet tons of inappropriate men, then just when I had given up on finding happiness and resigned myself to a life alone, *he* would come along and we would fall in love."

"So it's the timing that bothers you?"

Beth hated to admit that, but it was true. She nodded. "Why me? Why didn't I have to suffer?"

Cindy smiled. "Sometimes life just hands you a gift. Are you going to turn your back on it simply because it doesn't fit into your preconceived idea of the correct timing?"

"No. Of course not. It's just—"

"Stop it!" Cindy demanded, holding up her hands. "If you love him, be with him. If you don't love him, walk away. This isn't about Darren or the children or timing or what's right. It's about what you feel in your heart. Do you love him and do you want to be with him?"

Beth stared at her. Did she love Todd Graham? She

thought about his acts of kindness, the way he understood her, how they could talk for hours without running out of things to say. She thought about his patience with her children and with herself. How he was honest with her, even when being honest meant presenting himself in a less-than-flattering light. She thought of how he'd told her he'd never loved anyone else and how no one had ever taken the time to love him.

"Yes," she said at last. "I do love him."

"There's your answer."

"As simple as that," Beth said, and knew that Cindy was right.

Jodi and Matt stared at her expectantly. Beth wished she'd prepared notes or something before calling her children into a family meeting. But once she'd made up her mind, she'd wanted to talk to them.

"This is about Todd," she began.

Matt's expression turned worried. "He hasn't been over all week. Did you two have a fight?"

"Not exactly."

"He sent flowers," Jodi reminded her brother. "They look expensive."

"Don't flowers mean that she's mad at him and he's trying to say he's sorry?" Matt asked.

Beth shook her head. "Not in this case. I told Todd I needed some time to think and he's been giving me that." She ignored the flash of fear that said if he really loved her he would have called by now. She couldn't help feeling the fear, but after her talk with Cindy she'd vowed not to act on it so quickly.

Both children sat on the family-room sofa, with Beth perched on the edge of the coffee table in front of them. "I've been dating Todd for several months now and I wanted to talk about how you feel about him."

The teenagers glanced at each other. As the oldest, Jodi was the automatic spokesperson. "He's nice," she said. "We like him."

"Yeah, he's cool," Matt agreed. "At first I was kinda worried because he's so rich and stuff. Plus you're not real used to men like him. But I talked to him when I first met him and he listened. Even though I'm just some kid. I respect him, Mom. He's a good guy."

Beth felt her mouth drop open. She closed it and stared at her son. "You talked to Todd about me?"

"Sure. I had to. With Dad gone, it's up to me to take care of you."

She knew it was a guy thing and she didn't have a prayer of understanding it, so it was best to be grateful that she had such terrific children and let it go. "Thank you," she said. "I think."

"Are you two going to get married?" Jodi asked.

"I don't know," Beth answered truthfully. "I think we might be moving in that direction." Assuming she hadn't blown everything by taking so long to figure out how much she cared, she thought grimly. "How do you two feel about that? I agree that Todd is a good man. If we were to get m-married—" She could barely choke out the word. "Well, he wouldn't be taking your father's place. No one can do that."

She leaned toward her two wonderful offspring and smiled. "Your dad was a very special and wonderful person. We were all lucky to know him. No matter what happens for the rest of your life, you need to remember that. He loved you both so much. You meant everything to him."

"He loved you, too," Matt said.

Beth nodded. "I know. After he was gone, the memories of our lives together often helped me hang on. That and you two. If he hadn't died, he and I would still be together.

Our marriage was very strong. We loved each other.'' She paused. Now for the hard part. She wanted to explain things to her children, but without giving them more information that they would want or need. That delicate balancing act was made more difficult by the fact that she didn't understand everything herself.

"I thought I would be alone for a long time," she said. "I wasn't interested in dating. I have my job, I have you guys, I have a great life. I thought maybe someday I would look around for a man to go out with, but that wasn't important to me.''

She studied her children and their earnest expressions. Love filled her. If nothing else, her kids were a shining testament to her life.

"Then I met Todd. At first I didn't think we had anything in common.''

Jodi shook her head. "None of that matters. He's crazy about you, Mom. We can all see it.'' She wrinkled her nose. "With all my friends' parents getting divorced and stuff, I'm glad to know people really do fall in love. I like Todd.'' Her pretty mouth twisted. "I'd rather have Dad back, but I know that's not going to happen. So I say go for it.''

"Yeah, Mom,'' Matt agreed. "He doesn't know much about being a dad, but that's okay. We'll teach him.'' He paused as color stained his still smooth cheeks. "I kinda talked to Mike about him a while back. When we were over at their house for a barbecue.''

"You did?'' Beth frowned. Cindy had never mentioned it. Probably because Mike hadn't told his wife, she realized. Guy talk required a certain level of privacy and trust. She wasn't worried. She knew if it had been something terrible, Mike would have told her. He might tease her about a lot of things, but he was one of the good guys, too. "What did you two talk about?''

Matt shrugged. "Stuff. I was confused because I like

Todd a lot, but I love my dad. And I miss him. Mike said it was okay to let Todd into my life. He said that we can love a lot of people at the same time. It doesn't mean we're disloyal, it means that we're living up to our potential as human beings. The capacity to love and feel compassion is one of the things that makes us special.''

Beth was impressed. ''Mike said that?''

''Yeah. So, if you want to marry Todd, that's fine.'' He hesitated. ''The thing is, I'd want to keep Dad's last name. You know, for tradition and all that.''

She hadn't thought she had any tears left, but her eyes began to burn. Before she gave in, she swung around and settled between her children on the sofa and hugged them both close.

''Of course you'll want to keep your father's name. I wouldn't want it to be any other way. I love you both very much.''

They hugged her back. ''We love you, too,'' Jodi said.

Matt rested his chin on her shoulder. ''You think Todd will buy me a car?''

''No. I wouldn't let him. Besides, you're only fourteen.''

Matt grinned. ''Yeah, but I could go sit in it every day after school and all the guys would think I was so incredibly cool.''

''Not in this lifetime.''

''He'll buy me one when I'm sixteen.''

The kid was probably right. Todd would spoil her children because he loved them. Fortunately they were grounded enough to handle it.

''So when's the wedding?'' Jodi asked.

''I'm not sure.''

Beth sighed. One hurdle down and one to go. She'd talked to her children. Now she had to talk to the man who had offered her his heart, only to have her walk all over it. Was he going to give her another chance?

She realized it didn't matter. Regardless of what he said when she got in touch with him, she wasn't going to take no for an answer. She'd come too far and learned too much to give up on him now.

Mrs. Alberts, his secretary, walked into his office a little after five. She rarely came in without an invitation, but that wasn't what got Todd's attention. Instead it was the tuxedo and white shirt she held. In her other hand were a pair of his dress shoes.

"You'll need to get changed," she told him. "There isn't much time."

"Excuse me?"

She walked into the private bathroom off the left side of his office and hung up his suit. "I called the concierge at your building and had him get your tuxedo. The limo will be here in thirty minutes. That should give you enough time to shower and change."

He touched his computer keyboard until the screen displayed his calendar. He had nothing planned for the evening. It was Friday, nearly a week after his disastrous parting with Beth. He'd planned on calling her this evening. Despite her fears and her past, he was going to force her to talk to him, or at least listen while he explained how they couldn't turn their backs on each other. He'd spent his whole life looking for love and he wasn't going to give it up now that he'd found it. Somehow he would convince her that they belonged together.

In the meantime, he had to deal with his secretary. "I don't have anything on my schedule," he told Mrs. Alberts. Even if he did, he wasn't about to go anywhere except home to call Beth.

His secretary smiled at him. A warm, knowing smile he didn't think he'd seen before. "It's a last-minute thing, Mr. Graham, but I'm sure you'll want to go. As I said, the limo will be waiting downstairs at five-thirty. Beth is waiting for you at the Westin Hotel.''

He sat, stunned, unable to question her further. She gave him another smile and left him. When the door closed, he sprang to his feet to go after her, then fell back into his seat. Beth was waiting for him? Beth?

The cold dread that had settled into the corners of his life since she'd walked out on him the previous Sunday began to ease a little. She wouldn't be inviting him to a hotel to give him bad news, would she? That sort of thing could be shared over the phone, or even in a letter.

He knew there was no point in speculating. He would learn the truth when he saw her. Even so, hope flared inside of him as he quickly showered and dressed in his tuxedo. So they were going formal, were they?

Fifteen minutes later, he was on his way out the door. In his right front jacket pocket sat a small, black velvet box. Maybe he was setting himself up for more disappointment, but he couldn't resist taking a chance. She was all he'd ever wanted. Now that he'd found her, he wasn't going to let her get away again.

At the front desk of the luxurious hotel, he told the clerk his name and was handed an envelope. Inside was a room key and a short note.

I was promised a date with one of Houston's most eligible bachelors. Due to a case of nerves on my part, that date never happened. So tonight I request the honor of your presence for an evening that should have been, the very first night we met.

Her words made him smile...and want to believe it was going to work out for them.

Todd crossed to the elevator, then waited impatiently for the car to arrive. Minutes later he headed toward the top of the high-rise, then stepping into a thickly carpeted corridor and walking to the room number written at the bottom of her note. He put the key into the electronic lock and turned the handle on the door. It opened with a slight click.

The first thing he noticed was the soft music and the muted light inside the beautifully decorated suite. Flowers filled several vases and scented the room. The drapes had been opened, giving him a view of the city that was not unlike the one from his penthouse.

Something moved in the shadows. He turned and saw Beth standing there, watching him. She wore the same dress she'd had on at the charity function they'd attended together. Her expression was welcoming, but her fidgeting fingers betrayed her nervousness. Love filled him. No matter what, he had to convince her to trust him. She was all he'd been looking for.

"Thank you for coming," she said. "I hope you're not angry that I had your secretary help me plan this. I sort of wanted it to be a surprise."

He stood silently, looking at her, remembering what it was like to be with her. He knew her faults, her strong points. He suspected their life together wouldn't be anything he pictured, but the differences would be better.

She bit her lower lip, then shrugged. "I had this great speech prepared, but I think I forgot it."

"I remember mine. Want me to go first?"

She shook her head. "It's my turn to put myself on the line. You've done that enough in this relationship." She drew in a deep breath and met his gaze. "I love you, Todd. I'll admit that I'm a little nervous about loving you. There are several reasons, not the least of which is you're so perfect." She held up one hand. "Not a perfect man, but perfect for me. I will always love Darren. He will always be my first love. I can't change that and I wouldn't. But I see now that it's all right for me to love you both. The heart

oesn't rank the souls it embraces. When I tell you I love
ou, it's with my whole being. Nothing is held back. Which
means I'm going to love you with the part of me that also
oves Darren.''

He released the breath he didn't know he'd been holding.
'I wouldn't have it any other way.''

The corners of her mouth turned up in a smile that made
er face glow. "Really?"

"Really. I need you," he said as he crossed to stand
lose to her. "I want you and I love you. You mean the
vorld to me. I don't pretend it's going to be easy. We're
oing to have to learn to be a family. I've never been part
f one and you've already had one with your late husband.
Ve'll have to create something new. We're both going to
nake mistakes, but that doesn't scare me. I'm not afraid to
vork hard. I'm not afraid to promise forever. I'm only
fraid you won't give me a chance.''

She touched his cheeks, then his mouth. Her lips trem-
led. "Thank you for giving *me* another chance. I love you
o much and I've allowed fear to hold me back. I've been
fraid for a lot of reasons we can talk about at another time.
You're right, it's not going to be easy. Blending families
s a challenge, but I don't want to lose you, either. You're
othing like Darren, which is scary, but good. I trust you
o love me for always, even though I don't understand how
got so lucky to have you in my life.''

He absorbed the words, their meaning and then he hauled
er hard against him. "Stay with me," he demanded then
issed her. "Stay with me always.''

He kissed her again, plunging his tongue into her mouth.
he met his passion and fueled it with her own. Her hands
vere everywhere, as were his. They made it to the suite's
edroom while they tugged at clothing, his jacket falling to
he floor, her dress zipper being pulled down and the gar-
nent sagging off one shoulder.

He tasted her neck, her earlobes, then tugged down the front of her dress and fumbled with her bra. In the end, she had to unfasten it for him. It was only then that he realized his hands were shaking, too. Then her breasts were bare and he was licking her tight nipples, savoring the sweetness that was Beth.

They managed to pull off shoes and socks, pantyhose and trousers. His shirt and briefs, her dress and finally her panties joined the growing pile. At last they were both naked and tumbling across the bed.

"The lights are on," he said as he rolled onto his back and pulled her along with him.

"I know. You'd better get used to looking at me."

He drank in the beauty of her body. "I'll never get tired of seeing you naked," he promised. "You turn me on."

She straddled his thighs and reached down to stroke his arousal. "The feeling is mutual."

"Always a good thing."

Then he remembered something important. He reached for his jacket. Beth dug around in the same pile and pulled out a condom. "I found it first," she said as she slipped the protection on him.

"That's not what I was looking for." He felt the lapel of his jacket and followed that down to the front button. When he reached the pocket, he withdrew the jeweler's box.

"Marry me," he said, opening the velvet case and removing the stunning solitaire he'd purchased three days before. "Marry me and be my wife."

Beth couldn't believe what was happening. There they both were—naked as jaybirds—and about to do the wild thing. It was still light outside, which was so strange, she could barely stand it. And just to make the situation unforgettable, the man proposed.

What on earth could she say? Except— "Yes."

He slid the ring on her finger at the same moment he slipped into her body.

She started to cry and laugh at the same time. "How am supposed to tell people how we got engaged?" she asked.

"We'll make something up."

"Good idea. In fact..."

But he was drawing her close and kissing her. She went willingly, accepting his body as well as his heart. Knowing that she had been blessed a second time, blessed with a man who would love her forever.

Later they would make up an engagement story to share with her children. Later they would plan a wedding to be held at the end of the month. Later they would figure out where to live and what kind of car he was going to buy Jodi for her seventeenth birthday. Later she would tell him that she wanted to take his name for her own. Later he would tentatively ask if she'd ever thought about having another child and she would admit that the idea had merit. But for now it was enough to be in love, making love.

As they reached for their ultimate pleasure, the setting rays of the sun caught on her diamond ring and surrounded them with a light as bright as their future.

* * * * *

Silhouette® SPECIAL EDITION®

LINDSAY McKENNA

delivers two more exciting books in her heart-stopping new series:

MORGAN'S MERCENARIES
III
THE HUNTERS

handwritten: charlequen. Cm

Coming in July 1999:
HUNTER'S WOMAN
Special Edition #1255

Ty Hunter wanted his woman back from the moment he set his piercing gaze on her. For despite the protest on Dr. Catt Alborak's soft lips, Ty was on a mission to give the stubborn beauty everything he'd foolishly denied her once—his heart, his soul—and most of all, his child....

And coming in October 1999:
HUNTER'S PRIDE
Special Edition #1274

Devlin Hunter had a way with the ladies, but when it came to his job as a mercenary, the brooding bachelor worked alone. Until his latest assignment paired him up with Kulani Dawson, a feisty beauty whose tender vulnerabilities brought out his every protective instinct—and chipped away at his proud vow to never fall in love....

Look for the exciting series finale in early 2000—when MORGAN'S MERCENARIES: THE HUNTERS comes to Silhouette Desire®!

Available at your favorite retail outlet.

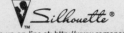
Silhouette®

SSEMM